"By the Eternal"

NETTIE.

"By the Eternal"

A NOVEL

By

OPIE READ

Author of

"The Son of the Swordmaker," "Turkey-Egg Griffin," "The Starbucks," "The Harkriders,"
"The Jucklins," "A Kentucky Colonel,"
"A Tennessee Judge," "The Carpet-
bagger," "Old Ebenezer,"
"On The Suwanee River,"
etc.

SPECIAL ILLUSTRATIONS

CHICAGO

LAIRD & LEE, PUBLISHERS

THEODORE ROOSEVELT once re-marked: "I was never more compliment-ed than when an old man called me a Jackson Democrat." And to that president, who, more than any other, has influenced legis-lation for the benefit, not only of his own people, but for all mankind—to this exponent of true democracy—to this man, not of the dim past but of the vivid present—to Theodore Roose-velt this book is most respectfully dedicated by the author.

PREFACE.

ANDREW JACKSON *was not only one of the strongest characters in American history, but one of the most striking individuals of all time. With him every narrowness was a farce and every prejudice an aggressive weapon. It is related that once when he spoke of appointing an obscure man to an important office, a member of the cabinet remarked: "But Mr. President, are you sure that he is able?" And Jackson answered: "Sir, all of my friends are able." In this lay his character. To be his friend was to be competent. His friends were right, and his enemies were all of them wrong. But there never lived a man of more integrity, and had he continued to live, a war between the North and the South would have been impossible. His duel with Dickinson, which in this story he is made to relate in his own words, was one of the most famous incidents in all the history of the "field of honor," and upon good authority it is told that while he was on his death bed, a minister sought to evoke from him an expression of remorse concerning the death of that popular young man. "General," said the preacher, "in looking back over your past life is there anything that you particularly regret?"*

iii

"Yes, there is," he answered. Ah, the confession was coming. *"I regret that I didn't hang John C. Calhoun."*

I was born not far from the *"Hermitage,"* and as a boy played on the ground where many of old Andrew's stirring scenes were enacted. I have listened to the talk of old men who were his intimates—*"able men,"* for they were his friends. But in reading the many lives of Old Hickory, and searching closely the many unpublished papers now in possession of the Tennessee Historical Society, I failed to find a number of *"facts"* which I have since discovered in my own book.   *The Author.*

CONTENTS.

CHAPTER.		PAGE
I	The Old Fellow With The Hairy Jaw..	7
II	They Whispered	14
III	His Respect For the Poets	21
IV	The Jolly Ferryman	28
V	At the Ball	33
VI	Arabella Crenshaw	38
VII	With Contempt	49
VIII	A Perfumed Night	57
IX	In the Interest of Another	65
X	Carrying the Message	76
XI	An Understanding	82
XII	Sneaked Out of the House	86
XIII	An Old Acquaintance from the Nursery	100
XIV	He Had Something to Tell	106
XV	At the Hermitage	113
XVI	Mahone Sees More Trouble Coming	129
XVII	In the Buggy	145
XVIII	She Begged Him to Let Her Stay	155
XIX	Grew Lighter at the Window	170
XX	I Am Denounced	176
XXI	He Did Not Regret	191
XXII	Mrs. Hilliard and Her Academy	202
XXIII	Just Waiting	208
XXIV	News That Was Not Good	225
XXV	A Taste of Fire	233
XXVI	Had Become Soldiers	249
XXVII	At Horseshoe Bend	261
XXVIII	A Message from Washington	275
XXIX	Twenty-Five Minutes	290
XXX	Conclusion	296

"BY THE ETERNAL."

CHAPTER I.

THE OLD FELLOW WITH THE HAIRY JAW.

A S SOON as I had mounted the stairway of that rude inn, I felt that the proprietor would attempt to murder me before morning. I was traveling, horseback from Jonesboro to Nashville, Tennessee, the new commonwealth that had just arisen out of the troublous, not to say desperate state of Franklin. The country was wild. Strong, moral men, unconscious poets, conscious patriots, with sentiment unto death in their powder horns, constituted the backbone of the recently built state. But the very current of their enterprise drew after it thieves and desperadoes; men to whom human blood meant no more than muddy water.

An adventurous youngster, not more than nineteen, late from an old field pine log academy in North Carolina, I had set forth to find fortune, with a vague idea that it lay somewhere beyond the hills. My parents had passed away some years before, my guardian had recently died, and now my possessions consisted of two suits of clothes, two pistols and a horse, bridle and saddle.

It was near the close of a day in summer. From the hillsides came the sweet and ever thrilling breath of June. The scenery about the place was a great and wasteful picture, with here and there a violent dash of color.

The proprietor, a grizzled old man in short sleeves, came out of the house, when I had dismounted, grunted a sort of welcome, gave over to a negro the care of my horse and led the way into the house. Taverns in those days and of this part of the country were rough indeed. This one was the roughest of its class. It was constructed of oak logs with the bark still on them. The two chimneys, one at each end, were built of sticks and plastered with clay. The floor impressed me, not on account of its rareness, but for a certain danger it held; it was laid in slabs riven from logs and was so thick set with splinters as to arouse within me a painful fear for my new calf-skin boots.

At an open fire place, a large, red-haired woman was cooking. She turned about, pot-hooks in hand, nodded, half smiled, revealing a tobacco-stained tusk, and apparently dismissed me from what I conceived to be her red mind.

The old man motioned toward a bench. "Set down," said he. "How fer have you come to-day?"

"Forty miles, I should think."

"Horse ain't blow'd much. Putty good cattle, I take it."

"Blooded," I answered with a youngster's vanity. The woman looked around at me. The man nodded and scratched his hairy jaw. I put my two pistols, in holsters, on a bed and sat down. As yet he had not aroused my suspicions.

In answer to an inquiry as to whether he had any other guests for the night, he said: "No, you happen to be the only one. The increase of travel has shut me out, somewhat; has caused the buildin' of

another house about two miles west of here. But I
don't reckon I'll starve. There's always a reward
fer the fellow that works hard and attends to his own
business. Puss, you'd better hurry up the gentleman's supper.''

"I'm gettin' it as fast as I can," the woman replied. "Meat don't fry no faster because you're anxious."

"Hit me on the top of the head," the old fellow re-
joined. "I reckon she's got more truths that you
ain't a-lookin' fer than any woman in the country.
Goin' out to the new settlements to start in prac-
ticin' law, young man?" And without giving me time
to answer, he added: "Yo' supper's ready."

I expected him to join me, as a tin plate, a knife and
fork had been placed opposite to those of their rude
kindred, which I was to use, but he did not; he remained in the background, talking continuously. The
woman stood in front of me, replying to the old man
when I failed to show interest in what he was saying. Once she addressed me: "You are putty young
to go wanderin' around the country by yourself; but
I don't reckon anybody's goin' to harm you very
much. There was a time when this country along
here was putty tolor'bl dangersome, but it has settled
down mightily within the past year. Why, it's
mother's milk now compared with what it was when
we came here. Why then, in that late day, a year
ago or more, folks would steal from you every time
you wan't lookin'. Stold my husband's Bible one
day right out of his saddle bags, they did; and if he
hadn't been one of the religiousest men, somebody
would 'a' got a good cussin'. And Sam'l could cuss,
too, before he j'ined the church and became an ex-

horter. Have some more of that bread. It ain't right
good fer there ain't no mill near here and we have to
beat the corn into meal with a hominy pess'le. Sam'l,
ain't you goin' to eat a bite with the young gentleman?''

"Wall, don't mind if I do," "Sam'l" answered;
and coming forward, he took a seat opposite me.

Through the window I could see the dusk-deepening
flush of the sun, now sunk beyond the hills.   The
evening was made sweetly melancholy with the songs
of birds; and from some distant valley came the sad-
dest of all love-calls, the notes of the whippoorwill.
In the sunrise, when the dew was sparkling, in the
noon-tide when squirrels reposed dreamily in the
grateful shade, I had mused with not much concern
upon what I was to do for a living, believing, in these
roseate hours of Nature's promise, that the very
brightness of the world was a prediction of fortune.   But in the sad, bird-choired, dun light of the
evening, my thoughts, like winged things, but with
no songs in them, flapped and fell against the dark
curtains of the Future. So now it was that I sat mute,
thinking in soberest mood; and in this life, no mood is
more serious than some of those that fall upon us in
youth, before we have climbed many of the hills, before many of the valleys have been crossed.

"You ain't eatin' much," said the old man. "Help
yourself, here, to some more of the fry. If you could
stay with us a day or two we could git you out of
the dumps that you 'pear to be fallin' into. Cheer up
fer you'll find everything over in the settlements all
right, I reckon; and then you can sail right along, and
when you're old enough, be elected a Justice of the
Peace—''

"He's mighty nigh old enough fer a constable now," the woman spoke up; and thus having flattered me she passed the bread.

"I was a constable once in North Caroliny," said the old man. "But I had to levy on property that belonged to poor folks, and I never could stand that sort of business; so I give it up and came out here and started a hotel, a feedin' of folks ruther than a takin' of bread out of their mouths. Well, Puss, he 'pears to have eat enough; and I reckon you might as well clear away the things."

There were no things to be cleared away except to remove a few tin plates; and this she did with a sweep of her great, red hand. Then she lighted an earthen lamp, with a rag wick, placed it upon the mantelpiece, sat down in a corner and began her evening's work, carding cotton batts. With a shovel, the old man covered up the fire, patting the ashes, like a sexton patting a grave, talking the while of the great improvement that had taken place in the country since his arrival. On the mantel shelf a battered old clock, with only the hour hand to mark the time, was ticking, louder, now that the birds had hushed.

I glanced at this ignorer of moments and the uncertain teller of the hours, and the old man said: "We lost one of the hands as we were movin' out here and I ain't had time to whittle out another one. Sorter looks like a waste of time, don't it?" And dropping his chin upon his hairy chest he laughed. "Wife there, has sorter stirred me up about it a time or two, but I always tell her we can do without another hand ourselves and apologize when we've got company. Young feller, you look like you might be sleepy. Yo' bed's ready fer you up stairs." He nodded toward a ladder that led to the loft. "You won't find no gold candlesticks up there, but you can take a hog-fat lamp, and that will sorter skeer off the darkness. Puss, light tuther lamp fer him, will you? We may economize as to the hands of a clock, but when it comes to lamps, why we are as wasteful as— now what do they call him? Hearn a preacher talk about him not long ago. Some sort of a son."

"Prodigal son," I answered out of my limited store of Scriptural learning.

"You hit it on the head, sir. Why, you're educated right up to the handle, ain't you?"

The woman lighted another lamp and gave it to me, and turning to the bed I took up my pistols.

"I can help you up with 'em if they're too heavy fer you," the old man laughed.

"I can manage them," I answered, throwing the holsters over one shoulder, dividing them like a pair of saddle bags. Bidding my host and his wife good night, I climbed the ladder to the room above. Then it was, and I couldn't have told exactly why, that the suspicion of murder crossed my mind. A shudder crept over me; a cold shudder, just alive enough to creep, frightening me with paralytic numbness. In the middle of the room was a legged slab intended to serve as a table, and placing the lamp upon it I looked about me. In one corner was a bed, a mere heap of straw spread over with a quilt. Near the bed was a low stool, and upon it I sat down to think. The pistols in the holsters were still across my shoulder. Suddenly the scene at the supper table arose before me. Why had the old man placed the bench so that I should sit with my eyes turned from the pistols on the bed? Why had he remained so long behind me, talking incessantly? And then, when he became silent, why had his wife sought so eagerly to seize upon my attention and to hold it?

I took the pistols out of the holsters and examined the priming. It had not been disturbed. But with ramrod I sounded the barrels. The powder and balls had been withdrawn. This was a complete confirmation of my fears. As quickly as possible I reloaded the weapons. Then, moving the stool over into another corner, as far as I could get from the hole up through which the ladder led, I put out the light, sat down and waited.

CHAPTER II.

TO WAIT was the utmost extent of possible enterprise. There was no window, no way to get out; not even through the roof, for I had noticed from the outside, that the riven boards that composed it were weighted down with heavy logs. So, to wait was all that I could do. In the floor were large cracks and up through them streaked the yellow light. The door below opened and closed. I could not through any of the cracks command a full view of what was taking place, but I fancied that the old man had looked out to make sure as to whether any traveler was passing along the road. Suddenly, I heard whispering, and placing my ear close to a crack, I had no difficulty in catching not only the import but the minutest accents of the words. "If you would make a crowd hear, whisper," I once heard an orator say; and now I thought of it, as I lay with my ear against the floor. Toward caution on their part there seemed to be not much of an effort. It may be easier to gauge the carrying force of a shout than of a whisper.

"There's no other way out of it," came from the old man. I could distinguish his whisper though I had never heard it before, but in it were notes identical with his wheezy laugh. "No other possible way. There won't be no blood to speak of. I'll just finish him with a stick of wood."

14

"But he's so young," the woman whispered.

"Wall, the younger they are the better prepared they are to go, I can tell you that. What are you so squeamish about now? Ain't gone off in a corner and 'fessed religion when I wan't a lookin', I hope. Wan't you sent to the penitentiary fer life in North Caroliny for murder, and didn't we both escape from there together, as man and wife should?"

"I ain't squeamish and I ain't weakenin'," the woman answered. "I jist want to be careful, that's all."

"Careful!" he repeated. "I'm goin' to be jist as careful as there's any use of bein'. All we've got to do after the job's done is to drag him off into the woods some whar, and when he's found, why it's the Indians that fixed him. There ain't such a hoss been along here in many a day," he added after a short pause. "And it ain't right to let him pass on and be rid around useless. A man's conscience will tell him, if he gives it half a chance, that a hoss ought to be put to good use."

"Is that stick you've got there heavy enough?" she inquired; and the old man answered: "Heavy enough to maul rails with and I reckon it ought to do for him."

"But don't you hate to do it, Sam'l—and at yo' age?"

"Weakenin' ag'in, are you? What's age got to do with it? Nothin', except to make a man set his gums instead of his teeth. And when a man sets his gums, I tell you he's got it in fer natur' right thar and then. When a man has lived beyond his teeth, life ain't fulfilled many of it's promises, I'll tell you that."

"You ought to have kept on preachin', Sam'l."

"I would if they hadn't proved it on me that I stol'd the hoss and started me down hill when I was tryin' to climb up. But there ain't no use for you to argy with me or fer me to argy with myself. The fact is that natur' made me a rascal and it ain't worth while to try to stand in her way."

Peering down through the crack I could now see him, standing with his back toward the fire-place, with the bludgeon in his hand. The lamp, on the mantel-shelf, to the left, shed light upon his countenance. It looked like an indictment for murder drawn in red. Civilization was marching, with its rifle, its plow and its prayer book, but in that day, as it may be on the day now most distant, depravity skulked in its train.

If I could find a place broad enough in the crack—no, he moved, and I could not shoot him.

"Ain't you goin' to take the light?" the woman inquired. "It's dark up there."

"No, I can see well enough. The moon is shinin' through the chinks. You can bring the light when I call fer it. I don't think there's any body else comin' along to-night, and we better have it over with. You might as well hold the light at the foot of the stairs, I reckon."

A shifting of shadows told me that she had taken down the lamp and was preparing to obey him. I heard them moving about; up through the hole in the floor, over against the wall, there came a yellow light, thick, like stagnant water, not dispelling the darkness, but showing where it lay. I heard his boot strike the ladder. The light thickened; he was ascending, obscuring it. With pistol leveled, I waited. There was light enough to direct my aim. His death was

"WITH PISTOL LEVELED, I WAITED."

sure. But suddenly he seemed to hesitate, and then I heard him say: "Take away the light. It will interfere with the moon."

The yellow flood sank down. Now all was dark, save for the moon-ribbons, streaming through the "chinks" of the wall; but to the left of the stairway, they offered no advantage to my pistol; and now I must estimate rather than aim. I could hear the ticking of that old, one-handed clock. Was it a mile up the stairs? If but a moonbeam would pierce that gloom! Were heaven-sent rays ever so unkind before? Was that a deeper darkness over there? The pistol flashed, fired; and with the pent up violence of the shock my very temples seemed to burst. And then a silence, as short as the pause between the drawing of a long breath and the escape of a sigh; and then, a cry as something heavily struck the floor below.

"Sam'l are you hurt?"

The answer was a roar that denied my victory: "Fetch me the blunderbuss and I'll blow him through the roof!"

At this moment there came a furious knocking at the door. Out went the light.

"Open this door," a voice demanded. All was silent within.

"Strike that light again and open this door."

"There's no other way," said the old man in his penetrating whisper, "I've hit on something." And then in a loud voice he answered the summons: "All right, in a minute. It will take some time to strike the light fer the fire has to be uncovered and there ain't no blaze."

"Be as quick as you can."

"Yes, sir, whoever you are, and I want to say that I'm mighty glad you've come. We've trapped a robber upstairs and we'll have to shoot him. Puss, can't you git that light?"

I heard the old woman blowing at the fire. The feeble light crept through the darkness. The door was opened. There seemed to be several men without. "You are under arrest!" I heard some one exclaim; and then it was the old man's voice that made answer.

"What fer, gentlemen? Because a robbber gits into my room up stairs and shoots at me? That's a putty come off."

And then a voice which I had not heard before spoke up. "Oh, we know you well enough, Brother Ferguson; we've got your pedigree, and we know where your company is most desired—over in the North Carolina penitentiary; and as I am an officer of that state, and have a warrant for you, I'll see that you get back there safe enough. Put on the irons, Jim."

"By the Eternal, not on the woman," spoke up the man whose voice had first demanded admission.

"All right, Judge, but she's a bad one."

"No matter how bad, sir, but still a woman, and therefore shall be treated with all reasonable consideration. But we are forgetting the old man's robber up stairs."

It did not require even a second hint to extract me from that dark loft; and when I had come down, a tall, grave man stepped forward, looked at me, smiled slightly and said: "A mere boy. Young man, I congratulate you upon your determined defense—and I will not add, upon the luckiness of our arrival, for your own bravery would have saved you, sir.''

I thanked him, and then in the dim light strove to get a good view of his features, but his countenance was as a page in Æschylus to one who did not know the text. In a moment, though, I was fascinated. His voice thrilled me. I felt that I would follow him to the frontier of any desperate measure; and in his slight smile, which made his face really graver than it was before, there was a something, a light, a more than a light, the dazzle of a great soul.

There were two other men in the room, and having merely nodded to me, as if I were one of the many necessary incidents that fell to their lives, they were soon busy with ironing the inn-keeper. The old woman stood by, wailing.

''We didn't intend to hurt you,'' she said to me. ''We had just been talking about what a nice boy you were, and Sam'l was goin' up to see if everything was all right in the room, and you shot at him, and then we thought you were a robber. Didn't we, Sam'l?''

''Shut up!'' the old man shouted.

''That is a poor recompense to her for all her fidelity to you, you infernal old brute,'' said the tall, grave gentleman. ''No matter how deep in crime she may be, she is better than you, and deserving of your respect. Madam, will you go along without any trouble? I should hate to see them handcuff you. But you must promise to behave yourself.''

Most fervently she promised that she would. He bowed to her, and speaking to one of the officers, cautioned him to treat her kindly. Then he addressed himself to me.

"Young man, there is a place a few miles further on, where we may find accommodations. If you wish it, you may come with me."

I thanked him and went on the keen bound to saddle my horse. The lustiest of shouting failed to draw the negro from his hiding place. But the stable door was not locked, and soon I was ready to take the road. My companion was splendidly mounted. For a time we proceeded swiftly, in silence. I was loth to break in upon his reserve. But curiosity was riding me with a sharper spur than the one bound to my own heel, and so I was prodded into inquiring his name.

"Andrew Jackson," he answered; and I asked if he would permit me to shake hands with him, there in the forest, with the moon sparkling upon us. How often has my mind flown back to the scene, the moment of that hand-grasp! And I can see him now as he sat on his horse, dark majesty, fated scourger of men who had never known defeat—men who were to over-topple Bonaparte and send him to Elba—Packenham's Nemesis speeding through the wild.

He was not unknown. I had heard of him, of his bravery as an Indian fighter, and of his term in Congress at Philadelphia, first representative from the state of Tennessee. But while his reputation laid just claim upon my admiration, yet that alone did not excite my wonder. I had seen Congressmen in North Carolina, at my father's house—had seen them drunk at our table; and as for bravery verging upon rashness, it was almost as common as caution is now. It was the man himself, name unknown, that laid strange hold upon me. Something told me that to know him was to be a part of history.

CHAPTER III.

HIS RESPECT FOR THE POETS.

A T AN inn not a great distance along the road
toward the west, we found what was in that
day "ample accommodations," which meant
not more than two in a bed. In consideration of the
fact that Jackson had served a term in Congress, he
was given a bed alone; and, commenting upon it, the
"circuit rider" who had been assigned to share a
bunk with me, delivered this impressive homily:
"Just see what comes to a man who accomplishes
something in this life. And no wonder there is such
incentive to be ambitious when fame is attended by
such reward."

"Fame not only lies alone but often stands alone,"
I ventured to remark.

"Yes," he agreed with me, "fame is lonesomeness,
I should think. Now, if I were a bishop—but I won't
permit myself to be ambitious. My aim is to persuade
men from noisy strife in the blazing light of the
devil's affairs, and to induce them in quiet, to think
upon their soul's salvation. That old man and his
wife had you in a close place. For a long time they
have been suspected. Recently, evidence became
strong enough, and so officers came with warrants
and in the nick of time, too, for you, it would seem.
Jackson didn't have anything to do legally with their
arrest, but happening to fall in with the officers, he
couldn't keep out of it—he never can. I suppose he

could keep out of a fight, but I don't believe he ever
tried. Among my different charges is a meeting-
house at Black Creek. Not long ago, I was holding
services there, and was pleased to see him enter the
room and become a part of my congregation. I was
selfish enough to hope that I might be the means of
his conversion. He's a great man, it is true enough,
but still he is a wanderer from the fold—fights chickens and occasionally knocks down a man who does
not happen to agree with him.''

"If he'd been meeker, we might never have heard
of him,'' said I; and my companion, turning over,
further away from me, thus replied:

"It would seem that you must have seen, yea,
looked into that infamous book by Thomas Paine. But
no matter, I will proceed with what I was going to
relate. In the neighborhood, as might have been expected, there was a very rough element, known as the
Simmon's gang. They had made their boasts against
me—said that they were going to break up my meeting. Not knowing any of them by sight, I had no
means of determining whether or not they were in
the congregation. But I wasn't long in doubt, for I
hadn't more than taken my text when a clay ball
came whizzing past my head. Pretending not to
have noticed it, I proceeded. Pretty soon there sped
another one, and with better aim. It struck me square
upon the bosom of my white shirt, the only vanity I
possessed, and the only white shirt, too, for that matter. A laugh broke out. Oh, any of them would
rather have seen a fight than to have heard a sermon.
The fight wasn't long in coming. I heard some one
exclaim: "By the Eternal!" Then I saw Jackson
in among a number of rough men, cracking their

heads with a cane, right and left. And when they made a show of resistance he whipped out his knife, and not only quelled them, but compelled them to come forward, take a seat on the front bench and listen attentively to my sermon.''

''That not only aroused your gratitude but must have challenged your admiration,'' said I, with the picture of the fight in my mind.

''Yes, but it had a sad termination. Jackson spoiled it all by a subsequent action. That very afternoon, I saw him with a game-cock under his arm going over the creek to have a fight. But I reprimanded him.''

''How did he take it?'' I inquired.

''With a slight inclination of the head and with his peculiar half smile. This attitude led me to believe that he was repentant; but he spoiled that, too, and by a very irreverant remark. 'Parson,' said he, 'if the Lord had made you as game as this bird, I reckon you could preach most anywhere.' That was no way to talk to me.''

''But there was truth in it,'' said I; and flouncing still farther away from me he declared with much irritation: ''Young sir, that is no way to talk to me. I bid you good night.''

Early on the following day, Jackson and I set forth on our journey to Nashville. He bade me good morning, and said nothing more for some time, and then he remarked:

''I like your modesty, sir.''

Not aware that I was modest this surprised me. But I made no denial; I bowed and waited for him to explain. He did.

''Last night when you inquired my name, you did

not give me your own. That was not like the youth
of the present day, sir; it was more like the self-sup-
pression of a day that has gone. Now, sir, on this
impudent rim of experimental time, a young fellow is
likely to shout his own name the moment he sees you,
believing that you cannot help but find interest in it.
What is your name?''

"Richard Staggs, sir.''

"Staggs, eh? Related to Potter Staggs?''

"He was my father.''

"Ah; you say he *was* your father. Dead?''

"Yes, sir, both my mother and father—were
drowned while crossing a river nearly five years
ago.''

"I am sorry. I remember him—he was kind to me.
Years ago when I was a boy, I stopped at his house—
bleeding, sir. Your father was very young, had just
been married.''

"You say you were bleeding.''

"I was. A British officer had ordered me to clean
his boots; and, by the Eternal, I told him that I
would see him in hell first. With that he came down
upon me with his sword. I warded off the blow, but
my hand and my head were cut. Your father dressed
the wound—cared for me until I was able to go on
my way. And now, tell me, what is it your intention
to do in Nashville?''

"It is my wish to be a part of that new community.
But as to just what sort of a part I don't know. It
was my father's aim, as I have understood, and I
know that it was the aim of my guardian, who died
recently, that I should be put to the law, and with
that end in view I went to school.''

"And you think that now you have education

enough to enable you to become a good lawyer, I suppose. But before you answer, let me assure you that I have never seen a young man go into study of the law with education enough. There is in Nashville a comparatively new institution and a very worthy one, known as the Davidson Academy. I am one of the trustees of it, and I advise you to go there for at least one term before beginning the study of the law. Do not urge, sir, that you are not able financially. I will arrange that part of it. So that is settled. Young man, it has always been the keenest grief of my life that I was not schooled so as to read of the great Greek and Latin heroes in the language in which their exploits were first recorded. Years ago, some one gave me Chapman's Homer, and when I read it, I wept bitterly because I could not read the original; and I struggled hard to acquaint myself with that knowledge, but the time was passed, my mind was too rebellious. Have you read the great poets in the original, sir?"

I answered that I had, after a perfunctory fashion, and ventured to add that so far as I was able to judge, the poets would take their own time in helping me toward any achievement in the practice of the law. Toward me he turned that strangely grave face; and he was in the sunlight now, but still a dark majesty. In his countenance there was nothing born of darkness —his eyes seemed gray, shooting blue spears of light; his hair, borrowing of the future, had begun slightly to turn gray, and yet to me a general view of him was dark. It must have been his avenging spirit that had taken hold upon my senses.

"Everything that teaches you human nature leads you to achievement in the law," he said. "Poetry is the blossom in the forest of human nature. Mark me, sir, I didn't say rhyme; I said poetry.''

"In your family, beyond the seas, there must have been poets," I suggested, and thus he answered, after riding for a time in silence: "In my family there has always been rebels against oppressive authority, and the poet may be the lawless champion of the human heart.'' Suddenly he broke off: "But in America, our poetry is not gentle measures, but heavy blows. Other countries may have reached the state where they may muse, but with us, it's—fight. And a man is but a part of the country; and to do anything—he must fight. If a man isn't willing at all times to die for what he believes to be right, then he is not fit to live. Honesty, not backed by courage, is but a one-legged virtue. A brave man will become honest eventually, if you give him a chance.''

I might not have agreed with him in all that he said, but I took no issue; I listened.

"If you would be a leader, you must inspire not love, but admiration tinctured with fear. We take persuasive issue with one we love; we are bold to tell him he is wrong, but if we fear him, we wait, half believing that he may be right.''

Was he experimenting with himself or with me? I have known men, great men, too, that experimented with themselves, seeking to draw themselves out, as it were, and sometimes I have fancied that they wondered as to what they might say next. No man lives up to or down to the discoveries which he makes in himself; no man wholly acts the better or the worse part of his talking self; and the mind is sometimes as aimless when we are awake as when we sleep.

Along toward noon, we halted at an inn near the

roadside. Here were gathered a number of men engaged in holding a local election. My companion was at once keenly alive. I was hungry and went straightway into the dining-room, but he remained outside, and when I returned to him, I found that he had canvassed the merits of the three candidates for Justice of the Peace, hitherto strangers to him, and was standing on a stump hotly advocating the claims of one of them. His assertions were dogmatic and his manner was violent. He swore that unless Joyce were elected the neighborhood would sink into moral nothingness. Hilton, another candidate, resented the interference, and then there was a fight. Joyce, who was present, showed the white feather; and Jackson, turning from him in disgust, threw his influence over to Hilton, who had stood up for himself—until he had been knocked down. The polls were not to close until four o'clock, and my companion would not listen to a hint at departure until the votes had been counted. Some of the men addressed him as General and some as Judge, and every one showed him great respect, especially Hilton, who had been introduced to two of his most active forces, his enmity and his advocacy. When the ballots had been counted it was found that Hilton had won by the handsome plurality of three votes, and then the General could not leave until after he had taken part in the celebration of the victory.

CHAPTER IV

THE JOLLY FERRYMAN.

IT WAS nearly nightfall when we mounted our horses again. Large quantities of whisky, greened with bruised mint, had been served, but the General had partaken sparingly, and his mood seemed to have been sobered rather than enlivened.

The moon arose and the graceful hills were flooded with light. The world seemed one great poem in accents of silver. In the sunlight the General had spoken of the poets, and I expected now to hear him break forth in rhapsody over them, now that we were in their natural zone, the moonlight, amid the shadowy, mysterious etchings; his mind, however, was not upon poetic hill-tops, but down in political jungles.

"The man who makes politics a profession may not be a good citizen, and still he is a far better citizen than the man who neglects to vote. In this regard, negligence is a crime. There are men, both North and South who already have begun to talk about a possible dissolution of this union. Such men ought to be hanged as high as Haman. Better that every man in the country should be dead than that the country should be divided. Power can come only from solidity. Richard, shall I tell you what is my life dream?"

"If you please, sir," I answered.

He turned his face toward me, and in the light of

the moon I could see the gleam of his strange, thrilling smile.

"Richard, with her sword old England struck me —a defenseless boy—a poverty-stricken boy; and, by the Eternal, it is my dream that she shall pay for it. With money? No, with her best blood. In a cabin in Ireland my people starved. Across the sea there lay a promise, and they left their endeared home, of starvation, and came over here, but the hand of oppression was reached forth after and clutched them—struck me with a sword, and to the grave I shall carry the scar, but I will make a scar on England's brow and she shall wear it."

I wondered if all great men were such egotists. That they are, years of subsequent observation have convinced me. The man of action must believe in himself. It is only the deep thinker that is made weak by a want of faith. This man's most quiet meditation seemed to look forward to action. That part of thought which is a sort of graceful sloth was not of him. His friends were to be many and blindly ardent, and his restless enemies were to inhabit the earth. Thousands of views were to be written of his character. I have read many of these estimates, some of them written by the ablest thinkers of the age. Acknowledging only average intelligence and deploring crudeness of expression, yet out of the vanity of my personal contact with him, I feel that here and there, I may discover in his character a light, a shade, a whim, that escaped the observation of those who looked wholly up or wholly down, gazing rather than searching. The university lays slow hold upon a violence of temperament and tones it down to hair-splitting polemics; and I believe that Andrew Jackson's violence in action was resultant from his inability to find at the right time the doctrinaire word. He expressed himself physically. This applies more particularly to the latter years of his life.

About eleven o'clock in the night we came to a river. The opposite shore, shrouded with shadows, seemed miles away. There was a boat, chained and padlocked to a tree. We shouted for the ferryman but there was no answer. Nowhere was there a light; but the General said that the ferryman lived on a hill not far away, and instructed me to go to his cabin and request him to set us over the river.

The house faced from the road, and I saw no gleam of light until I had gone around in front and then I discovered that a lamp was burning within. The door was open. I heard voices; and looking in I saw, seated about a blanket spread upon the floor, three men playing cards. Standing at the door, I spoke, asking if the ferryman were present. One of the men looked up and answered:

"He is, but he ain't doin' no ferryin' to-night."

"It isn't very late, and it is necessary that Judge Jackson and I should cross the river."

"Well," he answered, playing a card, "a man that's smart enough to be a judge ought to have patience enough to wait."

"Well put, Crutcher," cried out one of his companions. "I tell you, Crutch, he's got sense enough to be a judge himself."

"Much ableeged to you," said the ferryman, acknowledging the compliment; and then he added, speaking to me: "Good night, before the dogs bite you."

"HOLD ON, SIR, HOLD ON,"

"And must I tell the Judge that you refuse to set him over the river?"

"As I am feelin' particular well to-night, I don't care what you tell him. Pass the bottle. It's my drink, and Timothy's smell of the cork."

Just then Jackson passed me, with swift stride, into the house. I followed him. The ferryman was drinking out of a bottle.

"I don't mind visitors as a general thing," said he, putting the bottle aside and wiping his mouth, "but I don't like for 'em to be so infernal sudden. Anybody ask you fellows to take a hand?"

"No," answered the General, reminding me of a calm that was almost a silence, "but we ask you to take a hand and to put it to the oar. I beg your pardon for interrupting your game, but I take it that you are a licensed ferryman, and I therefore demand that you row us over the river or lend us your boat, just as you please."

"To that I could say all right, but I won't; I'll say all wrong."

"Meaning that you'll do neither?"

"You guess putty well."

That was all the guessing that was done. Jackson's pistols were out in less than a second; and giving the fellow a kick he said:

"Get up."

"Hold on, sir, hold on; that't just what I was thinkin' about doin' myself. You must be the Andy Jackson that I've heard 'em talk about."

He was up. "Timothy, you an' Dave run things here till I come back."

All three were on their feet. The one addressed as

Timothy appeared to be drunker than his companions.

"Crutch, I'll be hung, draw'd and quartered if I'd go down thar this time o' night unless I wanted to," he said.

"Now, Timothy, you wouldn't be so unaccommodatin', would you?"

"Lead on," commanded the General, "I'm waiting."

"Yes, sir, as soon as I find my key to the padlock. Here it is. Would have 'lowed that I left it in my other clothes, but happened to recollect that I ain't got none."

The General ordered him to go in advance of us, and he took the lead as cheerfully as if he had been conducting an expedition purely for his own pleasure. He broke out in song.

The river was swift, but Crutch knew his business and soon had us across. I thought that finally he would haggle about the price, but his mind had soared so high above such trifles that he insisted upon tendering our passage as a compliment due from himself; and when the General had forced him to accept his regular fee, he took it with a bow of deep gratitude.

"General," he said, "whenever you come along this way, no matter how deep I am in the game— whether it's my drink or Timothy's smell of the cork, you just holler and I'll be with you. Good night; mighty glad you dropped by to see me."

CHAPTER V.

IN THOSE days, Nashville was a small town, but to me it was a city. It was in the afternoon when we entered the place. The streets were crowded with buyers and sellers, and surely I had never beheld so busy a scene. There were great ox wagons loaded with tobacco, and the river was covered with flat boats weighted down with timber to be used in the construction of the many houses that were building.

As we passed through the streets toward the inn where we were to lodge, many of the people bowed to the General, and not a few of them came from the sidewalks, out into the mud, to shake him by the hand. The inn was a great structure, built of logs, and must have contained as many as ten rooms. In this hostelry there was a ball that evening, and I had an opportunity to look in upon the beauty and the fashion of the place. In the main hallway a little misunderstanding took place, concerning some women, I gathered; and a man was stabbed, but he did not die immediately, and thus what might have been a damper upon the gaiety of the occasion was happily averted. The sheriff came around to see the gentleman who had done the stabbing, but learning that it was in the defense of a woman's honor, bade him good night and returned to the livery stable, where the

two best known bulldogs of the community were to
fight, bets running high on each side.

Nothing further had been said concerning my mat-
riculation at the Davidson Academy, and believing
that I possessed sufficient education to fit me for an
immediate beginning in the study of the law, I hoped
that the General had forgotten having proposed it.
I was not, however, given much time for speculation.
On the following morning, while we were at breakfast
he said to me:

"Richard, to-day I am going to the Hermitage, my
home, about twelve miles up the river, but before setting out I will go with you to the academy to see
that you are properly entered there. As I said before, you must not take the expense into account.
Andrew Jackson never left a debt unpaid, never permitted an obligation to fade dim in his memory."

"But, sir," I interposed in the mildest manner possible, "what my father did for you he would have
done for any one else, and did not expect you to remember it as an obligation."

"Ah, and therefore the more generous, and the
more reason I should have to discharge the debt. Over
at Mrs. Crenshaw's, on Cherry street, you will find
an excellent boarding place. She was at the ball here
last night, and I meant to introduce you to her, but
just at that time something happened to distract my
attention. However, I spoke to her concerning you,
and all the arrangements have been made. If you
are diligent in the academy, as I know you will be,
you may, in a year's time, enter the law department."

"It shall be as you desire," I answered, and smiling he replied: "Becomingly meek for a young man
who owns two horse pistols."

I bowed my acknowledgments. "It is true that I have very little money at present," said I, "but I have—well, distant prospects in Virginia."

"We will not discuss them, sir, be they far or near. Did you mingle any in society last night? I left the ball rather early. It was a desperate fight—I mean the dog fight around at the stable. There was an English gentleman present, conceited to an unbearable degree, persistent in the assertion of his opinion that Cliff Robinson's dog would be the victor. I remarked to him that I might defer to his superior knowledge of ceremony, in a drawing-room in London, but that in an American livery stable I conceded nothing. Rather than to anger this seemed to please him, and taking out his wallet he remarked that he had a few pounds that he was willing to lay upon his judgment. I had some American money which did not seem fated to be taken out of the country by him, and I bet him one hundred dollars. Saveley's dog was the favorite, the better proportioned, and it surprised me, sir, that a world sportsman should choose the other animal."

"I hope you won, sir."

"I thank you for your interest, Richard, but that Englishman walked off yawning, with my money. Saveley's dog was killed; and, sir, I should not have minded it so much if he had died game. But he didn't; he howled before he died."

Ah, they have never succeeded in sainting this man. Nor have his enemies ever acknowledged the unostentatious but certain moral reformation that came upon him. Historians take into account the age in which a man has lived; the world grows more moral, gentler. But at the time of which I write, with the exception, perhaps, of New England, which was dark and intol-

erant under Puritanic restraint, society was loth to
condemn a man for drinking or gambling. And out
of this atmosphere there arose great men, not because of the taint in average life, but because they
were strong enough to withstand temptation or to re-
form; and I remember having heard an old fellow
say, "It ain't what he refuses to do in this life that
makes a man strong—it's what he quits doin'."

After breakfast we repaired to the academy, the
most pretentious school that I had ever seen, and here
I was solemnly entered as a student.

"And now," said the General, as I walked down
the hill with him, to see him on his way home, "remember that the harder you work the better you will
please me. I shall see you from time to time, as I am
in town every few days; and when Mrs. Jackson returns—she is now visiting relatives in Kentucky—I
shall expect you to come out and break bread with
me at my own table. Ah, let me see. There was
something else that I was going to say. Yes, I recall. Get along with your fellow students the best
you can, but always bear in mind that you are to
suffer no indignity whatever. 'Better be with the
dead,' sir, said a poet whom I *can* read in the original;
'better be with the dead.' "

He shook my hand and left me, striding slowly
down the gently sloping path, a picture of majesty,
as if he had conquered every inch of ground on
which he set his foot.

On this day I resumed my neglected studies. But
looking back, it seems to me that our system of education was most impractical; and the further back
you go, the more impractical it appears, until you
wander to the groves of Greece, where young men

were taught to memorize poetry and fancies called philosophy; and from these groves they were sent forth into the streets, orators, indeed, but exhibiting no advancement over their predecessors. In the rude states of America, education was little better than a rhapsody committed to memory. It was thought that the mind ought to be more graceful with vague theory before it should be strengthened with practical truth. My instructor was an Irishman, mellow with humor. His name was Mahone; and, what seemed strange to me, he was inclined to be a free thinker, a term which in those days meant a dark reproach. The circuit rider who had flounced over in bed from me had accused me justly when he declared that I had read Tom Paine, whom I believed a true worshiper of wondrous Nature's God.

CHAPTER VI.

ARABELLA CRENSHAW.

M AHONE made up to me at "recess," invited me to take a walk with him, and when we had reached a lonely spot down in the woods, he drew forth a bottle and bade me help myself. I declined, and he seemed hurt.

"Oh, don't be exclusive just because your sponsor here is one of the gamest men in the world to-day. Come, now, how are you ever to get at the spirit of the poets in Old Ireland if you don't take just a wee bit? And this came from the Old Sod. I'm sure the General himself would jump at the chance like a fish at a worm. That's right, drink it while you're smiling, for a smile adds zest to good liquor."

I took a swallow, and he clapped me on the shoulder. "Ah, surely now you have matriculated. The Irish poets would claim you as one of their own— brawny lad that you are. Ah, I have seen many a one of them set sail across the sea, for their only home, America; and one of these days they will go back again, I am thinking, with rods in their hands to scourge the oppressor. Let us walk down further on, in the valley, yonder where the grass is so green. Sure it is like the old home."

I went with him down into the cool depths of the green valley, and plucking up a handful of the rich grass he sprinkled it upon his bare head.

38

"I know your mother must have been Irish," he said, his eyes beaming upon me.

"She was," I answered.

"Ah, I could see it in your fine countenance, sir; blessed be her name." He turned about and looked up toward the schoolhouse, on the hill. "It is not all of them up there that hold Old Ireland dear in their hearts, sir; they are democrats, but they take pride in their English ancestry. I don't blame them for that, mind you, but no matter how great a country may be, no man should be proud of her lack of heart and sympathy. In England they sigh over the slave trade, but cry 'traitor' if one weeps over the suffering in Ireland. And now, in memory of that suffering, we will take just another wee drop—in silence."

"Not for me, Professor; with me the drinking of liquor would be a crime. It shoots through my blood and makes me restless; besides, there is not more than enough in the bottle for yourself. You'll need to sympathize again later in the day."

He clapped me on the shoulder. "Ah, what a broth of a lad. You would teach an Irishman to be provident; and, ah, sir, that is a degree that no university can confer."

He drank again, his sympathy showing in his eyes; and then he asked me to sit with him upon a green bank, beneath a red haw tree, to keep him company while he smoked his pipe—a bit of clay as black as any pot. With a flint and steel he struck a light, and for a time he smoked with a succession of loud smacks, seeming greatly to enjoy the exertion.

"I believe you are coming over to board at the Widow Crenshaw's," he said. Then he smacked his mouth louder than before. "There's a young widow among a million, sir; and I am sure that if her husband hadn't been killed he must sooner or later have died of joy. The likes of her eyes was never seen before, and her smile—" he took the pipe out of his mouth and slowly shook his head. "Shall I ever get over that smile? And the young fellows are all breaking their necks after her, bad luck to them; and I suppose you will be, too. Won't you now? Come tell me."

I strove to assure him that I was not much given that way, but he shook his head. "I have been trying to induce her to skip my looks and to center her beautiful mind on my spirit," he continued, "and sometimes I think she does, but not always, sir; she laughs, but I don't know whether she laughs at me or with me. But no matter. The man that takes her away from me will have a struggle to the end. I think you will have trouble with Lismukes, sir."

"Lismukes! Who is he?"

"The leading young man of our school. He expects every student to pay him homage."

"He needn't expect it of me," I hotly replied.

"There spoke a man. But he will."

"And he will find out that I won't."

"Ah, such beautiful talk cheers me to the soul of me," said the professor. In a way he was a scholar, but, above all, a native of Ireland. "Lismukes is off now on leave of absence," he continued, slowly smoking, "and will be gone as long as it suits his fancy. You might say that he runs things pretty much to suit himself, simply because no one cares to have trouble with him, knowing that it might be far-reaching in its results. His people, some of them, are educated

in a way, but the majority of them are tough custom-
ers. They have no fondness for Andrew Jackson.
They have come to remember him. He had trouble
with one of them while he was judge. The affair
is famous throughout this part of the country. The
fellow, a ruffian who in Ireland would have had his
head constantly broken with a blackthorne, committed
a depredation and swore that they shouldn't arrest
him. He came to the place where Jackson was holding court, and parading up and down in front of the
Hall of Justice, flourished his weapons and defied the
very name of law. The Judge ordered the sheriff to
arrest him, and the sheriff, who had no nerve at all,
went out and begged the ruffian to let himself be arrested, for the good of society; and the fellow, cock-
ing his pistols and raising his voice into a bawdy song,
improvised an oratorio to the effect that society might
be damned. This greatly humiliated the sheriff, for
he had a daughter in society at the time—was attending a quilting party that very day; and so he begged
the ruffian to revise and to modify his sweeping statement, but he wouldn't. The sheriff being a man of
few words, refused to argue with him, and, being
also a man of quick decision, decided to withdraw
from the contest and to report to the Judge that the
ruffian was in no humor to be arrested. Then the
Judge ordered that he himself might be summoned,
which was done; and out he went with a pistol in
each hand, walked up to the fellow who was entertaining a party of admirers, scared him into fits and
then arrested the fits. When asked afterward why
he didn't shoot the Judge, he said: 'I couldn't. With
his knife-blade eyes he had cut my nerves in two.'
Yet the fellow was game, for afterward he shot a

man under most unfavorable circumstances. I tell you this to show what sort of a faction you will have to deal with unless you pay homage to Lismukes.''

I felt my blood bubble with heat. I, the son of a man who, every one had said, did not know the meaning of the word "fear!" Should I stand in awe of this—this fellow, whatever his name might be? The Irishman enjoyed my anger. I wondered if Lismukes had been in Jackson's mind when he warned me to put up with no indignities.

"But there is one thing that we may both congratulate ourselves on, which is that Lismukes does not live at the house of the charming Mrs. Crenshaw,'' said the professor.

"It wouldn't make any difference to me if he did,'' I answered.

"Possibly not,'' the schoolman agreed, "but it would make a big difference to me.''

"How have you managed not to have trouble with this fellow?'' I inquired.

"For the reason that I made up my mind to put up with everything from him until after a certain event takes place, and then I will break every bone in his body and leave the country. The event I refer to is my marriage with Mrs. Crenshaw.''

I inquired as to what difference his marriage could make, and slowly he shook his head. "Ah, sir, they are distantly related, and it is singular, but out here in this wild country it would seem that blood is thicker than matrimony—much thicker than mine with her if I should have a fight with him beforehand.'' His pipe was out. Again he struck the flint and steel together, caught a spark in the fluffy tow and relighted it. My anger, stirred by the absent Mr.

Lismukes, had cooled—and this man's humors made
my nerves laugh.

"You will be moving into your new home about
supper time," said he. "And then, sir, you will see
one of the grandest sights that ever fell to mortal
view—Mrs. Crenshaw, sitting at the head of the table,
all unconscious of the fact that she is the most beautiful woman in the world."

Now he was becoming tiresome. Humor, individuality, character, all are alike when they prate of the
object of their love. All the world may love a lover
if all the world's in love, but I was not. I was one
of the few youngsters who had not fallen in love with
a dame almost old enough to be their mother.

Soon we returned to the academy, new shades of
ancient learning, and during the remainder of the
day I was busy with odes and philippics. In the
evening I returned to the inn, gathered up my scant
belongings, and repaired to the Widow Crenshaw's
home, the chief physical characteristic of which was
its construction of "frame" rather than of logs. The
mansion of the town, it was set back from the street
in the midst of a grove of graceful trees. Mahone
met me at the hall door and conducted me into a large
sitting-room, furnished, as you must know, to suggest
necessary economy rather than extravagance. On
the walls there were several portraits, one of a woman
stroking the head of a stag hound, and another of a
man with a hawk resting on his head. Mahone was
quick to tell me that they were family portraits, one
representing the widow and the other her husband,
which I surmised; but I did not quite understand the
significance of the hawk until my friend assured me
that the late Mr. Crenshaw was of a very ancient

house, dating back to the time when hawking was the favorite pastime of kings. Both portraits had been done about two years before by a Frenchman who had come up from New Orleans, and who had exchanged these works of art for six months domiciliary accommodations, as the professor termed it. Mr. Crenshaw's death had been sudden, if not instantaneous, he having been kicked by a horse that was much pestered by flies. It was a sad, not to say a mean, ending for a man whose kinsfolk had sent hawks sailing against the wind; still, it might have been worse, for the horse was a blooded animal and had been "complimented" by Governor John Sevier.

After a time several other boarders entered the room; Judge Black, who had been a Justice of the Peace in North Carolina, a young storekeeper named Harvey, and a woman who was looking for her husband, having heard that he had come down the Cumberland River on a raft of logs. She put on her spectacles, looked at me and slowly shook her head. Evidently, I was not her husband. Judge Black had heard of me—not that I was of good family or that I had done ought to commend myself to the public, but that I was the reputed owner of a fine horse. He shook me heartily by the hand and inquired the age of my horse.

"We welcome you to our rapidly developing city," said he, reaching for my hand again and giving it another squeeze. "We have need of young and enthusiastic blood. What will you take for your horse?"

I answered that I was not on the look-out for a purchaser, which, adding value to the animal, caused the Judge to smile upon me with renewed light. Soon there came the ringing of a bell, mellow as a cow-

bell rung at sunset—and the Judge, forgetting me,
and perhaps with a dimmer memory of my horse, hastened toward a door opening off into another room.
The bell had announced supper. Mahone took me by
the arm, led me to the head of the table and presented
me to Mrs. Arabella Crenshaw; and, as I bowed low,
the Judge brayed out: "The young man that owns
the horse."

Mrs. Crenshaw smiled and said: "I am much
pleased to meet you, Mr. Horse—I beg your pardon,
I mean Mr. Staggs."

The Judge clapped me on the shoulder as if I had
been complimented by the widow's mistake, and the
woman whose husband had been rafted away from
her, coughed and remarked that such "verbal mis-
haps" were most natural, as she had often made them
herself.

Mrs. Crenshaw laughed like a dove cooing, and
Mahone whispered to me: "Did you ever hear the
like of that?" It was music, melancholy and sweet;
and I looked into Mrs. Crenshaw's eyes, into the
great depths of them, where mischief sprites were
sporting in an azure sea. I said something, a foolish
something, of course; and down from a black cloud
floating above the sea, there shot one of the family's
ancestral hawks, and I knew that she had made a
witty reply, for I heard the company laughing and
felt myself grow red.

Some scribbler wrote, "a woman's glory-mark is
thirty." This woman had not reached this golden
age. It seemed that she was just old enough for what
she was, a charming widow, a conscious wringer of
hearts. But in those days I was ignorant. Ah, and
who shall say that as man grows older he grows wiser?

It is true that he knows more of man, and it is true, also, that he may know less of woman.

Nature said to the mathematician: "I will give you a problem which you cannot solve." Time passed; and the mathematician, in the ripeness of his victorious years, inquired of Nature: "Where is the problem you were to give me—the one I could not solve?" And Nature smiled and thus made answer: "I gave it to you years ago—your wife." And the mathematician bowed his head and was mute.

The widow laughed, and spring-time waters were loosened in the hills. Well could I now catch at the spirit of the schoolman's infatuation. She passed the bread, and I felt that she had knighted me; she smiled, and for a moment I knew that I wore a crown.

"General Jackson has spoken so highly of you, Mr. Staggs, and we are so pleased to have you with us," she said, and I whispered to the Irishman: "Did you ever hear the like of that?" And it seemed that his eyes groaned in jealousy as he looked at me. Was I in love, too? Oh, no; but for her sake, I would do homage to Lismukes, her ruffian kinsman; with reverent hands I would tallow his rawhide boots, curry his horse, give him my own.

"Don't you think we have a charming city for so new a place?" sweetly she made remark, passing a platter of fried venison; and with a lump of gold in my throat I answered: "Madam, while approaching it, had I seen all its charms, I should have thought it the new Jerusalem, coming down out of the clouds."

"Oh, you blasphemous boy," she cried, and perhaps I said it, perhaps dreamed afterward that I did say it to the Irishman: "Sweep me a place on the floor, that I may fall there and at her feet expire in humiliation.'' Waving my knife, and doubtless at my own throat, I shouted that I was not a blasphemer but a worshiper. At this moment Judge Black's voice hammered at my ear:

"Is your horse a single footer?"

"Oh, yes, do tell us something about his accomplishments," cried Arabella. I could no longer think of her as Mrs. Crenshaw, no matter if the kings who had the honor of establishing her husband's family hawked the skies.

"Madam," I answered, bowing low over the gravy, "to-morrow you shall ride him—ride him to the place of your nativity, the end of a June rainbow—if you promise to come back to us."

She dropped a napkin to clap her hands, and that which had been a dip candle but now a Jove-torch, seemed to sweep my cheek with its flame. She told me that I was not eating anything. How could she have said that? Eating! I was eating *her*. She handed a glass of milk to the Irishman, and I wondered as to the exact time on the following day when I should kill him.

When we returned to the sitting-room, Harvey, the merchant, asked me if I would like to walk down to the store with him. Store! My pistols were not within reach, and so, I did not shoot him, except with a look that ought to have been fatal. And what was it that Arabella was saying? "Oh, I think you would enjoy a visit to Mr. Harvey's store—it's such an emporium of trade."

Trade at this time, when there should be no barter save the exchange of sentiment, the swapping of poetry! She said that she would like to go, and Ajax,

Hercules—could not have held me. I swore that I was charmed with emporiums, loved them; and when she bade me tie the ribbons of her bonnet beneath her chin, I did not believe that I could possibly live through it, or wish to survive it. She laughed at me; declared me awkward; and as we were going out it is a thousand wonders that I didn't butt my head against the door, so completely had I lost control of it. The Irishman stepped forward, offered his arm; and she took it—and I walked with the "emporium."

CHAPTER VII.

SOMETIMES beneath a lamp hung in front of a door, she would turn her face back toward me, and at such times the Irishman would hasten her forward into the dark again. Through black gaps I reached the store. The proud young merchant lighted the candles and showed us his stock of goods, brought in wagons and on pack mules from distant Philadelphia. How her eyes sparkled as she viewed a piece of silk; and the sordid wretch, the merchant, stood there and saw her covet it—looked on without emotion—did not fall upon his knees and beg of her to accept it. Ah, but if he had, surely I should have slain him and set fire to his house.

I cannot recall an incident of our return, except that walking with the Irishman she looked back at me. I don't know how I got into the house, up the stairway, into my room. I remember dropping down upon the bed, hillock of feathers—remember staring at the ceiling till the candle burned out, and then, of gazing upward into the dark. A wink and it was still dark; another wink and the sun was shining. I sprang from the bed and looked out through the window, down into the front yard, and there was Arabella, with sleeves rolled up, watering the flowers. She looked as if she had slept in the moon, brought down about her head the raveled dawn, and absorbed the early sunbeams with her snappy eyes. There

49

came the sounds of rapid hoofs, and then a majestic figure was at the gate—General Jackson. She waved a kiss at him as he dismounted; and then he took her hand and gallantly touched it with his lips.

"You are just in time for breakfast," she said. "There's the bell now."

"You townspeople are lazy. I breakfasted more than two hours ago," he answered. "Ah, my young friend Staggs—isn't he up yet?"

She said that she thought not, slowly walking with him toward the house.

"He is a fine and spirited young man, madam."

Why didn't she speak out so that I could hear? What was that? An amusing boy? Oh, and was that all? And this, after my devotion. Now there was but one course for me to pursue, to treat her with the contempt she deserved.

The General greeted me cordially as I entered the sitting-room. Arabella—or rather the widow of that pretentious fellow named Crenshaw—was not present, and it was just as well for her that she was not. What difference, however, could it make to me? I had dismissed her from my mind. Perhaps she was right. Her age warranted the remark that I was an amusing boy, but after this she would not find me so amusing. I would humiliate her with her own ignorance.

"Of course you haven't had time to get your bearings," said the General, "but how do you like your school thus far?"

"I am much pleased with it, sir."

"I am glad to hear you say so. I never attended one half so good."

"But to genius, sir," I answered, "one school is as good as another."

He smiled, and I can see him now as he stood on the hearth, his back toward the fireplace. "Young man, genius is will. Creative force is will. The meek tell us that God is love, but I know that God is *will*. And they who have within them more of will for good have inherited more of the spirit of the Master. Some of the mightiest minds have been impatient of the minutia of learning. There was many a drill sergeant that could give Washington points, and I cannot imagine Shakespeare tying the wing-tips of his soaring mind with that hempen string—a rule in grammar. Just now, sir, you paid me a high compliment, inferring that I am a genius. I am not; I have had a disappointment that convinced me. I had thought that to take a seat in the United States Senate would surely develop certain latent powers that I felt within me, but upon attaining this exalted position I found that I was out of place. Able men arose and contented themselves with the splitting of hairs when, by the Eternal, I had thought to see them break chains. I felt myself out of place, and so I resigned my seat and came back home. If I am to be quiet, let me be quiet in private life."

At this moment, the widow appeared at the door, and smiling upon me—but it was lost—asked me if I would be so obliging as to walk out to breakfast. The General said that he would come, too, and take a cup of coffee.

"There is one thing when I am ill that I always tell the physician," he remarked as he seated himself at the table, "and that is that he may save himself the trouble of ordering me to give up coffee and tobacco. Dr. Robinson once told me that I had to leave off my pipe, and on this occasion I came near doing it, not because of his advice, but because Mrs. Jackson decided in his favor; but, happily, I won her over to my side. There is nothing so sweet as an old pipe, and when a man, who for years has tasted of its sweetness, gives it up, he lives the remainder of his life in impenetrable solitude. He may attain riches and see his ambitions rounded out to full measure, but he will be alone, with nothing to look forward to; he will live in the past. Therefore, Richard, don't wed yourself to the habit of smoking."

"Bravo!" cried the Irishman; and Judge Black looked up and remarked:

"Yes, and good liquor is right hard to quit, too."

"But I should think," said Crenshaw's widow, "that a man could give up anything for the woman he loves." The Irishman's jaw dropped. She appealed to him: "Don't you think so, Professor?"

"Surely, surely," he answered, looking forward to his pipe beneath the trees after breakfast.

"What do you think, Mr. Richard?" she asked of me.

"It may be an evidence of a man's love when he gives up everything, but it's no proof of a woman's love when she asks it," I answered.

"Very reasonable, sir," the General spoke up, and instead of showing resentment, which I thought she would, the widow looked up with a smile.

"But," she said, "a woman must know whether or not a man loves her before she gives herself to him, and she can't take merely his word—men have so many words for women, you know. Don't you think so, Professor?"

"Surely, surely," cried Mahone.

"How easy it is to be a coward," I whispered to

him, and in a whisper he answered: "And, sir, at times how impossible not to be."

I kept my eyes off the woman. I was free now. Cool judgment had emancipated me; but there was such music in her voice that whenever she spoke I felt myself trembling.

I thought that the General might have something of particular moment to say to me, but he had not. As we were walking out beneath the trees after breakfast, he said that he had come to town on business, as he did nearly every day. "And no matter what your aspirations are, you must not despise business, Richard," said he. "Such a disposition has ruined many a lawyer. When I was a candidate for Major General of militia, it was brought against me that I had kept a country store, but I made no denial of it." He halted in his speech and smiled. "I was keeping a country store at that time. The necessary attention given to any sort of business makes us executive, and the most successful kings have been men of business. So, don't think that success in the practice of the law depends wholly upon oratory. I was thinking that it would not be a bad idea for you to go down to Harvey's store, of a Saturday, and help him out, just for the experience."

Gratitude sometimes makes a liar of a man, and I answered that I thought it an excellent idea. This pleased him. And what was it I would not have done to have won his approbation?

He walked with Mahone and me toward the school. The poetry of the morning and a smile from the widow gave exuberance to the Irishman's spirits. The man who is easy to cast down is easy to elate. It is stubborn virtue that stands cool upon a knoll of the middle ground, knowing not moments of supreme happiness because unacquainted with the depths of misery. Mahone knew both extremes, and I believe nearly all Irishmen do. If they do not, charge the failure to their nearness to Scotland.

"You seem to be happy this morning," said the General.

"I am that same, sir," Mahone answered.

"Creditable to a good night's rest, I presume."

"Ah, to a good morning and a look, sir."

"The Widow Crenshaw?"

"The same, sir. She has as good as confessed that my love is not in vain."

"You are hopeful," said the General, and in a second it seemed that the uplifting spring fell out of the Irishman's walk.

"Do you think it was only my hope, sir? Do you think that? I thought it was the look that gave me the hope, forgetting that out of my own hope might have come what I thought to be the look. You gentlemen walk on. I will return to the house just for a moment, to satisfy myself."

We halted and the General apologized. "I have discouraged you, sir, and I regret it."

"Oh, not at all," the Irishman declared, but I could see that his heart was low. He turned back, and we walked on, slowly. "She will never marry him," said the General. I was silent, wondering whom she would marry. "She was never happy with her husband," the General remarked.

"You surprise me, sir. I thought that she and her husband were devoted to each other."

"Oh, no. She was much Crenshaw's superior. And besides, he was not a brave man. No matter how

timid a woman may be, she has a contempt for a man
when she discovers that he is wanting in physical
courage. One night at a ball a man asked Mrs. Crenshaw to dance with him. She declined and he said
something rude to her. She told her husband. He
demanded an apology from the fellow. It was not
given, and Crenshaw—took his wife home, sir. After
that they did not get along well together. She has
her faults, but Mrs. Jackson and I are very fond of
her. If she were faultless, she would not seem so
much a daughter to me. I have never known but one
faultless woman—Mrs. Jackson, sir; and Heaven sent
her to me, not as a reward for any good I may have
done, but as a stimulus toward good in the future.''

He halted and looked back over the pathway.
''Well, I will leave you here, with another assurance
that as soon as Mrs. Jackson returns, you shall break
bread at our house. Ah, one word more concerning
Mrs. Crenshaw: I take you to be a sensible young
fellow, and therefore it may not be necessary to warn
you, but you must know that she is careless with—
hearts. Here comes your friend.''

He bade me good morning, striding down the hill
as he strode before, as if he had conquered every foot
of it; and I waited for Mahone, observing long before he came up to where I stood that his spirits were
heavy.

''I walk on the earth a dead man, Master Richard.''

''Yes, but your death doesn't give you the leave to
call me *Master* Richard. I am nearly twenty years
old, sir.''

''I beg your pardon, Mr. Richard, but a dead man
ought not to be accountable for what he says. I
went back there and she killed me. She says, says she,

sitting on a chain with one pretty foot on a stool—a
negro girl brushing her hair—'oh,' says she, 'why
did you come back so soon?' All of my wits flew
away, and like the fool that I was, I said that I had
come back after my pipe; and she pouted and tapped
her foot upon the stool and answered: 'Oh, I thought
you told me you'd quit smoking.' It was then that
I became a corpse—a most ordinary and uninteresting corpse."

We were now near the school and he slackened his
pace, remarking as he dragged his feet along: "Last
night for a time you made me sick with jealousy, but
then I discovered that she cared nothing for you."

"You did, did you? And I wish you to understand
that I don't give a snap for her."

This did not offend him. Indeed, he was so grateful that he halted and insisted upon shaking hands
with me.

"IT WAS THEN THAT I BECAME A CORPSE."

CHAPTER VIII.

A MONG the members of my class in a very pretentious study, and of which we learned but little save a few names—in our class in astronomy was a young fellow named Atcherson. We sat at the same desk where we could look out through a window upon the green country. On this, my second morning, Atcherson said to me: "The Irishman is deep down in the valley to-day. The widow must have winked at you. And she'll wink at anybody. There's no more sympathy in her heart than there is in a catamount's. Oh, I know her—I had my whirl with her—I wasn't much over seventeen, but I had my whirl, just as you will have—just as everybody has. I boarded there for a week. I was born· and brought up in Philadelphia, and necessarily must have seen a good many women, but I never saw one to equal her."

"But she's ignorant, isn't she?" I ventured, and he answered: "Don't you fool yourself there. She's read more than either of us ever did. She is the dove that's as wise as the serpent. Cal Lismukes is a sort of cousin of hers, but she wrung his heart like wringing the neck of a chicken—and they say that he lay down on the ground and actually bawled."

"But," said I, with a sore spot in my mind, if not in my heart, "I believe she will marry Mahone."

"He's got just as much chance in the next world,

57

where they are not given in marriage. I'm sorry for
him, for he's a good fellow and as game as a pea-
cock."

I was not happy during that day; I was sorry for
Mahone. As for myself—why, I was thoroughly
cured. That night there was company in our sitting-
room, young women and young men, but I gave to
them none of my attention. I gathered my book and
sat down in a corner alone; but I tore out a leaf and
chewed it up, hating all the world, and especially
that woman who stood smiling in her devilish grace.
After a time she came over to me and said:

"Old Luke, the fiddler, has come and we are going
to have a dance. Won't you please join us? Please,
come on and dance with me, won't you?"

I didn't wish to create a scene; I hoped that I was
a gentleman, so I yielded. And when the company
were all gone and I was lying in bed, I mused in deep
self-reproach that I had been exceedingly happy.
Then followed days when I did not seem to know anything. I sat with Atcherson, and in a sort of skeleton
way I walked with Mahone, of an evening, but all
was vague.

One evening—it must have been a week later—the
Irishman's services were required at the school, and
I was left at home, alone with Arabella. For a time
the stupid Harvey had sat about, contributing an occasional husk, some bit of fodder, relative to trade;
but finally he went down to the emporium, thinking,
doubtless, that he might possibly sell a yard of red
calico. And now we were alone, I and this princess.
How I had misjudged her; how envy had slandered
her. It could not be denied that she had wrought
misery, but this was no fault of her own; it was the

fault of the riot that nature had run with her, of the
wasteful glory of her hair, the re-caught and intensi-
fied Paradise light in her eyes. We walked across
the room to look at a picture that I had seen a hundred times, and returning, shoulders touching, sat
down together on a sofa. The windows were up, and
from a garden of roses nearby, there came a breeze
ladened with a perfume rich almost to intoxication.
Had there ever been such another night? The moon
was at the full, and birds that had followed civilization from the older haunts of men, poured forth their
melody—tribute to this most wondrous hour of sky
and air.

"At one time you were angry at me," she said,
and a stupid, intoxicated calf replied, "At you?"

"Yes. For days at a time you scarcely spoke to
me."

And a liar answered: "I was deep in the study
of my books—to make myself more worthy of your
regard."

"How aptly spoken you are. You must already
have studied hard."

"No, for not until lately did I have an incentive."

"And where did you find one lately?"

"In this house."

"This house," she said looking upward, her eyes
throwing light upon the ceiling, "it is not old, but it
has a history. It was to this place that Mr. Crenshaw brought me—a girl, a mere child—"

"Oh, let us not talk about him," I moaned.

"Why not, pray? Wasn't he my husband?"

"Yes, and that's the reason I don't want to talk
about him. Arabella, listen to me, I—"

"Why *Richard!*"

"You must listen—you shall. In your sight I may be only an amusing boy, but I shall soon be a man— I'm growing old very fast now—have been for some time, and I have prospects in Virginia that will make me rich. I love you and I offer you everything."

"And your horse, too, Richard?"

"Oh, everything—my life."

"But what am I to do with all this? What use am I to make of it all, and what compensation can I offer?"

"Is it possible you don't catch my meaning?" I groaned. "Arabella, you must be my wife."

"Oh, Richard, how you shock me. Marry you! I couldn't think of such a thing. Why, what would General Jackson say?"

"He would say that you'd make a man of me. Arabella I—"

"Oh, but Richard, I haven't time to be making men out of boys, you know."

"But if you did not intend to marry me, why did you encourage me?"

"Encourage you! Why how can you say that? Of course I have encouraged you in a way, because I do think so much of you—more of you than of anybody in the world, so there, doesn't that satisfy you?"

Satisfy me! It brought about a greater hunger, a starvation; and I dropped upon my knees. Suddenly she sprang to her feet with a cry: "Cousin Cal Lismukes, where did you come from?"

Before I could possibly spring to my feet—and I was not slow—I saw him, standing at the window, holding the curtain aside, looking in upon us. Arabella flew to the door, opened it and called him, but he continued to stand at the window, with his eyes fixed on me. She went out after him, brought him into the hall-way and led him into the room.

"Cousin Cal Lismukes, this is my young friend Richard—I mean Mr. Staggs."

He gave me a short nod. "How are you, Mr. Staggs?"

I gave him a nod as short as his own and told him that I was well, a fact which I expected soon to be compelled to prove to him.

"Please be seated," said Arabella. "Cousin Cal, you sit over here on the sofa by me."

He sat down beside her, and she looked up at him with a smile that made me sick at heart; and meeting her look he said:

"Don't shut off your smile, Arabella. There's no harm in it for me now—I am cured. But I see you are up to your old tricks. How long have you known this fellow? Ten minutes?"

"Sir!" I exclaimed, but with mellow laughter Arabella drowned me into silence. "Why, Cousin Cal, he lives here—goes to the Academy."

"Oh, he does."

How I hated him! How my blood stewed as I looked at him.

"I have just returned," said he, "found my room-mate drunk, the inn stocked up two in a bed, and I'd like to find lodgings here tonight."

"I haven't a spare bed, Cousin Cal, but perhaps Mr. Richard wouldn't mind sharing his bed with you. I know he would to oblige me."

"Surely," I cried, in imitation of Mahone, but my cry was weak.

"No, we won't put things to that strain," he said. "I'll go over on the hill and if Jim isn't sober enough

to sleep with, I'll throw him out. Good-night, Mr.
Staggs," he said, showing no disposition to depart.

"Yes, good night, Richard," she rang in her silver
bell to chime with that cankered brass. "I'll see you
in the morning. Pleasant dreams!"

Thus was I driven out, and fuming I trod my way
up to bed. In the dark I stroked my pistols, with my
mind on that brute. How any woman could think of
loving him—how any woman could call him even
cousin! Tall, high shouldered, angular, with a snarl
for a mouth and two evil lights for eyes, he was a
man to be shunned. I say a man, for he must have
been nearing thirty, and I couldn't see what object
he had in attending the school, but soon I learned
that he was there only as a student of the law. The
Irishman's assertion that I was likely to have trouble
with this fellow was not to be wondered at, for now
in my heart I felt that I should be compelled to kill
him. I heard him take his leave of her. I went to
the window and looked down upon them as they
stood on the flag-stones that paved the way from the
front door to the gate.

"Oh, I'm not going to have any trouble with him,"
I heard Lismukes say, as she stood near him, seeming-
ly looking up into his face; and I knew that she had
been pleading for me. "Why should I?" he went
on. "It's nothing to me how much any fool thinks
of you. You didn't care anything for me and were
honest enough to tell me so. Why don't you be equal-
ly honest with him?"

"Why, Cousin Cal, he is a mere boy."

"Then why don't you box his jaws if he's too young
to understand what you tell him? You can tell some
people plainly enough."

"I told you I loved you as a cousin," she answered in a voice sweet and low.

"Oh, that was all right," he answered. "I got over it in a day—hurt my pride a little at first and that was all. I am not a man to favor any woman long— I'm not put up that way. The best thing you ever did for me was to refuse to marry me. Why, the man that marries you will have to shoot some fellow at least every other day—or night."

"If I didn't know you so well I should feel insulted. But," she laughed, "having to kill a fellow every other day—or night—wouldn't inconvenience you; it would be to your liking."

"Would it? Well, I haven't committed murder yet, and that's some little credit."

"You have shaded it pretty close, however, Cousin Calvin. It took you some time to explain to a very easy court why you killed young Nevins; and I've heard that if General Jackson had been judge at the time you would have stretched hemp. These were the words of—"

"Jackson himself, I reckon," he broke in. "But that's all right as far as it goes, but it doesn't lead to anything. The question is, are you going to let me have the money?"

"I would if I could, cousin, but I really cannot. I should have to mortgage my house."

"Well, that would be all right. I'd take it up on time."

"No, I will not risk it."

"Then I withdraw my promise."

"What promise?"

"That I will not seek trouble with that young fool."

"Oh, Cousin Calvin, you couldn't have chosen a

poorer way to threaten me. Good-night. Let us part friends, won't you?"

"I must part with a better understanding concerning the thousand dollars. I tell you I must have it, to save the old home in North Carolina."

"Good-night, pleasant dreams," she said.

"Good-night, and no promises," he answered, turning abruptly from her and striding rapidly toward the gate.

CHAPTER IX.

IN THE INTEREST OF ANOTHER.

WHEN a fool is suddenly cured, it would seem that the days of miracles were not yet over. On the following morning, I went down the stairs cured, not of my admiration for Mrs. Crenshaw, but of my blind folly toward Arabella. On this day there was no session of the school, the day being Saturday, and I sought an early opportunity to "explain" myself to the widow. There was nothing to explain, it is true,—nothing to say except to assure her that I had been foolish, of which there was no need; but it seemed to me that I had something of almost desperate importance to say to her. And as I sat at the breakfast table, staring out into the yard, I wondered if the world would look the same after I had said it. Would that bush with its pink flowers be just as bright? Would that robin's song be just as full of melody? Then I wondered as to what I was going to say to her, and then sat speechless as to what I could possibly say. At the head of the table, in her short sleeves—and somehow I could always see her arms—she poured the coffee, and her voice belonged to the sweet clear notes of the morning, and her eyes were of the garden where the dew was sparkling. Yes, I came down the stairs cured of my folly; still I didn't exactly like the smile she gave to the Irishman.

Remembering the General's suggestion regarding

my holiday employment at Harvey's store, I spoke to
the merchant, who sat opposite me, offering my services. He had not the graciousness to thank me, but
he did not appear displeased, and so long as Commerce does not frown, you have not committed against
it an unpardonable sin.

"Oh, you can come in whenever you feel like it.
Glad to have you and all that, but I can't use you—
got two clerks already."

"I should think it would be charming to sell
goods," said—well, I had determined to think of her
as Arabella until after my final "explanation" with
her.

"Don't you think it would be just as charming to
buy 'em?" Judge Black spoke up.

"To wear them," she suggested, beaming in turn
upon us all.

"The woman spoke that time," said Harvey; and
I wondered if he were quite as much mutton-head as
he looked.

"What do you know about women?" the Judge
inquired.

"What do I know about them? Funny question to
ask me, Judge. I know all about them. I am a business man."

"But does that give you any particular insight into woman's character?"

"Of course. For woman, with all her sentiment is
—business."

The brute. I looked at Arabella, and had she given
me the slightest encouragement I would have thrown
him out of the dining-room.

"Mr. Harvey hasn't a very high opinion of us,"
she said.

"Oh, yes," he answered. "Woman is very necessary."

"Is it possible!" she cried. "What an admission."

"Sir," gallantly roared the Judge, "woman rounds
out and completes the glory of creation. Sir, your
mother was a woman."

"Yes, a fact attested by my own recollection, by
tradition and the family Bible. She is still living, in
Virginia, and adorns a charming circle in society.
And whenever I meet a woman with as many as one-
third of her virtues I'll marry her or find out the reason why I can't."

The Judge bowed. "You have redeemed yourself,
sir," he said.

During this time the Irishman had said nothing.
Now he spoke. "The Anglo-Saxon turns to his mother
with affection and admiration—the Irishman turns to
his mother with love and with tears. He recalls her
sad song as she labored from morning till late in the
night, battling against oppression, starving herself to
give him a start in life. And if there had been no
heaven, justice would have created one for her."

Mahone had spoken with much feeling, and it
pleased me when Arabella smiled upon him, which she
did as a reward, and I saw him tremble and I knew
that his great heart was arising strong within him.
But after breakfast I wished that he would go away,
to give me an opportunity to explain. When the
others had taken their leave, he and I sat in the shade
on the front veranda. I asked him if he had seen Lismukes.

"No, has he come back?"

"He returned last night and I met him, and he insulted me."

"He couldn't have helped that, sir. His mere presence was quite enough for that. He is a desperate fellow, and you must pocket up a wrong or cock a pistol."

"I have two," I answered.

He placed his hand upon my arm. "To fight for cause is a virtue, but patience is a virtue, too. Remember that."

"Yes, and I'll have patience until the time comes, and then he will force me to kill him."

"He is a fine shot, Richard. You can't shoot him down in the road—you'll have to meet him according to custom. And when you do, escape on your part will be almost a miracle. It is well enough to be brave, but it's a crime to throw your life away."

"But he is going to pick a quarrel with me. I heard him say as much, to Arabella, as he was taking his leave of her last night, standing out there near the gate; and she pleaded with him in my behalf."

"Angel that she is," he replied. "Ah, did you see the look she gave me this morning? And surely, Richard, in that look there must have been love."

I was willing that he should be "characteristic," but he was never interesting when he speculated upon Arabella's looks or intentions—relative to himself. From some distant part of the house came her voice, singing; and looking at this man, my friend, I saw his blood leap. With regard to my feelings toward her I was deceiving him. But I would do so no longer.

"Professor—my friend," said I, "you have shown me your heart, with Arabella pictured upon it, but I have not shown you mine, with that same picture there in purple. Last night I declared my love for her, but this morning I am going to withdraw it and stand as advocate of your cause."

He clutched my arm, and we sat staring at each other, earnest and "mottled fools in the forest." He muttered, and I knew that his grateful heart, muffled in its own emotion, was striving to express gratitude. Man, drowning in the sea of love not only clutches at the straw, but at the fleeting shadow thrown by the insect's gossamer wing. "Leave me alone with her for a short time this morning," said I; "go over into the valley and smoke your pipe beneath the red haw tree."

Simultaneously we arose, moved by the resolve of one great purpose. He grasped my hand, and doubtless in unconscious reminiscence of some old Dublin play, he said: "I go."

I went with him to the gate and opened it for him. He passed through but halted and faced about. "Yes, I go." The distance was not more than half a mile but it was a "sentimental journey," and the significance of such journeys is not measured by the county surveyor. "Richard, in your hands I place my future. I have not had the courage to tell her of my love, but you tell her. She has a high opinion of your veracity and I think she will believe you. Withdrawing in my favor you show the unselfish nobility of your nature. I would have done the same for you— will do it now if you say so."

He made as if he would open the gate, to re-enter the yard, but in his eyes there was a look that begged me to shove him out into the road, to knock him down, to keep him from the sacrifice.

"To the red haw tree," I commanded. 1 had seen a play myself, in Raleigh, done by a company that brought medals from London and exhibited them on a board, leaning against the front entrance of the livery stable.

In violent gratitude he grasped my hand, pressed it against the top bar of the gate and said: "I thank you." With that he turned quickly and hastened away. Now had I taken upon myself the greatest mission of my life, and slowly I walked back toward the house. I heard Arabella singing as she came down the stairs and going into the sitting-room I waited for her, bold in the magnanimity of my cause—until she entered, and then my hands fell off into embarrassed fumblings, and I squeaked that I had something of importance to say to her.

"But for pity sake don't be so scared about it," she answered, plucking a rose from her hair and playfully throwing it at me. Confound it, could woman never be fair in her dealings with a heart? I caught the rose and pressed it to my lips. The despot laughed. She sat down on the sofa and bade me sit beside her. Through the window a ray of sunlight streamed and revealed a yellowish spot on her cheek. How slight a defect in woman will sometimes serve to make a man strong with her!

"Arabella."

"Sir!"   .

"Mrs. Crenshaw."

"Yes, sir."

"Last night I was very foolish."

"With my Cousin Calvin?"

"With you. Your Cousin Calvin doesn't exist, so far as I am concerned."

"Sophomoric declaimer, they will send you to the legislature. But proceed. You were foolish with me, and now you are going to be foolish again. Eh?"

That "eh" was a pop to a silken whip. "No, I am going to be strong with you."

She shouted with laughter, snatched the rose out of my hand, plucked off a leaf, puffed it towards me, like a thistle-down, and asked me if she should bring the rope.

"The rope? What for?"

"I didn't know but in your strength you were going to tie my hands."

"I would rather tie your heart."

"Now you are getting weak again," she said, pretending disappointment. "I hoped you were going to be strong—I like to look at men when they are strong."

"I am not going to be weak, Mrs. Crenshaw."

"Oh, then you are going to disappoint me. I didn't think you'd do that. Are you going to tell me what an old fright I am? That's the way men are strong with women. What are you going to do?"

"Arabella."

"Yes, sir."

"Last night I told you I loved you."

"Did you? Oh, of course you did, just as Cousin Calvin appeared at the window. How embarrassing that must have been—for you."

"Will you please be serious with me?" I implored, and she answered: "Not if you are going to be serious with me."

"But I am going to be serious and, therefore, sensible with myself," I insisted. "You persist in regarding me as a mere boy, and—"

"As a boy somewhat overgrown intellectually," she broke in—"as a pedantic boy. And don't you

know that such boys can make themselves very disa-
greeable to women?"

"Mrs. Crenshaw, I am not to be driven from my
purpose."

"Gracious me, child, then let us get at it, whatever
it is."

"I don't like that tone."

"Of course not, but the purpose. Let us get at it."

"I am here to acknowledge that last night I was
exceedingly foolish."

"Yes, go ahead, but you have already acknowledged
that."

"Well, then, let me now accent the acknowledgment by withdrawing from my former position."

"Why then, you don't love me any longer?"

She plucked at my sleeve and I knew that her eyes
were searching for mine, but I knew that to meet them
would mean surrender, and so, bowed over, I gazed
down at the floor.

"No one can help loving you," I said. "You are
surely not the handsomest woman in the world, but I
do believe you are one of the most powerful. You
have a thousand little traps, baited with graces, and
these traps are constantly snapping; but I am reciting
to you your own primer."

"Your own poem, Mr. Richard."

"Snap went another trap," I replied, and my blood
danced to the music of a jingling rhyme—she was
laughing. When she ceased laughing she said that
she was listening. That is a way a woman has of
assuring a man that whatever he may say can possess
no interest for her.

"Mrs. Crenshaw, let us be friends."

"Yes, dear friends," she answered quickly, and

again she plucked at my sleeve, but I did not look up at her.

"Entertaining the sentiment of friendship rather than the sentimentality of love," I said.

"Put aside Clarissa Harlowe and tell me what you mean," she replied.

"I do not need to put aside something which I have not taken up, but I can tell you what I mean. I am now talking in the interest of another."

"I should not have suspected it."

"But I am—of a man who loves you down to the depths of measureless devotion; a man, the most honorable of his—of his sex—Professor Mahone. I have crushed myself to withdraw in his favor, and I urge you to listen to his suit."

"You silly boy, look at me and let me tell you something."

"I must not look at you. If I did, you could tell me only one thing to make me listen—that you love me."

"What a March hare you are; but if you withhold your eyes you will at least grant me your ears. Perhaps in many respects I am the silliest creature you have ever met. I love admiration—it seems my very air, but at times I can be sensible and I am going to be sensible now. I know that my time is slipping away, and that I should be making the most of it, but I am not. I am shaking the dewdrops from the honey-suckle—trying to catch them in my mouth. No matter how much I might love you I couldn't marry you. You are only an intoxicated boy, threatening even now to open your eyes and to find yourself sober."

"But I am not asking you to marry me."

"Ah, you are sober."

She plucked again at my sleeve and I looked into her eyes and they were laughing at me.

"You are a charming, great, big, awkward boy, Richard, and one of these days the community's finest woman will be proud to call you husband. And now, after I have told you so much, won't you promise me something—that you will try in every possible way to avoid trouble with Calvin Lismukes? Oh, you don't know how desperate he is. Human life doesn't mean anything to him—not a thing; and he is one of the deadliest shots in the whole country."

"But to tell me how deadly a shot he is can have no weight in keeping down trouble between him and me. I may be a deadly shot, too."

In my mind there was no memory of prowess with the pistol. But all boys, as indeed nearly all men, are gamblers with Fate, standing ready to shake dice with her.

"Oh, yes, of course," she said, "but being a good shot could only inflict harm upon the enemy. It could not save yourself."

"Let us talk about Mahone," said I.

"Oh, yes, about him when you have promised. And you do promise, don't you, because you like—love me."

"I am a fool again and I promise."

"Thank you so much, and I know you will keep your word, for who is it that cannot see in you the soul of honor? And now about Mr. Mahone! He has been most kind and attentive to me, but how do I know he loves me when he has not told me so? But wait, he must not tell me so—now. If he has any such intention let him wait—a little while longer."

"But why should he wait?"

"Oh, you don't understand."

"No, I am willing to swear to that fact."

"But you must not be so ready to swear. I must have time to think, you know. I am almost certain that I shall—consider him favorably, but he must wait two weeks. Doesn't that seem reasonable enough?"

"No, it seems out of all reason. I don't see why he should wait—unless you have some one else in view."

"How can you be so heartless as to say that? Of course I have no one in view. Now go and tell him."

CHAPTER X.

F EELING that I had not been wholly worsted, I hastened out to find Mahone. My heart was not light and yet it was not heavy. Regarding myself as a hero, having yielded to sacrifice, as one who had given up everything for his friend, the humiliation of my own personal loss was not crushing. That yellow blemish on her cheek was a strong feature in my consolation.

I saw Mahone walking up and down, near the red haw tree. With a start he caught sight of my approach and came hastening to meet me. As he drew near I smiled, and then he came running, with his arms held out as if he would gather me from the earth, but I held up my hand and he stumbled into a walk.

"Don't tell me," he said.

"There is nothing bad to tell."

His eyes brightened. "Then tell me."

We walked back to the red haw tree and sat down upon the green bank; and when I had told him, adding encouragements of my own as I proceeded, he put his arm about me and pressed me to him.

"It will be a long time to wait, it is true, Richard," he said, "but when I have waited—oh, when I have waited! I believe it is because she wishes to study her own heart. It can't be that she wishes to investigate my prospects, for she must know already

76

that aside from my energy, I have none at all. Some
times I have been most woefully cast down, but I
have always believed that she is to be my wife. And
now, my boy, what can I do for you?''

"You can be my friend, that's all.''

"I shall be that, until death. Ah, here comes Lismukes.''

My mortal enemy, for only as such could I regard
him, came swinging along down the path. In his
hand he carried a switch and was lashing at his legs.
He whistled, and a dog that had been smelling about
for a rabbit, came out of the briars and ran up to him
and with his switch he lashed the trusting creature
and roared with laughter; the dog howled.

"He's got a good voice,'' said the brute as he came
up to where we were sitting—the two-legged brute,
for compared with him the dog was a Wilberforce in
gentleness and a Chesterfield in manners. "If he
hadn't debased himself with rabbits he might make
music after a fox.''

He halted and stood in front of us, but I did not
bestow upon him the recognition of even a nod.
"Staggs, I believe,'' he said.

"My name is Staggs,'' I answered.

"Yes, met you last night.'' He laughed.

"I believe so.''

"You believe so. Trying to forget, eh?''

"A man that would not try to forget some things
and some people has but a poor opinion of the uses
of his own memory,'' I answered, and rather pleased,
too, I was for what seemed to me a sort of inspiration. Was I forgetting my promise to Arabella? Her
cousin Calvin whistled.

"The dog will not trust you a second time,'' I

could not refrain from saying. Ignoring me he spoke
to the Professor. "Mahone, your little school is getting to be too stupid for me. And I don't know but
I'll find the law just a trifle dull. I am thinking of
joining the army. It would give me scope for my accomplishments, you know. I am better trained in
shooting than in argument."

"You are well trained in both, Mr. Lismukes," the
Irishman answered.

"Yes, but argument is too slow. It takes too long
to convince. Well, I'll bid you good morning.
Staggs—" and he looked hard at me—"I'll see you
again."

He strode away, and when he was beyond the reach
of a low tone, the Professor said:

"Trouble, Richard; I can see it coming."

"And I am not going to humiliate myself in order
to avoid it," I answered. "I promised Arabella, but
I also promised the General that I would put up with
no indignity; and my promise to him was made first.
Why, my father would turn over in his grave—and
my Irish mother, too, if I were to let that hound yelp
over me."

"Yes, I know, but I wish you could put it off two
weeks." He said this in a tone of such comical distress that I had to laugh. He shook his head sadly.

As we were nearing the house we heard Arabella
singing. Mahone grasped my arm and whispered
that she seemed to be happy. She came into the room,
in short sleeves, those graceful arms still showing;
and at the moment of her appearance, Mahone gasped,
as he always did. I thought it a part of my heroism
to leave them alone, and I would have quitted the
room but she gave me a look that commanded me to

stay. She spoke of the beauty of the day, slowly rocking in a chair out of which she had shaken the household cat, and Mahone, sitting beside me on the sofa, whispered in my ear: "Poetry from the Old Sod."

Then she inquired: "Did you see my cousin during your walk?"

"Yes, Madam," Mahone spoke up, "we had a charming talk with him beneath the red haw tree."

"Oh, did you—beneath the red haw; and how appropriately that tree is named, for more than once its roots have been stained with blood. It was there that Anderson shot Pruitt, and there, also, that Menifee fell, shot by Colonel Caruthers. A dueling ground, and so close to a seat of learning."

"At Heidelberg, Madam, and I might say at old Trinity, where merry Oliver got through by the narrowest squeak, they fight in the very halls of learning."

"Professor, I hope you don't defend dueling."

"Ah, Madam, I deplore it from—from the bottom stratum of my soul. It is unchristian."

"How glad I am to hear you say that. You speak of it being unchristian. What church do you attend?"

"The—the Methodist, Madam."

"Are you quite sure?"

"As certain as that I am sitting here, Madam. And it was my mother's hope that I should be a minister."

"How interesting."

"Yes, Madam, and I often regret that her wishes could not be carried out, but the drouth came and I was forced to make my way to America."

"It is not too late yet," she said with a sharp look at me; and this big-hearted liar, believing that all was fair in love, told her that he spent much of his spare time in the study of theology. Again I made a motion to quit the room, but she restrained me with a look.

It was now about noon time, and I was not sorry to hear the Judge's heavy tread upon the veranda. He came in, soon followed by Harvey. The young merchant spoke to us in a business-like way, took a notebook out of his pocket, made a few figures in it, and asked Arabella if dinner were nearly ready. She said that she would see, and went out, and the Irishman gave Harvey a look that was quite enough to over-topple any man not braced and strengthened by business. The Judge asked Harvey if trade were good, and with a swell of pride the young man answered that it was so rushing as to necessitate the early adding of a shed-room to his already extensive establishment. Arabella, who had just re-entered, caught this last remark, and clapping her hands, her sleeves falling back upon her shoulders, she cried out: "Oh, isn't that grand news!"

"Yes," said the merchant, "and the next week's number of the newspaper will have a long account of it."

"And I have some news," the Judge spoke up. "You doubtless recall the lady that was looking for her husband who floated away from home on a raft."

"Yes," said Harvey, "what's become of her? The fact is, I didn't blame her husband for leaving."

"Sir!" cried the Judge, "be careful. She discovered that her husband had been drowned up the river.

She is now at the house of a friend in this town and —sir—is soon to become my wife.''

. "Then, sir, I beg your pardon," said Harvey.

"That is easy enough," the Judge snorted, "but I'll have you to know that men have been called out for less than what your remark implied, sir."

"Gentlemen, gentlemen!" cried Arabella, "remember where you are."

The Judge bowed to her. The business man nodded. The Irishman, student of theology during his spare time, stood fuming, ready to knock some one down for Arabella's sake.

"Yes," said Harvey, "men have been called and some of them had the moral courage not to go. I apologize for making the remark, it was thoughtless, not to say ungentlemanly, and I humbly beg your pardon."

"Spoken like a man," shouted Mahone.

The Judge bowed. "I accept your apology, sir, and am free to express my gratitude that I am not compelled to take further steps in the matter."

"Walk out to dinner," said Arabella.

CHAPTER XI.

A T SCHOOL on the following Monday, Lismukes granted me the distinction of paying no attention to me, and thus it was during the week. A number of times he passed me on the play-ground, our eyes meeting the first time, but we walked on without recognition, and after this we did not so much as look at each other. Atcherson, my desk mate, remarked one day: "Oh, Lismukes is likely to break out when you least expect it. He knows you are not afraid of him, and he's saving you as food for his temper whenever he doesn't happen to feel well. That's a part of his peculiar disposition. It's the way he served young Bethpage; and when the time came he tried to force a challenge. Bethpage was a Quaker and had scruples against fighting. When Lismukes found this out he posted him as a coward and the real cowards nagged the poor fellow until he had to quit school. But you're not a Quaker."

"No more than Mahone is a Methodist," I answered. I had told him of the Irishman's apostasy. And in this we had agreed he was not worse than the great poet Dryden who changed back and forth to suit the humor of that day, when pensions were dearer than the heart's true sentiments. It was just after this talk with Atcherson that the Irishman, at play-time, said to me:

"Only a few more days now to wait, Richard. And

in her precious mind I think she has decided already.''

"But, Professor, what will she say when she finds out that you're not a Methodist?''

He answered with his feet on the "Old Sod": "Begorry, how is she ever to find it out? I can play Methodist as fast as she can ply questions.''

"But you can't deceive her always.''

"Ah, trust true love for deception, sir. And besides, she ought to think more of me to know that I have risked my soul for her. The truth is, friend Richard, that I am not a communicant of any church. Begorry''—with his feet again thrust back upon the "Old Sod"—"for her I could become not only a preacher—but a highwayman, if she insisted. However, neither of the two will be necessary, for when we are married she will find me an ideal landlord.''

"But is she to continue keeping boarders after her marriage?''

We were walking in the green valley. He placed his hand on my arm. "Richard, the feeding of the hungry is a pleasure, and sure it is a brute that would deprive his wife of a harmless enjoyment. Didn't I tell you about her as she sat at the head of the table, a veritable queen? She would adorn any position, but here her grace is supreme, and sure it is a husband's duty not to restrict his wife's graces. In this respect I am not at all jealous. And it's only a week, now.''

"What if she should decline? Have you thought of that?''

He gripped my arm. "I have thought of it Richard, you may well know, and while my belief in the devil is not strong, yet I have thought that it might please him, evil one that he is, thus to punish me for saying that my mother wanted me to be a preacher. Speaking of the evil one, here comes Lismukes."

We were not far from the school building when we met him, and a number of the boys were near. He halted and said:

"Staggs, I have something to say to you."

"Very well, sir, I am here."

"I understand that you have been talking about me."

"Did you understand what it was I said?"

"I understand enough."

"Then that ought to satisfy you."

"It does. It convinces me of something I might have known the moment I saw you—that you reflect the spirit of your sponsor."

"You mean General Jackson? I should like to re- flect his spirit."

Several of the boys came up and stood about.

"Ah, and you say this without a blush. You wish to reflect the spirit of a blackguard and a wife stealer."

"Wife stealer," I echoed, for a moment forgetting myself to muse upon the strangeness of his accusa- tion.

"Oh, you needn't marvel at it—it is well known here. Jackson was boarding at the house of a Mrs. Donaldson, and her daughter Rachel, Mrs. Robards, came from Kentucky to visit her—with her husband. Jackson persuaded her not to return with him, and after a time he took her down to Natchez and brought her back as his wife—said she had been divorced when every one knew that it was a lie—that she was not his wife—that he has her now, another man's wife, and is living with her, in defiance of the law. This man is your champion here, the cause of your being here, you pauper, and you go about, you liar, talking about me.''

I slapped his face.

There was a general outcry. Some of the boys ran away. The Irishman stood beside me. Lismuke's hat had fallen. He stooped to recover it, and as he straightened up I saw an evil glint in his eyes. I had done what it was his aim to provoke. He smiled. He was cool. The perfect understanding had come.

''I suppose you will be in your room this evening,'' he said.

And with a forethought which I imagined did me credit, I answered, ''Not at Mrs. Crenshaw's—at the inn.''

''Very well. Boys, I shall hold personally responsible any one that makes neighborhood news of this little affair. Good-day, Mr. Staggs.''

''Ah, at times he can be almost a gentleman,'' said the Irishman.

CHAPTER XII.

SNEAKED OUT OF THE HOUSE.

AT THE supper table I was pleased to observe that no one seemed to have got wind of the "little difficulty." Arabella was gracious, with her sleeves shorter than ever, the merchant was full of business and the Judge sentimental.

"Mr. Mahone," said Arabella, "you seem to be very thoughtful this evening."

"Ah, Madam, if I appear so, it is because I am restraining myself to keep from being too hilarious," the Irishman answered.

"Were your duties in school pleasant to-day?" she inquired.

"As heart could wish, Madam."

"You are not in the law department, but you must have met my cousin Calvin somewhere on the grounds?"

I began to wonder if she had heard anything.

"Had a very pleasant talk with him in the afternoon. He is a fine talker, Madam."

"Yes, but I wish you wouldn't call me Madam every time you speak."

"I thank you for the suggestion," he said, and this unblushing lover of prevarication proceeded to add: "I had thought of it myself, and as we were coming on home I said to Richard that I didn't much like the word Madam when applied to you and that I should be much pleased to call you Miss."

"Oh, thank you, and if you wish you *may* call me Miss."

"It would tickle me to the soul, Miss, and I shall take the first opportunity of doing so."

"What tomfoolery is all this," spoke up the merchant.

Arabella seemed hurt, and in the Irishman's neck I saw the veins begin to swell. "Say the word, Madam—Miss, I beg your pardon—and out through the window he goes," Mahone exclaimed, striking the table with his fist. She laughed, and the quick perceiving son of Erin bowed to the merchant and begged his pardon. "I wouldn't injure you for the world, sir," he declared, and then added: "And as they say in old Ireland, may your soul be in heaven before the devil knows you're dead."

After supper when Mahone had gone to my room with me I said to him: "You are not to act as my second in this affair. They would turn you out of the school, and besides, Arabella would never speak to you again."

"That is all very true, sir, but when that fellow kills you, you'll find Dan Mahone standing beside you. Didn't you make a great sacrifice for me? Didn't you go to her like the man you are and withdraw in my favor without any hope of reward? You did, sir, and where's the gentleman that could have done more?"

"Dan, my sacrifice amounted to nothing. I had only discovered that she didn't love me, but what is more, that I didn't love her."

"No, sir," he persisted. "You are simply trying to make it easy for me. Then let me make it a little easier on my side. I have discovered that I don't—

don't love her, either; and as for the school, I was thinking about quitting to-morrow—on my soul, yes.''

"Glorious liar," I said to him.

"The truth, Richard, if I ever told it," he declared, but his voice shook and his eyes were cast down. "And besides it all, sir," he continued, "wasn't your mother an Irish woman, and over here far from her native home didn't she sing the old songs to you? And what sort of a traitor would I be not to stand by you now?''

I put my arms about him, there in the candle light where the shadows were dancing. We heard Arabella singing and I felt him quaver against my breast.

"No, Dan, it cannot be," I said. "It would be an insult to Atcherson. I have already put the matter in his hands, and he will meet me at the inn.''

"Are you sure, Richard?''

"On my honor, yes.''

"Then of course I am out of it. But I want you to know—''

"I do know, Dan, and with my last breath I shall thank you, and tell you how true I know your heart is.''

"But I'll go to the inn with you—out to the meeting to see that every thing is square. You can't object to that, and neither can the rest of them.''

"I cannot decline that service, Dan. And it's time now we were going to the inn.''

I brought out my horse pistols and putting them on the bed, stood looking at them, stroked them, wondering which one of them should end their master's life.

Mahone shuddered. "By the Lord, are they to be used?"

"Yes, I have no dueling pistols."

"But they are cannons!"

"Yes, but they give me some shadow of hope, for not being rifled and less true of aim than regular dueling pistols they lessen the difference between that fellow's skill and my awkwardness."

"If you could only shoot with as much directness as you talk! What you say is true—and he'll bat his eyes when he sees these blunderbusses. See, I can almost get my thumb in the bore. Have you got bullets to fit them or will you load them with buckshot?"

"Bullets to fit tight," I answered. "You'll find them in my saddle-bags hanging over there against the wall. Get out half a dozen, please. We'll have to sneak these pistols out. You carry one under your coat and I'll manage the other."

We passed down the stairs and sneaked through the hallway without attracting attention. Nothing would have been thought had we walked out boldly, but the secrecy of the mission built out of every shadow the substance of detection. Out in front sat a man in an open-top buggy. Wondering if it were Atcherson, I spoke, and Harvey, the merchant, answered me.

"What do you suppose he's doing there with that rig?" Mahone remarked as we passed on. "Do you think he's going to take Arabella out riding?"

"She wouldn't ride with him—she has a contempt for him," I answered. "He must have come to take the Judge over to marry the up-river woman—to make stronger his apology for having spoken slightingly of her.''

"Forget your grammar, Richard, and strike at a better explanation. He has come for Arabella. And if this belief in me were a little stronger, I'd walk back and cut his traces. What impudence in him, the calico measurer, to drive with her, and in the night, too.''

Shortly afterward a buggy passed us, but in the dark we could not determine whether it contained one or two persons. Mahone, however, swore that it was Arabella with Harvey. "And to think that I declared myself a Methodist for this," said he. "And I warrant you they are going now to hear some cane-brake preacher roar over his creed. If I had a horse I'd follow them. Richard, I wonder why it is that a widow, no matter how beautiful and pure and high-minded, is full of tricks.''

"She must have learned them from her husband," I answered.

"Ah, you are a wise young dog yourself.''

Atcherson had engaged a room at the inn and was waiting for us. The importance of his office conferred upon him a degree of exceeding gaiety. He seized my hand and congratulated me. He assured us that he had, after paying an extra price, rented the best room in the hostelry, the bridal-chamber, and with many a flourish he conducted us to it, commenting upon the fact that the table had carved legs and that the walls were actually papered.

"Sit down," he said, "and make yourselves at home. I suppose Lismukes' friend will be here pretty soon—Bill Vance, I believe. Of course you know him, Dick. He has acted before and will know exactly what to do—was Lismukes' second when he shot a young medical student over in North Carolina. There is one thing, Dick, you won't have to fear—being crippled. Professor, you'll find that rocking chair more comfortable. Gentlemen don't forget to notice our furniture. Won't have to fear being crippled, Dick. Lismukes is not a maimer—he does complete work.''

"You are very complimentary to the furniture and woefully discouraging to our principal,'' Mahone replied, seating himself in the rocking chair.

"Ah, not at all,'' Atcherson disclaimed. "When all parties know the truth there is no use in attempting to disguise it. Why, Lismukes can't miss Dick. Out of the force of habit he could hit him with his eyes shut.''

"And,'' said I, "with no force of habit, I may possibly kill him with my eyes open.''

"Oh, yes, you've got that to encourage you; but I suppose you've made your will.''

"No, I hadn't thought of that.''

"Well then, you'd better attend to it at once. Professor, would you mind pulling the bell-cord for a lawyer? Hello, we haven't a bell cord; but gentlemen, you must remember that this is the bridal and not the dueling chamber. But there are a score of lawyers about the hotel. Professor, would you mind looking for one?''

The Professor went out. My second continued. "Are those the pistols over there on the bed? Whoppers,'' he exclaimed, taking up one of them. "What is the legal bore for a pistol? Strikes me that this— this hollow log is a little beyond precedent. What would you call this thing? Artillery? Are you

going to load with stones as they did at the battle of
Crécy?''

It did not strike me that he was heartless, for the
age was an age of false gallantry, of hollow laughter
that comes of desperation—an age of morbid honor,
and no matter in how great a degree a man might
stand in abhorrence of death, on account of his re-
sponsibilities here upon earth, to give evidence of it
was a weakness which all gentlemen deplored.

"My father is a Presbyterian, you know, and for
me it was an easy jump into fatalism. So, if your
time has come you might just as well accept it good
humoredly,'' said Atcherson, smiling.

There came a tap at the door. Atcherson opened
it, and with a bow which it seemed he must have
practiced as he came along, Bill Vance entered the
room. He shook hands with me, with Atcherson and
sat down. He spoke of the weather, of the scarcity of
corn, complained of the farmers, and then taking
from his pocket a paper neatly folded, handed it to
me. I glanced at it and passed it over to Atcherson.
Vance arose and with another practiced bow took his
leave. Shortly afterward, Mahone came in with a
lawyer, but before giving my attention to the will, I
drew up a brief answer to the significant communication brought by Vance and gave it to Atcherson,
who withdrew, also with a bow. The lawyer wasted
no time with bowing. He was there on business and
from him was not expected the luxury of over politeness. My will consisted of no long list. For ownership of a few cherished books, my pistols and my
horse, I named my friend Mahone, and my prospects
in a dim Virginia estate I willed to General Jackson.
The lawyer said that five dollars would be enough for

his services, and as Mahone and I between us could
not raise more than three dollars, I was inclined to
think so, too. But the lawyer, being young and accommodating, accepted our meager silver as discharge
in full of the obligation, and withdrew.

"Richard," said the Irishman, "I feel uneasy."

"Quite natural under the circumstances, and still
it can serve no purpose. If my time has come, why
it can't be helped."

"I mean that I'm uneasy about that infernal
buggy. I believe Arabella was with that counter-
jumper."

"But what of it, even if she was? He'll have to
take her home when the time comes."

"Yes, I know, but I don't want her to be riding
around with him. He may not be able to talk silken
but he owns silk, and that goes a devilish long ways
with—a widow. You may talk buckskin to a girl,
but to the majority of women that have been married no oftener even than once, why it must be bright
goods of fine texture. Ah, but what am I growling
about? Didn't she give you her word for me, and
won't she give me her blessed answer less than one
week from to-night? And Richard, you shall be my
best man."

"I may not be here," I answered.

"I beg your pardon, I forgot."

He did not attempt to give me hope; he sat, silent,
slowly rocking himself, tapping his heels on the floor.

"Of course you left all the details to Atcherson,"
he said after a silence that seemed to come from afar,
out of the dark night, settling in the room.

"Yes," I answered, looking toward the pistols,
their brass mountings gleaming in the candle light.

"Ah," said Mahone, "and he goes about it as cheerfully as if it were a Christmas pie, baked by his grandmother. But it's just as well, for whatever you've got to do, do it with a vim. Would you mind if I'd light my pipe?"

"Not at all. Why do you ask?"

"Well, my old clay is pretty fetching and I didn't know but it might disturb your thoughts—on this solemn occasion. Were you ever at a wake? Ah, there's where you encounter more pipes than can walk about the room. The guests are supposed to smoke the new pipes furnished by the host or the hostess as the case may be, but they don't—they puff the gags they bring with them, desiring to feel comfortable and at home. I remember Jerry Ragan. There was a man, Richard. Fight a duel! He wouldn't leave breath enough in a man's body to challenge him. Well, when he died they brought out every old pipe in the neighborhood—and you could smell that wake for ten miles or more. It was the night my father fought with Gorman, a pretty good man, too, Gorman was, but even if he had had no whisky he couldn't have stood up with Dan Mahone, senior. I can't remember much about it, but my mother often told me it was a beautiful fight. That must be Atcherson at the door."

Atcherson came in, his face as bright as the brass on my pistols. He threw his hat on the table and said that everything had been arranged in a most satisfactory manner. The time for the meeting was to be sunrise on the following day, and the place, the red haw tree. "Many is the time I have smoked my pipe there," said Mahone, "but I am afraid that I shall have to avoid that nook hereafter. It was there that Richard and I had our first talk—when I told him of the beautiful widow.''

''It is even more historic than that in my affections, for it was there that I first met Mrs. Crenshaw,'' Atcherson replied. ''I was coming along just before sunset one evening, and there she was. She had playfully thrown her bonnet up into the tree and couldn't get it down.''

''Don't,'' said the Irishman, putting up his hand, ''don't—the picture is too strong for me.''

''And for a long time it was too strong for me, too,'' Atcherson declared. ''Ah, I beg your pardon, I believe you are in love with her at present, Professor.''

''Yes, sir, and shall be till the sun goes down for the last time. But Richard will need sleep and we are keeping him from it.''

''Yes, that's a fact. You are thoughtful, Professor; and as this is one of the times when a man would naturally prefer to be alone, we'd better leave him to himself. Dick, we'll get another room, and don't you be afraid to sleep, for I will call you in plenty of time.''

''One moment,'' said the Professor. ''Did you see Lismukes just now?''

''Yes, he was in the room while Vance and I were completing the arrangements.''

''How did he seem? Regretful?''

''That fellow? I never saw him in as high spirits. He walked up and down the room and whistled, leaving off occasionally to make some pleasant remark. He may be a beast but he's not a coward. And I never saw a man with such confidence in himself. One of the boys told me in a whisper that he went out late

in the afternoon and took a few practice shots with his
pistols.''

"But little good that will do him," Mahone replied.
"And I warrant you his jaw will drop a bit when he
catches sight of Richard's fuzees. He may practice
tills doomsday with rifled barrels and that won't give
him much of a call with these old smooth bores. They
are as whimsical as a woman, and the more powder
you put in, the more they act according to their own
notion. Richard, my boy, we'll see you in the morning. Let the justice of your cause sustain you.''

"Don't try to sustain yourself with anything but
fate," said Atcherson. "Just consider yourself as
having never been born. That's the proper way to
get at it.''

"Our young friend here," remarked Mahone, halting at the door, "has just attained his atheistic majority, which means that he has not cut his philosophical teeth. You'll be a preacher one of these days,
Atcherson.''

"I'm already a preacher of truth," my second
answered. Then he turned to me. "Good night, old
fellow. Dream as pleasantly as you can. This is not
a formal leave-taking, understand. We'll see you
early to-morrow morning.''

Mahone went out last, looking intently upon me
and then carefully closing the door. And now for
the first time a sensation of weakness flew over me,
and I seized hold of the table to steady myself. It
was not fear, it was a weakening wonder if my time
had really come, a flash of cold speculation as to
whether I was prepared to meet it. Suddenly I heard
footsteps approaching my door, heard a voice which
I recognized, and opening the door I stood face to face

with General Jackson. Just behind him stood Mahone. The General held forth his hand with that dignified cordiality that made him so winning both with women and with men.

"I was surprised to learn that you were here, Richard," he said, entering the room. "Why did you quit Mrs. Crenshaw's?"

I offered him a chair, but he remained standing. "Why are you here?" he asked before I had answered him.

"I am here only temporarily, sir."

Just then he caught sight of the pistols on the bed. He looked at me, at Mahone, and then fixing his eye on me, he said:

"I demand to know, sir, what this means? Why have you quitted your abode to come here to nurse pistols at this time of night?"

"The pistols, sir," said I, have been put to bed to be aroused at daylight. Mr. Mahone, I will leave the room while you explain to the General."

I hastened out, glad to escape from the necessity of explaining, because I dreaded to repeat in his presence the words of Lismukes. Not far off I stood waiting in the hallway, intending to give Mahone time enough, and thinking that I had, I was returning when I heard the General exclaim, "By the Eternal!" Then I knew that the climax had been reached. Just outside the door the General met me—gripped me tightly by the arm, drew me into the room. "Richard," he said, and there was that strange smile, but now as cold as frost, "Richard, this affair is mine—I must assume it—I demand it as my right."

"That is impossible, General. The arrangements

have all been made. No, I must meet him to-morrow morning, and if he escapes—he may answer to you. He has insulted me time after time—met me first with an insult, has done everything he could to bring about a meeting, believing that my blood is within his easy reach. Mahone said at first that there was bound to be trouble—Mrs. Crenshaw knew it was coming and made me promise to do everything I could to avoid it, but I could not put up with his insults.''

He took my hand and pressed it hard. ''Richard, for years I have kept on my mantelpiece two pistols, cocked for just such scoundrels as this fellow. And he shall die, if not by your hand, by mine. Richard, and you, Professor Mahone, it is not necessary to explain to you, but I will. In the case of Robarts and his wife, the legislature of the State of Virginia granted a divorce. On this subject that is all I have to say, except that she is as pure as a heaven-sent angel; and when any man breathes suspicion against her fair name, be he Governor or President, I will send his soul to hell. But my brave boy, enough of this. It is of no use for me to tell you to keep your courage up. You will not falter. And when the times comes, aim at his breast, rather low down. Don't risk his head. Those are old army pistols, are they not? I have better ones.''

''They might be better for him and not for me,'' I answered.

''That is true enough, sir. You are thoughtful. Ah, I had come to tell you of Mrs. Jackson's return and to invite you out to visit us, but in this life we can foresee nothing.''

He walked off from me, as straight between the

shoulders as an Indian chief, then returned, and in his eye there was a deadly fire, but with it all a tenderness for me; and I felt my heart swelling with gratitude toward him, so much do the really great demand from us.

"Richard, forgive my harshness in demanding from you the surrender of your right to avenge a gross insult. But you understand my motive."

"I do, General, and appreciate it."

"I thank you. And now we will bid you good night. I shall see you in the morning."

CHAPTER XIII.

AN OLD ACQUAINTANCE FROM THE NURSERY.

IT was now past midnight. I went to the window
and looked out. Nowhere was there a light. I
heard the heavy tread of the watchman, slowly
pacing his round. The candle was burning low, and
I lay down, without undressing, and gazed at the
flickering light as it rose and fell. On the wall the
shadows danced. Suddenly all the world was one
great impenetrable shadow. The candle's flame had
died. I strove to fix my mind on serious subjects but
they eluded me. I thought of a rabbit that I had
caught in a trap, many years ago; of an early play-
mate, a stammering negro boy. My lips fashioned a
prayer, but in my mind there arose a foolish tune I
had heard a boatman whistle. Then there came
nursery rhymes and I wondered why Jack Sprat
could eat no fat. If he were hungry he might have
eaten almost anything. I offered him a piece of meat
on a toasting fork, but he shook his head, declaring
that it was fat. But his wife took it and thanked me,
too. What an engaging creature she was. Of course,
I had met her a number of times, in a casual way,
but somehow this was my first opportunity to get a
good look at her. I asked her why she had married
such an obstinate clown, and she said that it was
because he signed a contract to milk the cow. I inquired as to whether he had kept his agreement, and
she answered that he no doubt would have done so,

but that thus far he had failed to provide the cow. Then she turned her face fuller toward me and I saw a blemish on her cheek. Why, this Mrs. Sprat was Arabella, and she laughed when she found that I had discovered her, and taking down a pair of shears from a nail on the wall she cut off her sleeves, threw her bare arms about my neck and told me that she loved me, had loved me long before Crenshaw's fore-fathers, the kings, had sported with hawks on the downs of England. She kissed me and I asked her why her lips were so cool, and she answered that it was because she had just whistled to a man that had ice for sale. This explanation being satisfactory I permitted her to kiss me again. Then she sprang away from me with the cry, "Cousin Calvin Lis-mukes, where did you come from?" He stood at the window holding the curtain aside, looking in upon us. She led him into the room, and suddenly he was no other than plain Jack Sprat. But he said that I had taken his wife from him and that I should have to pay for it, and when I protested my innocence he swore that I had taken her down to Natchez and brought her back as my wife, and that he was going to shoot me; and with that he snatched a blunderbuss down from the wall and fired—and I jumped off of the bed. Some one was knocking at the door.

It was Atcherson. I opened the door and a flood of light poured into the room. He had brought a candle.

"You're already dressed, eh? It's well enough as we haven't any time to lose. The General and Ma-hone are down stairs, waiting."

He gathered up the pistols, concealed them under his coat, and I followed him down the stairs. The General came forward and took my hand and held it for a few moments. "Your nerves are strong, sir," he said. The sleepy clerk followed us to the door and inquired if we were going out for a hunt.

"For a wolf hunt, sir," the General answered.

The streets were dark, but in the east the sables of night were laced with gray.

Mahone had gripped me by the arm, as was his habit, but had not spoken. After a time, as we walked briskly along, he said:

"I dreamed that Arabella drove over me in a buggy, Richard. On more accounts than one of them my heart is heavy this morning. Did you sleep?"

"Dozed. But I feel strong."

"May the saints make you stronger."

I spoke to the General, who walked just in front of me: "I should think, sir, that it would be best for you not to be seen at the place of meeting. Report would associate you with the arrangements and the conduct of the affair, and that would injure the academy."

"Spoken with Supreme Court precision," laughed Atcherson.

"And with quite as much thought, sir," the General replied. "You are right, Richard. I will halt just a little this side. But remember that I will be near."

"This will be a notable day in the recollection of young Hanie," remarked Atcherson. "He is to be one of the surgeons, and this is his first case."

It was now just light enough to observe that upon saying this he looked back at me.

What an outcry the neighborhood roosters were making. At the edge of the pathway I trod upon a

stick, and it snapped, like a pistol missing fire. From
the river came the song of the early ferryman. I
could hear him plying his oars. It was now Glen-
dower's time, "As is the difference betwixt day and
night, the hour before the heavenly-harnessed team
begins his golden progress in the east."

"I will halt here behind this clump of bushes,"
said the General. He knew the red haw tree, knew
where it was—knew that its roots had been dyed with
blood. Facing about he placed one arm on my shoulder and with the other one took mine. "Richard,"
he said, "I believe in God. Put your trust in Him,
and your aim will be steadier. In England it was
the steadfastness of that trust that enabled the people
to chop off a king's head. Remember, aim low. Ten
bullets fly in mid air where one strikes the ground."

"I shall remember, sir."

He pressed my hand, and we left him, and looking
back I saw him standing near the edge of the thicket,
a majestic statue, carved out of the night and set
there in the graying dawn.

Our party was first to arrive. Atcherson said that
it was because Lismukes always liked to defer a pleasure, to make it last longer.

"It's time now to leave off your joking," Mahone
replied.

"Joking! I'm as serious as a mourner's bench."

We sat down beneath the tree and I asked Mahone
if he wouldn't light his pipe.

"No, Richard, I have smoked here for the last
time."

"There's the rim of the sun," said Atcherson—
"and yonder come the others, surgeons and all.

Steady, everybody. You're making history, and
that ought to be a painstaking business."

Lismukes came up, dressed jauntily. He shook
hands with Atcherson, and offered his hand to Mahone, who declined it with a bow. I did not suppose
that he would grant to me even the heed of a nod, that
he would appear loftily unaware of my presence until
he drew his bead on me, but he could not refrain from
an insult. · "I believe I've forgotten your name," he
said. "Stubbs, is that it? Oh, yes, Staggs. Well,
Mr. Staggs, I am at your service." His second
stepped forward and protested with him. "All
right," he said, "but why this delay?" But he
frowned when he saw my pistols, lying on a shawl.

In position there was no particular advantage to
be sought. The ground was stepped off, ten paces.
The pistols were carefully loaded. We took position.
The rising sun was to my right, his left. One of the
weapons was given to me. I saw that Lismukes had
the other, looking at it—seeming to weigh it. The
signal was to be, one, two, three—fire. I wondered
why I was not more nervous. Had Atcherson's fatalism struck in upon me, and had I perforce accepted
this as my time to die?

Before leveling my pistols to take aim, during that
hour-minute, it seemed that Lismukes was sometimes
close to me, sometimes afar off, on the very edge of
the horizon. When I sighted at him, along the barrel of the pistol he was far away, but coming closer
as the slow counting began. "One" seemed to fall
down out of the sky; "two" came up out of the
ground, from beneath my feet—"three" was weak,
coming from a great distance. And "fire" was a clap

of thunder. Then! All my breath burst out in a gasp, and fainting I fell to the ground. That was all I knew. I remember the gasp, the fall, but nothing more.

CHAPTER XIV.

HE HAD SOMETHING TO TELL.

IT seemed that for hours I was struggling in a continuous attempt to open my eyes. Sometimes there came a low hum into my ears, and once I thought that I heard the General's voice. Then there would fall deep silence and deep darkness. And then it seemed that after a lapse of interminable time my eyes were suddenly torn open; and through my mind a bird, a hawk, was flapping its wings—flown consciousness flying home. I was lying on a bed, in a room not wholly strange to me as I looked about—the bridal chamber of the Nashville inn. My mind was now perfectly clear. General Jackson was standing near the bed, looking down upon me—I heard the rip of some sort of cloth, and then into my nostrils came a scent that turned me deathly sick. But from this I soon rallied—drank something that was given to me in a large spoon. I recognized Hanie, the young surgeon, and observed that he consulted an older man who stood near.

"Do you think he can stand the journey?" General Jackson inquired. And the older physician answered:

"Made as easy as possible, I hardly think it will lessen his chances of recovery."

"Richard," said the General, "I am going to take you home with me. The doctors say you can stand the journey. Out at my house you will receive the

tenderest and most loving care—care that can but in-
sure an early recovery.''

''Yes, sir, I shall be glad to go. Where is Mahone?''

''He comes to the door every five minutes to ask
how you are—he can't stand it in here, looking at you
long at a time, though we have assured him that there
is no immediate danger,'' Dr. Hanie answered. ''Here
he is now.''

The Irishman entered the room. He looked like a
ghost. But he smiled upon seeing that I recognized
him. ''I have something to tell you, Richard,'' said
he.

''But not now,'' the old doctor spoke up.

''I should like to hear it,'' I insisted, but the physician shook his head. Then I asked how long I had
been lying there and the answer was, ''Since the day
before yesterday.''

''Why is the church bell tolling?'' I inquired.

''You must not ask,'' said Mahone.

''That is as bad as telling him,'' said the old doctor.
''At the church they are holding services. It is the
funeral of Lismukes.''

I saw General Jackson's cool smile. ''Did you
kill him?'' I asked.

''You killed him, Richard.''

''I aimed low, as you instructed.''

''But your bullet struck him almost squarely between the eyes. He fired a second before you did, it
seemed. They tell me that your weapon was not dis-
charged until after you were struck.''

''Is this what you were keeping from me, Mahone?''
I asked.

He shook his head. "Something worse," he answered.

"Tell him," said the old doctor. "He seems to be able to stand anything."

Mahone sat down on the edge of the bed, took my hand and proceeded to make such a demonstration that the old physician cautioned him.

"The world has come to an end," said Mahone. "The widow *was* in the buggy with Harvey; and he took her out into the country to the house of a Justice of the Peace and married her. I went to her house the next morning, and that old fossil, Black, that calls himself a judge, was walking up and down in front of the house, just as if nothing had happened, to pinch the vitals of this old earth; and he told me. Then, sir, the devil rose up within me, and I asked him if she were in the house, and he said she was. 'Then, sir,' said I, 'present to her the compliments of Daniel Mahone and assure her that he had the exceeding satisfaction of seeing her cousin Calvin's soul fly away to the devil about sunrise this morning, sir.' And now they may go to the funeral on their wedding journey."

"There," commanded the doctor, "you have said enough."

I was fully alive to what had been said, and I sympathized with Mahone, with, however, a feeling of humor stealing through me—into the right side of my breast, where the wound was—pulling at me sharply, there, and then my mind dwelt upon the man I had killed. It was not, however, with a feeling of regret. Now, in this latter day, when in exultation men crush one another in the financial fight and send women and children weeping to the poorhouse, it may seem that I was wanting in Christian training; brutal. But to my conscience I turned for no palliation of the deed. I had been provoked, I went out to kill him if I could, had killed him, and there were no apologies to be made.

My wound was serious, you may well believe, but not so dangerous, as the physicians, especially the younger one, at first made it appear. The bullet had ranged round, had missed the lung, and had been extracted near the shoulder blade.

The weather was fine, and the journey, twelve miles, up the river to the Hermitage, was not a hardship, after I had been placed on a boat manned by half a dozen able-bodied negroes. The young surgeon accompanied the expedition, pleased to assume entire charge of a patient who necessarily had created a sensation in the neighborhood.

"Am I to go? Mahone inquired, looking with sad appeal at the General, but stepping aboard.

"Yes, sir," Jackson answered, "and you are to remain there until our young friend is thoroughly recovered."

"But what about your duties at the academy, Professor?" I inquired.

"Ah," he answered, "I no longer have any duties there. They informed me this morning that they could manage to get along without my services. They made my—my active sympathy with the duel a pretext for my dismissal, but it was only a pretext, for when I pinned them down to it they declared that I was incompetent, anyway. I told the man that said it that if he would step outside I would give him an example of physical competence that would keep beef on his eyes for the better part of a week, but he declined my invitation, although I assure you it was given in the best possible spirit.''

"You need not worry as to future employment," said the General. "On my estate I need just such a man as you are, and will pay you more than you received at the academy.''

"I thank you, true gentleman that you are and a competent General, too, if it ever comes to the test. I will attend to your affairs the best I can, but you must know, sir, that grief holds me down to the earth. I shall not live long, sir.''

"Let me feel your pulse," said Dr. Hanie.

"Feel of them, sir, and not much good can you get out of them," Mahone replied, thrusting forth his hand. "Weak as a bird's, sir.''

"Strong as an ox," said the doctor.

"I hear you say so, sir, but I know it to be one of the many mistakes of the medical profession.''

General Jackson smiled and remarked: "Perhaps you need bleeding.''

"Ah, General, badinage may be good salve at times, but not for the heart when a woman is its concern, sir.''

"I beg your pardon," said the General. "Those who do not know how to joke should never attempt it. I beg your pardon. The rapid improvement in our young friend here, led my spirits astray. I beg your pardon.''

"Ah, and it was joking that you were with me! I beg your pardon myself for misunderstanding you. I am the last man to feel hurt at a joke. It is joking, sir, that has kept old Ireland's heart from breaking; but as to my own individual heart, it is beyond the medicine of fun. You know the woman well, sir.

the Mrs. Crenshaw that was, and you know what a
fine wife she could have made me if she had only been
a mind to. Then there wouldn't have been any question at the school as to my education and fitness for
the position. But it is too late now; and I have seen
my best days, all of my days, in truth, except a few
remaining dark ones.''

The General appeared to be greatly moved. He
had cause to worship his own wife, for her temper
was sweet, her nature devout; but concerning women
at large, or rather, I should say, in society, this great
man had no judgment whatever. The fact that she
wore skirts, that her eyes were ready to weep—the
fact *in* fact that she was a woman established her in
his mind, if not an angel, as a being but little less in
grace. In his presence no one was permitted to repeat a scandal against a woman, no matter how frail
she might have proved her own character.

"I do not think that Mrs. Crenshaw meant to deceive you, sir," he said. "There must have been
some misunderstanding. Perhaps she looked upon it
all as the mere play of an idle hour."

"She did, and without a doubt," Mahone was quick
to reply. "As her own play and her own hour—all
her own twice over. And if it wouldn't have the
awkward appearance of suicide I'd jump into the
river now."

"God made no man, marking him out for self-de-
struction," said the General. "And whenever a man
does that, regardless of what the cause may be, he insults his Maker."

"But suppose a man is brought face to face with
the fact that he has no further end to serve here upon
earth," Mahone suggested. "What must he do then?"

"He must wait, sir. His sight is too short to penetrate the future, even to the extent of one day. Let him wait, for, by the Eternal, the morrow may bring an obvious duty to be performed, a duty that shall revive his hope."

"If I thought that," said the Irishman, "I'd sit up all night, waiting for to-morrow's sun to rise. But ah, sir, the broken mind may be mended, like a spider mending his web, but there is no mending of a broken heart. The mind has many lives, like a cat, but the heart has only one."

"Sir," said the General, "there is a noble woman waiting for every noble heart. Bide your time."

The boat reached the landing at the Hermitage in the cool of the evening. A negro boy had been sent, horseback, to apprise Mrs. Jackson of our coming, and she was down at the bottom of the garden to meet us. She came forward, embraced the General, and then with gentle touch placed her hand on my brow, walking beside the mattress as they bore it along the path.

CHAPTER XV.

FROM my window I could look out upon the river, and the cool banks upon the opposite shore. It was from those shades that the birds came in the late afternooon to present their opera, in the garden, like Handel driven by neglect out of London to give the Messiah in Dublin. This was Mahone's fancy. "I have read about it, but I have heard my uncle tell of some of its phases not to be read of," said he one evening as he sat beside my bed. "It was a fact, hardly as historic as some facts taken account of by kings, but nevertheless historic, that my father, Daniel Mahone, senior, was in Dublin at the time. What did he know about Handel? Blessed little, I assure you; but he heard that there was to be a show, given by a great man, and that was enough for him. So in he goes, and the first thing that attracted his attention was an understrapper who volunteered the information that he couldn't smoke his pipe in there —one of those country wake pipes, I'm telling you. Now, my father being a polite man, thanked the obliging understrapper, but went right on pulling at the gag. But for a time only. A big six footer came up and knocked the pipe out of my father's mouth, and it was then that the performance began. And my uncle who was present and therefore somewhat mixed up in it assured me without boasting that for a time it was the liveliest opera ever given in the town. It was a great—Richard,'' he suddenly broke off, gazing through the window. "Richard, have you taken note of that young girl here—that beauty? I was talking to her, out in the yard this forenoon. She is very distantly related to Mrs. Jackson and has been adopted as her niece. And sure, St. Patrick would claim her for a niece of his own. Her name is Nettie Blakemore, and she asked me to-day—as true as I am sitting here, how long it would be before they would let her come in and sit here and read to you. Have you taken note of her?''

I had, but I did not know but that she was one of the dreams that had passed through my mind. Since my coming a week had gone by; a week, not of much pain but of weariness. This, though, was made bearable by the kindness, the gentle solicitude of the General and his wife—of every one. And this girl! Then she was not a dream. I thought that she had stood near my bed, smiling upon me, that she had put the hair back out of my eyes, but with the thrill of her touch I seemed to awake, and was alone.

"No, she is not a dream, and yet she can be nothing else," said the Irishman. "She is as yet little more than a child—not sixteen, I should think—with scarcely any of the ways of a woman about her—talks just as if Adam hadn't been turned out of Eden. Let me lift you up and you can see her as she stands now, beneath the plum tree. Now, can you see her?''

I could see her, my dream—with hair blacker than the first night that had fallen on Adam after he *was* turned out of Eden. She wore no bonnet. And when suddenly she leaped to run away, I saw that she wore no shoes.

"She jumps and runs not that she desires to leave

one place to go to another, but on account of the life that is within her," said Mahone. "If a painter could catch her his fortune would be made in any court in Europe. And to think that when you are well enough she is to read to you! Begorry, with such a reward in store, they might shoot me to pieces."

"Dan, have you forgotten the widow?" I asked.

"Sure, sir, and didn't the General command me to? And being employed by him, must I not take his orders? But, confidentially, I will tell you that I have not forgotten her. I loved her, but this young girl—no one could love her for being lost in awe, sir. Aside from the extreme youth of her, I don't see how a man could think of making her his wife. She is an elf, out of the woods, and they must have caught her where the vines were thickest. But, changing the subject, would you mind telling me something? But it is a delicate question."

"I will answer it if I can."

"And you won't feel offended or shocked?"

"I think not. What is it?"

"Well, sir, lying here alone in the dark, when every one else is asleep, do you ever imagine that you see Lismukes?"

"I have dreamed about him a number of times."

"And does it frighten you to dream about him?"

"Not at all."

"How does he look to you?"

"Always insulting. And when I wake, I am never sorry that I killed him."

"And in the dark, too? I should be afraid of him."

"I wasn't afraid of him while he was alive."

"And I should think that he has found that out

himself by this time. Oh, I've some news. I was out
walking on the road this morning and here came driving along Judge Black and his wife—and in that same
buggy, too, I warrant you, that took Arabella away
from me. That was a bad night, Richard. He drew
rein and I had the hardihood to ask him how the
widow was getting along with her new husband—and
the woman laughed right out—she whose husband
came down the river on a raft. And it was a delight
to her to volunteer the information that Arabella
was perfectly happy. And this may be true, but I
wanted to call her a liar. But the news I wanted
to tell you is this: She does not take the death of
her cousin much to heart, neither does she blame you.
He told her he was going to kill you, and when she
asked him why, he answered—'Oh, just for the fun
of seeing him fall!' A lot of fun he got out of it.''

Mrs. Jackson entered the room, followed by a
negress with my supper.

''I wouldn't have him talk too much, Mr. Mahone,''
said the prudent woman; and my friend answered:
''I was just telling him, madam, that he must be
very careful. I have been a student of medicine myself.''

''And gave it up for theology,'' I suggested, determined to punish him for his lying to this gentle,
motherly woman. His jaw dropped. ''There, don't
remind me of my foolish escapades, Richard,'' he
said. ''I have a good deal to answer for, but don't
compel me to answer until the times comes. Ah, here's
the General, fresh from town with all the news.''

The General came in, bowed to his wife as if he
were in the presence of a queen, and then embraced
her with most loving tenderness. I have been an ob-

server in my time, have noted relationships among men and women in society and in the family circle, but in my judgment there was never such unabated consideration, such congeniality, such constant affection as that which characterized the home of Andrew Jackson.

"Mr. Jackson, our patient is doing finely," said my hostess, my nurse, indeed—my mother.

"Coming out like a vine," the General answered. He drew his chair up near the bed, asked me several questions concerning myself, and then addressed himself to Mahone, to discuss affairs on the estate. Here business had many features, planting, boat building, the breeding of fine horses and a mercantile trade of no mean dimensions. It was here that the famous race horse "Truxton" was bred. Jackson's passions were varied, his love for the turf being among the uppermost.

Mahone had been assigned to duty in the general plantation store. It was thought that his "student habits" at the academy would fit him for the almost solitary confinement of book-keeping, but as this did not require all his time, he was promoted to the position of salesman and general manager, to rely upon his own judgment in the event that no one else happened to be near. His first exercise of this function of judgment, or at least the first that marked his initiative inclination, was patriotic in a way. Over the mountains from Philadelphia had driven a book peddler, a young fellow named Billings, afterward known to nearly every school boy in Middle Tennessee. Billings was a literary pioneer, drove a covered wagon, heavily laden with fancies, Walter Scott, from whom the South was to receive her romantic

tone, and the earlier poems of Tom Moore. Mahone
felt under deep obligations to his employer; through
the woods at night he had walked, wondering as to the
quickest and best methods of discharging by a show
of his own worth his debt of gratitude; so from Billings he bought a hundred volumes of Moore, and
stacked them upon a shelf, just above speckled calico
and just beneath brown jeans. The General did not
care particularly for Tom Moore, a melodist rather
than an exponent of action, but his strictures were
not severe. He simply remarked to Mahone that if
business became active in the autumn he might possibly dispose of half of the Moore books, provided
that counterfeit money were accepted. The Irishman grieved for a day, wondering how he could redeem himself. And on this day, not long before the
General returned from town, he had, in his own
opinion, more than succeeded.

"General," said he, "I have worked up a fine trade
to-day."

"I am pleased to hear it, Professor."

"I have, and there's no mistake. I sold one bill for
two hundred and ten dollars."

"You surprise me."

"But it is the Lord's truth, or, rather I should say,
the Saint's truth, since the Lord takes no cognizance
of such matters. Along in the afternoon to-day,
while business was as slack as a rope with nothing
tied to the other end of it, I sat out under the syca-
more tree for a few whiffs at the pipe, when along
came an old gentleman that might have been the
governor of Virginia. He got out of his gig, ah-
hahing a good deal and asked me if I had any water
handy. I told him that as all of the negro boys were

off fishing somewhere I had compensated a white boy
that had ambitions to rise in the world—compensated
him to the extent of giving him a hickory cigar to
fetch me a pail of water, which was still fresh and at
his service. I went with him into the store—I tell
you all this to show you that I am gradually master-
ing the necessary details of trade.''

"Proceed," said the General, "I am listening, sir."

"I thank you. Into the house with him, and after
he had satisfied his thirst he looked about and said
that we had a fine array of goods, and I acknowledged
to him that we had that same. Then he began to ex-
amine our stock and before he could make his escape
I succeeded in selling him a bill of two hundred and
ten dollars' worth, which he carried away himself, to
satisfy my suspicious nature that the sale was genuine. He resides over the river not a great distance
from here, and he said he would settle the account on
the presentation of the bill. He is no other, sir, than
Colonel Lavite Bradshaw.''

I was looking at the General as Mahone concluded.
The master of the Hermitage bowed to his wife and
said: ''Mrs. Jackson, if it is not asking too much,
will you please leave the room while I tell this Irishman that he has played hell!''

"Why, Mr. Jackson!"

"Mrs. Jackson, I humbly beg your pardon."

Mahone's eyes were popping out. "Is it possible
that I have made a mistake, sir," he gasped.

"Only to the extent that you have given my goods
to old Bradshaw. He owes me three hundred already
and is law proof.''

"Will you think of that, now!" cried the Irishman.
"Law proof, and he looked like the law itself! If he

were a younger man, General, I would compensate you."

"If *he* were a younger man?".

"The same, sir. I would go over and take it out of his hide."

It was not often that the General laughed, but he laughed now; and Mrs. Jackson's face beamed with pleasure to see her solemn lord diverted. In that merriment, slight though it was, the Irishman read the pardon of his fault. But he was not wholly to escape.

"Professor," said the General, "I value your services highly, but hereafter when your judgment tells you to do one thing, do the other."

"That is not a bad suggestion," Mahone agreed, heartily accepting it. "My father, Daniel Mahone, was almost a failure till he adopted that same idea with regard to himself."

Mrs. Jackson withdrew and the General said to me: "I have some news for you. But first let me remind you that you have not seen Atcherson since the morning of that unfortunate affair."

"That is true, and several times I have thought to inquire about him, but something always came up to eliminate him from my mind," I answered.

"His grammar again," the Irishman murmured.

"Well, I now have news for you concerning him," said the General. "I met him in town to-day, and a more changed young man, both in appearance and in voice, I don't think I ever saw. The part he played in the duel wrought so heavily upon him that for several nights afterward he couldn't sleep. Just about this time he met a Methodist preacher who was conducting a revival meeting in a church over on the hill; and what did Atcherson do but go over—and drop upon his knees at the mourners' bench. In due time he professed religion and now he is studying for the ministry.''

"I told him so before he knew it himself," said Mahone. "I saw it coming, sir. I can always see such things coming. It is then, sir, that I don't have to depend upon reverse judgment for correctness of view. And I'll warrant you, sir, that he'll make a very troublesome preacher. I don't mean quarrelsome, but persistent, always pulling and hauling, you understand—one of the narrow sort that can never see anything good outside of his own creed.''

"We must give him credit for sincerity," said the man whom they have never succeeded in sainting.

"I shall do that, sir, and at the same time request him to let me walk my own way. Yes, sir, when that fellow was so glib, I thought we should have trouble with him.''

After a time when the General had given me a few words of his usual encouragement, he withdrew into his sitting-room, and soon I heard his wife reading the Bible to him. It was known that she had greatly "reformed" him. He had game cocks on the place but he discouraged their fighting—on Sunday; and it was said that of late the wagers he laid at horse races had much diminished. Within him she had awakened an admiration, if not a love, for the Bible, but it was apparent that his fondness for Moses and the warlike leaders was more pronounced than for the quiet and poetic musers. In truth, he did not care to be led beside the still waters, but to stand where roared the cataract.

After the General had quitted the room Mahone re-

marked: "Richard, I have made the discovery that
I am not an egotist; and this naturally leads me to
the acknowledgment of the fact that I am not a success as a business man.   Didn't I read in an Irish
newspaper that the American people loved Tom
Moore? I did.   Don't business men read market
reports and follow them in their buying and selling?
They do.   But when I buy goods, why, it is soon
discovered that I made a mistake.   What is a man to
do? If you can't reduce trade to some sort of system,
what is to become of commerce?   And that old party
in the gig!   How did I know he was proof against
the law when he bore no evidence of it?   Why doesn't
the law compel such men to wear signs, setting forth
the fact?   Richard, I think I am better fitted for law-
making than for business.   Ah, see the failures and
the humiliation Arabella put upon me!   What is it
that a woman can't do for a man?   She could have
made something out of me—the ideal landlord of the
community; in time we could have established a fine
inn, and our children might have amounted to something, but as it is, what can be expected of them?   It
it not a matter for laughter, friend Richard, although
I assure you it does me good to see you laugh.   I ex-
ercised your horse this morning and he seemed proud
of the fact that you are getting well.   And that little
barefooted elf they call Nettie!   Ah, but you've got
something in store for you."

On the following day, just after I had eaten breakfast, the elf came into the room. She was not more
than a child—sixteen Mahone had said—she peeped
in at me with those great Italian eyes and inquired if
I were well enough to see her—then slammed the door
to, opening it again slowly, peeping at me.

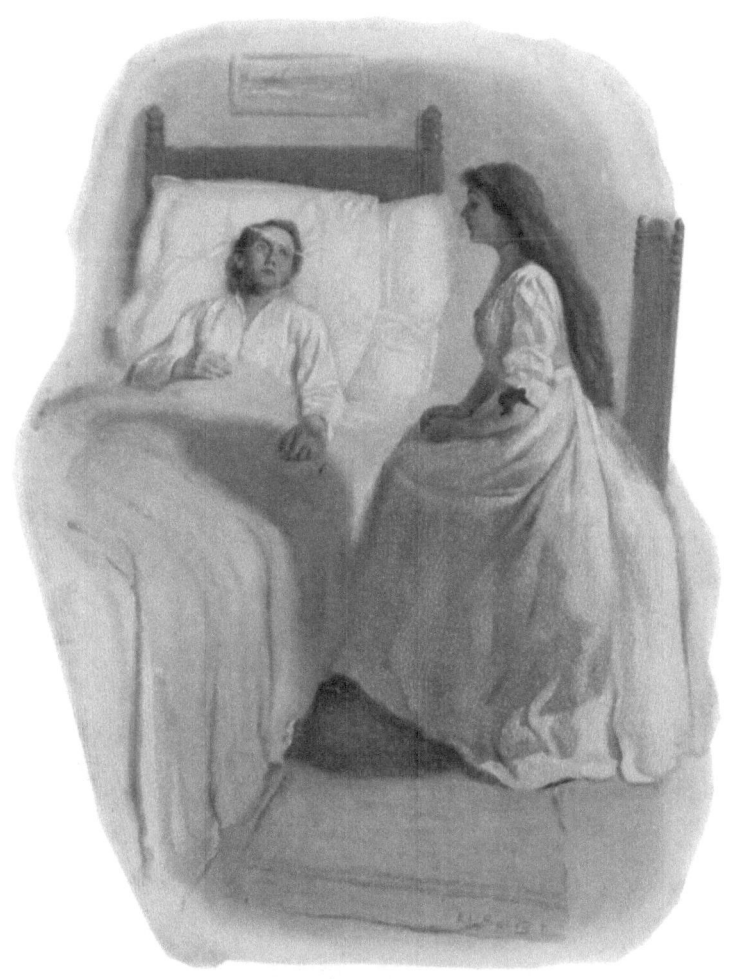

"SHE LOOKED AT ME."

"Yes, come in," I called.

She came, shaking the dew from her hair as she nodded at me, and I asked her if she had spent the night in the trees with the birds, and laughing as she drew a chair nearer toward the bed, she answered that she had slept in the house, but that she had gone out early to see them haul the hay. She sat down. "I have been wanting to come in here, oh, ever so long!" she said. "But Aunt Rachel was afraid I'd bother you. I did slip in once, though. Mr. Mahone —and he's so funny—well, he said you was a regular grammar; and then I was afraid of you, but I asked Aunt Rachel and she said you wasn't any grammar at all, so far as she could see. Then I said I'd come some time and read to you, whenever they'd let me. I didn't bring my book this time—I came this time so we could get acquainted, and when we do it won't make any difference much whether I bring a book at all or not, for we can talk, then. I've got on new shoes. Uncle Andrew brought them from town yesterday, because there wasn't any in the plantation store good enough for me, he said. When they told Aunt Rachel about you fighting the man, oh, how she did cry. And Uncle Andrew said as loud as he almost could—'I've always got two pistols cocked for such scoundrels.' Why did you want to fight the man?"

"Because he insulted me," I answered. She looked at me, studying my face, shrewdly searching for my conscience through my eyes, it seemed. But in her gaze there was naught that was embarrassing on either her part or mine. I felt as if she were pouring something deliciously warm upon me; a cordial into my mind.

"How did he insult you?" she inquired, and her eyes seemed to repeat the question after her lips.

"He called me a pauper, a liar and a coward."

"But what was it he said about Aunt Rachel?"

"Oh, nothing at all."

Again she searched for my conscience through my eyes. Then she shook her head and sighed, this beautiful mid-way woman; ah, how women have shaken their heads with tears in their eyes, and how they have sighed at the window in the night, peering out into the dark, waiting for men to come, striving to understand why love when it was so free to come home should remain away.

"My father was killed like that," she said. "I can just remember it; and I have heard them talk, and I know that my father challenged the man, because he had said things about my mother. My mother came here, when she was a girl, from away off—from Italy; she was a music teacher. My father and Uncle Andrew loved each other, and when Uncle Andrew does love, he loves harder than anybody, but he doesn't say much about it."

I let her wander along, desiring that she should give me her history in her own way. "My father and Aunt Rachel were—were almost kin to each other."

That reminded me of Mahone, and I smiled. "Yes, they were," she insisted, "almost kin. Why do men say things about women that have to make them be killed or kill somebody?"

"Because some men are scoundrels," I answered.

"Yes," she assented, nodding her head, "and that is the sort Uncle Andrew says he has his pistols cocked for."

As I looked at her, studied the radiant harmony of her features and the blue-black thicket of her hair, I wondered why she had not been more spoiled, in that age, when to flatter gracefully was thought to be one of the highest qualities of the gentleman. The era of the hair-trigger was also the era of compliment. But this creature, to whom nature had willed so much of beauty, although she was approaching womanhood, seemed unconscious of her extravagant inheritance.

"My name is Nettie Blakemore now," she said, smiling mischievously at me, "but it will be Nettie something else when I am eighteen. Then it will be Nettie Page. Ah, hah. Wilbur Page is my third cousin, and is more than twenty-one now, and I am to marry him. That was all made up a long time ago, and I promised my mother before she died."

"But you may not love him when you are eighteen," said I.

"Oh, yes, I will, for I have promised."

She had promised! How like the fate of woman! "Nobody could keep from loving him," she went on. "And he is going to be a doctor and cure people. Doctors don't have to fight duels as much as lawyers do. They don't have to argue so much. Lawyers get mad so easily. Uncle Andrew has quarrels with them nearly all the time. I wonder why they keep on trying to fight him when they know he can whip them. One time not long ago we were driving in the carriage, me and Aunt Rachel and Uncle Andrew, and we met a lawyer on a horse; and Uncle Andrew told the driver to stop, and he took his cane and beat the lawyer, and then we drove on. After quite a long time Aunt Rachel she says, 'Mr. Jackson, may I ask what was the trouble between you and the man back

yonder?' And Uncle Andrew he smiled dry and said:
'It was no trouble, I assure you, Mrs. Jackson—it was
a pleasure.' "

Her eyes glowed with humor; her lips were buds of
mirth, ever bursting into the rose of full blown laughter. It was as Mahone had said: She was not to be
fallen in love with; and for two reasons, one because
she was in years a child, the other—I don't know
what, unless it was that the constantly startled heart
beat too fast, beat itself out of all the gentler paces
of love. But my mind was on that young doctor.

"How long has it been since you saw him—the man
you are going to marry?" I asked.

"Oh, Cousin Wilbur? A long, long time—nearly
a year, I should think. And he had on the prettiest
shirt you ever saw—all ruffled, without a speck of dirt
on it. He wanted me to kiss him, and I told him I
would as his cousin, but couldn't as his sweetheart
until it was nearly time for me to marry him. He
said he didn't want my cousin kisses; he said he could
get them most any time and most anywhere, as he
had kin folks scattered all up and down the river. I
told him them was the only kind I had. He's got
curly hair and some gold on one of his teeth."

"And you know you will love him when you are
seventeen?"

"Oh, yes, for how could I help it when he is my
cousin now and to be my sweetheart for a month or
two, and then—to be everything. Of course, I'll love
him. Do you want me to get my book and read to
you?"

"I'd rather you would talk to me."

"About Cousin Wilbur? All right. I know you
will like him. I was at his house one day and he

tried to ride a calf. It was the funniest thing, for a little while, and then it wasn't, for the calf threw him over into the hog lot and nearly killed him. His eyes are blue. What color are your eyes? They are brown, ain't they? Yes, they are. That was what Aunt Rachel said when I asked her; and then Uncle Andrew said the color of a man's eyes didn't make any difference—it was what he saw out of them that counted. Did you think your time had come when you stood up waiting for that man to shoot at you? Of course, you must, for you and everybody else knew he was a good shooter. You have heard about Uncle Andrew killing Mr. Charles Dickinson, a long time ago, haven't you?''

Before leaving North Carolina I had heard of this famous duel, the most famous ever fought in the Western country. In nearly every household there was a copy of the Nashville Impartial Review, now growing old, in which was set forth an account of that sad affair. I had been close to Jackson's heart, on the morning when he walked with me toward the place where I was to take life and to shed my own blood, and I knew that he held me strong in his affections, but to me he had never mentioned the Dickinson duel. Accounts of it had been printed everywhere throughout the country and in England as well, and every detail of it was familiar to me, but what would I not have given for the story, told by the General himself? The newspapers had begged him for his ''statement,'' meaning his recital, and the preachers, some of them his warm personal friends, had begged him to express his regret, for the influence that it might have among young men, but he had remained silent and grim. But it was my hope that he might unbutton his almost echoless breast to me—kin, almost one, in this instance, because it was Mrs. Jackson's name that had caused both the death of Dickinson and of Lismukes. The public, let me explain, did not know why, in my case, the "field of honor" had been measured. All parties were close of mouth and the details had been withheld from the newspapers— it was a student quarrel. I may say here that the courts took a side-glance notice of it, that constructively I was a prisoner to await trial, but that the trial was never called, mainly because every one believed that the death of Lismukes was good for the community.

"What are you thinking about so long?" the girl inquired.

"Of the time when you are to be eighteen."

This pleased her and she laughed; and I wished that I might be permitted to kiss her, even as a cousin, or even as a grandfather.

CHAPTER XVI.

IT was a day of encouragement when the physician permitted me to get out of bed and to put on my clothes. In a rocking-chair I sat, near the window, looking out upon the river. In this home was a bright and rosy boy, relative of Mrs. Jackson, taken when an infant, given the name of Andrew, and adopted by the General as his own son and heir. Of his own, the General had no child, but as Mahone remarked, he could not have loved his own twins more than he loved this mischievous youngster. He used to race through the house on a crutch horse. Surely there never was a household where crutches were more abundant. They appeared to be standing behind every door, in every corner. And it seemed that there were not many months at a time when the General did not require a set of them. So, in his line, young Andrew had the finest stable in the country. There was one crutch at least six feet high. This with its mate, now lost, had been sent to the General by an admirer who had never seen him but who imagined him a giant eight feet tall. This crutch-horse the boy named Truxton, after the General's famous race horse. His race course lay through my room, out upon the veranda. On the morning of my getting out of bed he won a great race and had come in to tell me about it. He said that they had tried to drug his

129

horse and that if he found the fellow he was going
to shoot him. This was an echo from the real stable.
While he was talking to me I heard Nettie Blakemore
utter a cry, and then I saw her run swiftly down the
veranda, and into the yard. Andrew, scenting adven-
ture, seized his corn-cob pistol, mounted his horse and
dashed after her. I would have followed, but was
too weak. I leaned out of the window, straining to
discover the cause of the girl's excitement. It was
not long a mystery. A young man had dismounted
at the gate; and now she was coming toward the house
with him, clinging to his arm. Not even instinct
was needed to tell me that the young doctor had arrived. And now my first feeling toward him was
generous, I thought. I was resolved not to hate him.
The General was in town, Mrs. Jackson busy somewhere with her numerous duties, and so, the exuber-
ant miss conducted him into my room, and in a warm
glow of pride introduced him to me. I stood up to
shake hands with him; and, as he had heard something of my case, he began at once to talk about gun-
shot wounds, telling me that formerly on the field of
battle they had poured hot oil into them—"the
wretched barbarians," he added. The girl smiled
and shook that cluster of clouds, her hair.

I was resolved not to hate him, but Christian duty
did not demand that I should actually love him. His
face was too pale, his forehead too white. He as-
sumed a carelessness of learning, mispronounced a
word, accenting it to show that he knew how it ought
to be pronounced. He wore with his other finery a
"westcut," flowered with green vines and yellowish
blossoms. They might have been herbs from which
he intended to extract his medicines.

He asked me what sort of medicine I was taking,
and I nodded toward a phial on the mantelpiece. He
arose, took down the phial, uncorked it, held it to his
nose, shook his head, recorked it and sat down. It
was evident that my physician was giving me the
wrong stuff. He asked Nettie if she were glad to see
him and she said yes, and told him that she knew
where there was a bird's nest, but that she wouldn't
tell Andrew. The boy, listening, jumped upon his
horse and galloped forth to find it.

"How are you getting along at school?" the young
doctor inquired.

"I get along better when I'm not there," she answered. "I don't like school. It makes me sleepy."

He frowned. "You musn't feel that way. I expect you to study, so that you may grow into a smart
woman."

"But I don't want to be smart, if it makes me
sleepy," she replied. "What's the use of smartness,
anyway? Smart people don't have any fun. They
have to argue and then quarrel and then fight. They
say Mr. Staggs is a grammar, but he had to kill a
man and be shot himself. Oh, I know that ladies
don't have to fight, but men have to fight about
smart women. I don't like fighting, except roosters.
Last Sunday morning me and Uncle Andrew were out
by the barn, and a dominicker rooster kept on jump-
ing up on the fence and crowing just because there
was a red rooster walking about over in the lot. Uncle
Andrew looked at the dominicker and said: 'Old
fellow, with your crowing you have drawn attention
to the fact that you are a strange bird and don't
belong here.' Then he opened the gate and shood
him through to where the red rooster was, and they

were making the feathers fly, when along came Mr.
Peter Cartwright, the preacher. Wasn't he fretted
to see Uncle Andrew standing there watching the
roosters fight, and on Sunday, too! My, but he was
mad, and he began to scold.

"Uncle Andrew likes Mr. Cartwright, because he
knocks sinners down when they disturb the meeting,
so he didn't get mad. He just said, 'Brother Cartwright, the red rooster will whip him in less than ten
minutes.'

"Mr. Cartwright took off his hat as he sat there on
his horse and blowed his breath like he was tired, and
said, 'I need about ten logs to finish that new church
up the river. I never bet, of course, but I'll lay five
barrels of corn that have just been given to me against
the ten logs I need for the church, that the dominicker
whips him.'

" 'Taken,' said Uncle Andrew.

"Then Mr. Cartwright said to me, 'Sissy, you run
on into the house,' and I told him I would as soon as
I saw who won, and he frowned at me and said I
mustn't talk about winning, and then sat gazing at
the chickens. After a while the dominicker got the
red down and pecked him and pecked him until he
was dead.

"Then Mr. Cartwright said: 'Well, Brother Jackson, I've got to go on over to meet my appointment.
I wish you'd have your darkies cut those logs as early
in the week as possible, as we are anxious to get the
new church done.'

"Uncle Andrew said he would; and when he was
gone Uncle Andrew said to me: 'Old Peter is a
smart man. He knows how to get logs.' ''

"But my dear child, I don't care to hear all this,"

said young Page. "I would much rather you'd tell me something from your school books."

"But," she answered, "you can take up my books yourself and find out all there's in them, but you never would have known about this if I hadn't told you. You wanted to hear about it, didn't you, Mr. Staggs?"

"I was delighted with it," I answered; and at that moment there was a look in the doctor's eye that told me he could never be my friend. I wondered how long he might remain a guest at this house, where I was compelled to stay; and I remember having had a feeling that the air, with him nowhere in sight, would be easier to breathe. Among other things that I did not like about him was his smile. It looked like an apology, never willing to come out with complete acknowledgment of good humor. He had a sort of rice-pudding countenance, with no firmness of crust; and I know that he had been a "mammy boy" and flattered, for occasionally he would lean back and look to catch his reflection in a mirror that was hanging on the wall.

"I suppose, sir, that you have settled upon a profession," he said, giving me a weak smile—a thin crack in the rice pudding. I answered that I had decided upon the law.

"Law," he repeated. "But don't you think that it is already overcrowded? It is so easy to pass an examination for that profession, you know. A few commentaries read, a few rules committed to memory and there you are. Nettie, bring me a drink of water, please. A profession questioned by geographical lines, for a man may be a good lawyer in one part of the world and not a lawyer at all, in another part, while medicine is as universal as man himself.''

''But,'' said I, ''it is narrowed down to man's body and wholly misses his mind, except to deceive him as to the nature of his disease. When you have dissected a man you don't know anything about him except to the extent that he is a machine.''

Nettie brought him a dipper of water. He drank, thanked her with a hair-line crack in his countenance, and turned a more decided face toward me. He frowned. ''The law couldn't keep you out of this sort of trouble, but surgery steps forward to save you.''

Nettie stood by, shaking the dipper at us. ''Smart men getting into a quarrel,'' she said.

''Not at all,'' Page answered. ''We are just arguing a point.''

''Yes,'' she replied, ''and that is what they do with Uncle Andrew at first. Come on with me, Cousin Wilbur, and I will show you the bird's nest.''

''But we should be leaving our friend alone,'' he said.

''Oh, don't mind me,'' I spoke up quickly. ''I shall not be alone, for here comes my friend, Professor Mahone.''

He arose to go just as Mahone entered the room. I introduced them. The Irishman bowed stiffly but took the doctor's hand when he offered it. They exchanged a few words, and when Page had gone out with the girl, Mahone sat down, silent for a few moments, and then he blurted: ''More trouble, Richard.''

''With that fellow? Oh, no, Nettie loves him.''

''Begorry, and that will be the cause of it.''

"Why, Dan, you don't mean—"

"I do mean that same, Richard. It can't be otherwise; it must come. Lord love us all, what a world! When we are thick in the head we sit in the shade and nod, and when at last we are clear of brain we look up with keen eye and see a quarrel coming; but let us be cheerful over things that can't be avoided. She will be more than worth every blow you deal to win her."

"But I thought you said no man could love her as he would a sweetheart or a wife."

"Surely I did, and meant as she is now, but she will grow out of the elf and become the most magnificent of women."

"But am I to fall in love with her on that account?" I sparred. "Must I fall in love with every woman because she happens to be beautiful?"

"Oh, no, but you are to love, begorry, to the death when along comes a woman with Fate in her hair and her eyes. Mind that now."

"Then your warning won't help matters any."

"Not at all," he answered. "All the warning of all the saints wouldn't have kept me from falling in love with Arabella. Mind that."

"You have almost forgotten her, Dan."

"Forgotten her when I would water the flowers on her grave, and that gladly every day, if she only had one. And willingly would I make her one if she needed it. Richard, you could no more drive the thoughts of her out of my mind than you could drive a flock of geese, headed by an obstreperous gander, across a windy plain. Did you ever attempt to drive geese in the mind? Try it once and you will see the force of my illustration. I wish you would make haste with your recovery," he continued, having fallen for a few moments into a dream. "I get very lonesome in the heat of the day, over at that store, not a soul passing along, and with dazzling heat dancing away down the road as I sit out in the shade, looking drowsy-eyed down the road. The birds are then hidden among the leaves with their songs tucked away into silence. From the blue of the distance into the white dazzle overhead shoots the briar-eyed hawk, a feathered hunger, a winged famine; and the birds looking down from among the leaves see an awful shadow, cutting through the sun-blaze lying on the earth, and they shudder in fear. It is a lonesome time of day then, Richard. Tom Moore drops from my hand, and then I know nothing till I hear a thump from the inside of the store, and then out runs a stray dog, with a sugar-cured ham by the shank. It is not a lonesome time of day for him. Mind that. And after I have tried to pull up the root of a tree to throw at him—after I have followed along, whooping at him till he has disappeared down in the woods, I muse, 'that's all right, old fellow, I don't blame you much,' and then return to the shade. That reminds me. I have disposed of one copy of Moore's poems. Yes, sir—to a young woman. I presented it to her, with my compliments. And we can't tell how fast they'll go now that they've got a start. But am I tiring you with all this?"

"No, you entertain me."

"Richard, I thank you for that lie. But don't fear to take any of the conceit out of me. In truth, what little I had left is gone from me. Beneath the tree yesterday, I looked back over my past to see how —how very unlearned I am. And I said to myself,

'What, sir, have you ever said to make any man think?' Put your mind down on that, Richard. To make any man think. What is the worth of one man to another? Not to lend him money, not to help him materially, but to make him think. That is the use of books—the whole of education. But as I looked back I couldn't see that I had made any one think. And I said to myself, 'You shallow Latin poets and you incomprehensible Greek tragedians, what have you done for me? Through me you have transmitted no thought to my fellow man.' I make men smile, but they smile when a fellow's hat blows off. I shall soon be thirty-three, and here I am without an occupation. The trouble is I have not been able to make men think. Why is a Scotchman successful? Because he cannot make people laugh. Sometimes he may make them think he is a dull ass, but they have to stop and look at him to do that, and when they do he sells them something.''

The brass knocker at the front door cut him off from his recital. ''There's no one besides ourselves in the house, and you'll have to see who that is,'' said I.

He hastened to the door and I heard him cry: ''Ah, who can this be but yourself! Come in.''

The visitor spoke but I did not recognize the voice other than that it was the tone of a man. ''You will find him inside, sir, sitting up like the lark he is.''

In came Atcherson. He smiled in a manner becoming to his new course of study and sedately shook hands with me. ''Mr. Staggs,'' he said, and the ticking of a midnight clock could not have been more solemn, ''the Lord has forgiven me.''

"Let us join in with that hope," the Irishman replied. "But in the meantime, kick off your braided
slippers and out of consideration for us stand in the
shoes of a man."

It was so much in accord with what was in my own
mind that I laughed. The sprouting Reverend, smiling, made answer: "I stand in the shoes that walk
the narrow way."

"Begorry, if you stand you don't walk," said Mahone. "Sit down and rest while you're standing."

"Brother Staggs," Atcherson began, and the
Irishman cried: "Put your mind on that, Richard."

Atcherson, now in the rocking-chair with the tips
of his fingers pressed together, smiled faintly at him
and then proceeded to address me: "Brother Staggs,
I have been exceedingly busy with my studies or I
should have been out to see you sooner. And I may
say now that I am much pleased to see you doing so
well—in the flesh, this heavy flesh of earth."

"His flesh is not so heavy as it was," answered the
Irishman. "They have extracted the bullet."

Again Atcherson smiled at him, though weak and
feebly. The Irishman gave him a broad, good humored grin.

"Brother Staggs," said the embryo preacher, "I
have come out to have a little talk with you, and my
hope is that it may be profitable."

Mahone asked if he did not think that he ought to
have deferred his talk until I should be stronger, but
to this he did not accede. He shook his head slowly
and addressed himself to me.

"Brother Staggs—"

"Atcherson," I broke in upon him, "you called me

Staggs at school. Don't bother with calling me brother now.''

''Forget his rhetoric,'' murmured Mahone.

''Oh, be it as you wish,'' said Atcherson. ''But from my present point of view Staggs sounds harsh.''

The Professor spoke up. ''From points of view things *appear*. They do not sound.''

''As you wish, sir,'' Atcherson agreed.

''Not as I wish but as it is.''

''Very well, sir; but no quibble shall keep me from my purpose. I wish to talk—to Richard concerning his soul.''

The Irishman bowed. ''It is man's privilege, not to say his province, to talk on subjects of which he knows nothing.''

''Atcherson,'' said I, ''as to my soul, it is in good hands—in the hands of its Creator, and the mere fact that you have been stricken with remorse, does not make you better acquainted with it than I am.''

''Richard,'' said he, ''do not say stricken with remorse but repentance; and the man who repents is nearer unto grace than the man who does not.''

''Well, what is it you want me to subscribe to?''

''I solicit no humiliating subscription, Richard, but I do yearn to see you humbled in repentance.''

''Atcherson,'' said Mahone, ''it hasn't made you humble but arrogant. You may not know it, but it has. I believe you are sincere—mind that—but as yet there are a few weeds growing in this new garden of yours, and you ought to root them out before you come it too strong with other men. It is easy enough for one that has been of us to come around and to declare that he has vomited up his part of the devil, eaten for us all by old Adam. And we accept his pal-

lor and his cold sweat as the evidences of his violent
wretching. That is well enough. But we can't help
seeing that he is proud of his humility, and as the
dramatist says, 'This gives us pause.' Wait till your
new garments settle better upon you before you demand of us that we shall follow your fashion. Tell
us some news, Atcherson. What is going on in town?''

Atcherson's countenance had undergone a change,
had softened into an expression of charity. "Professor," he spoke, "there is truth in what you have just
said. And I feel already that I am going to profit
by it. We are too much inclined to make a boast of
our humility. There is a better way of getting at
each other's faults than by assuming a moral superior-
ity; it is by the true fellowship of gentleness and for-
bearance. And, Professor, I am beholden to you."

"A good old accommodating word, beholden," the
Irishman replied, his countenance brightening. "And
I thank you for taking what I said in such good part.
You have never been a bad fellow, Atcherson; I told
you so the day when I took the knife out of your
hand, and kept you from stabbing Foster Pryor. But,
of course, you have repented of all such little whims,
and when the time comes for you to preach, we will
all be there, and begorry, we'll cry 'Amen' upon the
first word—and thank you for the last one. Now that
we have got back down into the low ground of human
nature you can tell us the news, I hope."

"The town is becoming a city very fast," said Atcherson. "And morality is striving to keep pace
with material progress. They have passed a law
against billiards, and we hope after a while to get an
enactment that will effectually prevent dueling. The
forthcoming numbers of the weekly newspapers may

record these things, together with the fact that night
before last John Slater shot and killed Moses C. Tabb,
the difficulty arising out of the disputed ownership
of a negro man, Slater claiming to have won him.
But Tabb persisted that Slater had filched a card
from the deck and—''

''Meaning thereby,'' broke in the Professor, ''that
the transfer of property right was irregular.''

''The same,'' said Atcherson. ''And you remember
Brad Royston, don't you?''

''Very well,'' Mahone answered. ''The last time I
saw him we had a dish of cove oysters together. Does
he own that greyhound yet?''

''I am sorry to relate that he doesn't own anything,
and that is what I was going to speak about. He was
usually a peaceable fellow, except when in his cups
and—''

''In his half-gallon measures,'' Mahone interrupted.
''Mere cups were too shallow for him.''

''Yes, he drank deep or not at all. Well, he was
drinking deep when he and Nat Roscoe met; nor was
it long before they drew and fired. Royston fell on
the sidewalk in front of Harvey's store and—''

''And the Harveys, sir, how are they getting
along?'' Mahone broke in. ''Do they keep boarders,
or does Mrs. Harvey that was or rather Arabella
that was and Mrs. Harvey that is—does she stand in
the store, giving to silk a smile for a shimmer? Tell
me about her. Never mind Royston. It is enough to
know that he's dead, saints rest his soul. Does she
look happy?''

''I thought so when I saw her the other day,'' said
Atcherson, dropping the Royston tragedy. ''She appeared in excellent health.''

"A fine compliment to me," the Professor replied. "But tell me, does she seem to be fond of that counter jumper? Don't disguise the truth from me. I am prepared to stand it."

"I should think you would be," I remarked.

"I am, sir, and there's no mistake."

"She is devoted to him," said Atcherson.

"Easy, now, easy," the Irishman warned him. "I can stand much but not everything. Easy. Such assurances, sir, rob me of my last vestige of hope."

"Why, what hope could you have had after she was married?"

"I could have that very natural, that human nature hope, sir, that she might be miserable. Does her husband look strong?"

"He is not fat, but he looks well."

"Tell me no more. So Royston is dead. He was a good fiddler and the community will miss him. Well, as I left the store open and as there's no one to look after things it is time I was getting back. Atcherson, I am much obliged for your news, and I am glad you took in good part what I said to you."

After Mahone had gone, Atcherson began to sound my conscience. He asked if it did not weigh upon me dreadfully that I had killed a man, although it could not well have been avoided. He seemed disappointed when I assured him that I had lost no sleep.

"It was my hope," said he, "that you might turn as I have and become a preacher of the Word. Then together we could go throughout the country, doing a great work. I feel that I have been called."

"And when I feel that I have, I shall go," I answered.

"But, perhaps, you have been called and do not

yet feel it. It may be that I shall interpret that call
to you.''

"Atcherson, I accepted something of your former
faith—in Fate, and I believe that she has singled me
out for some other purpose. From instant death I
was almost miraculously saved, and for a purpose
which after a while will be made plain to me. If it
be to preach, I shall accept it. Whatever it may be
I shall take it up. In yourself have all possible faith,
but let me warn you not to believe you have been appointed to convert me.''

"Then my coming has been vain.''

"Not at all; I am glad to see you. Tell me something about the school.''

He arose to take his leave. In an after year, amid
fire and smoke, I saw him stand just as he stood now,
thoughtful, youth in the habiliments of deep solemn-
ity. From the hallway his retiring footsteps were
still echoing when in ran Nettie, the elf, with her
hands full of dew-berries; and she insisted upon
feeding them to me, one at a time, her purple fingers
touching my lips.

"Cousin Wilbur saw Uncle Andrew coming and
went to meet him and they have gone out to the pasture to look at the colts,'' she said, standing beside
me, slowly putting the berries into my mouth.
"Cousin Wilbur asked me if I wanted to go, too, and
I told him I had to come in here and give you these
berries, and he said I mustn't be foolish. And you
know what he said to me? That I must go away off
somewhere to a boarding-school. He said his mother,
Aunt 'Riah, wanted me to—here's another one, big
one—and I told him I loved Aunt Rachel better than
Aunt 'Riah. That's what I told him. Here's the

last one. And I have come to like you, now," she said in her innocence. "We don't want to go away just as soon as we like anybody, do we? Of course, I'm ignorant, but I don't want to be smart—it's so dangerous. Would you fight for me if I were smart?"

"What nonsense are you talking?" I heard from without, and looking up, I saw Page standing near the window.

CHAPTER XVII.

IN THE BUGGY.

WHEN I awoke on the following morning, after a night not wholly of sound sleep, my first thought was in the form of a speculation as to how long that fellow Page might remain. In some way, he was distantly related to Mrs. Jackson, and this was quite sufficient to endear him to the General. I had no right to wish him to go. I felt that any excuse I could find for my dislike of him must be contemptibly petty. So, I was still resolved not to hate him. I compromised with—not to like him. Of course, at the proper time he would marry the girl, as was his right; nor had I aught to say or to feel against this arrangement. It was not possible that I could so soon be in love, after Arabella, and that, too, with a child. But how different were the two situations! Arabella had come at me with the perfected art of an experienced woman, and I yielded to it, but this girl had no art at all. Indeed, I had not really known what this art was until she taught me what it was not. My admiration for Arabella could have been none other than vanity on my own part. To bring out her smiles, mechanical as they were, had thrilled me—with my own sex prowess. And when I was on my knees at her feet, pleading for her love, there was somewhere within me a contempt for myself. But this girl! When one by one she was placing the dew-berries to my lips, I felt that she was feeding to me bits of her own sweet nature.

As I was sitting at the window, she came down the veranda, or gallery, as we then termed it, books in satchel, moping her way to school in unconscious grace. She halted, looked back and then spoke to me:

"They said I had to go and I must. Ain't you sorry for me?"

"Yes, I am," and I told her the truth. "I am as sorry for you as I am for all imprisoned birds."

"Thank you so much. But Cousin Wilbur is looking and I must go. Good-bye."

She pretended to run away, looking back, and her bud lips burst into a rose.

Not long afterward Page came into the room. "How that girl hates to go to school," he said, sitting down. "I suppose you know she is to become my wife at the proper time."

"Yes, I have heard so."

"Family arrangement," he said. "But a very good one I am inclined to think. I believe somewhere in the Bible it says that a soldier is better accommodated than with a wife, but it does not say a physician."

"Bible your grandmother's cat," exclaimed Mahone, of whose presence I had not been aware. "It was spoken by Bardolph, one of the immortal disreputables, with reference to his master, Sir John, tallow ketch, larder of the lean earth."

"I am still in the woods even after all that lucidity of explanation," the doctor acknowledged. "But I beg your pardon, I did not know that I had been addressing you."

"No offense, I assure you," answered the Irish-

man. "Richard, the General says I am to have you
lifted into the buggy and to take you for a drive."

This was delightful news, and I felt strong enough
to walk out to the gate, but two negroes came in to
carry me. Page followed along, with words of caution. The General stood out by the horse-block. He
had just come in from a fox chase, and his hounds
were gathered about him, some of them stretched upon the ground, weary with their night's work. One
old fellow, a veteran, sat gazing up at his master's
face.

"I thought that a drive would do you good," said
the General. "But wouldn't you feel safer with Dr.
Page?"

"I have been a medical student, sir," Mahone spoke
up. "But of course we will leave it to Richard."

It was rather an awkward position, but I decided
almost instantly. I said that as the Professor and I
were old friends and therefore had many things in
common to discuss, I preferred him. "And very naturally so," Page good humoredly answered.

"I was afraid that courtesy would influence your
decision against me," said Mahone as we drove along.
"I knew that fellow would spoil it all for you. See
that rabbit hop over there with the sun shining
through his thin ears. Ah, if everything were all
right and there was nothing to worry over, what a
glorious thing it would be to live. By the way I
have succeeded in disposing of another copy of Tom
Moore. You remember I told you of my giving one
to a young woman. Well, she came back, so pleased
she was with her bargain, and said she wanted another copy, for her aunt. How does this air make
you feel?"

"As if I were flying. But why are you turning off into this lane?"

"Ah, do you see that little house over yonder beneath the big trees? Well, that is the school-house."

My heart jumped.

"And we are going to drive by there slowly and perhaps stop for a moment or two," said Mahone. "It will be recess by the time we get there and I want you to see a beautiful sight, the elf racing about on the grass. I've been over before—I made them a speech; and the one that clapped hands the loudest was the elf herself. But let me ease your mind. I shall never be in love with her. No, sir. In the case of Arabella you sacrificed yourself in my favor, and now I shall do as much for you. And it does me good to see that you are stealing her heart away from that fellow who never had it at all. See, they are piling out of the door, and there she is—I could tell her a mile off. Richard, she is a child, but you are in love with her."

"Dan, I must beg of you not to talk that way. You must never do so again. I should be a wolf to attempt to steal her love, and I could not possess it in any other way."

"Surely not. Who ever possessed the love of a woman that he didn't steal it? A woman expects her love to be stolen, when she leaves it exposed, and little respect she has for a man if he does not steal it. Mind that. Ah, she sees us and is coming out to the fence."

She came, bonnetless, her hair a blue-black blaze in the sun. "Oh," she cried, "did you come to see me? Thank you so much. Mr. Mahone, you get out and let me drive Mr. Richard around, just a little bit, won't you please?"

"I will and there's no mistake," Mahone answered. "Ha, if she hasn't climbed the fence like a squirrel."

Mahone got out and she was in the buggy before he could assist her. "You must let me drive," she said, catching up the lines. "Oh, I'm a good driver. Good-bye, Mr. Mahone. Give our love to everybody."

Was there a music of the spheres? Was that sweet melody the hum of this old earth?

The lane led out into the grassy woods, a river emptying into the sea. I spoke this fancy, and pointing to a moss-covered log she said: "And there is an old whale resting himself."

"After having had to give up Jonah," I said, and holding the lines with one hand she made as if she would stop my irreverent mouth with the other.

"It is wicked to make fun out of the Bible," she declared. "But Jonah must have felt awfully queer, there in the dark, for a whale hasn't any lights, like an animal has." She bowed over the lines and shrieked with laughter at this conceit. I joined with her, and looking up she said that we ought to be ashamed of ourselves.

"Oh," she cried, "I know where some dew-berries are, over by the fence at the edge of the woods; and we'll drive over there and I'll pick them for you."

"But I'm afraid we shall not have time," I protested, weakly, hypocritically. "The bell will ring pretty soon."

"Yes, but we can't hear it from there," she laughed. "And they can't blame us if we didn't hear the bell. Oh, isn't it fine to be out here? There oughten't to

be any winter, ought there? Winter comes after the
year has gone to school and is smart."

"You are poetry, like a blossom," I said.

"If Cousin Wilbur talked to me like that I'd be
sorrier when he goes away. I love poetry because it
doesn't try to teach me anything. But Cousin Wilbur may talk like that after a while, when we are
married and have a house of our own."

If she had wanted to escape from him she did not
seem to think that there was any possible way. The
plan of her marriage to him was engrafted upon her
very nature. It was to come as naturally as that a
birthday should fall, a yellowed autumn leaf. Woman, the necklace of pearls and of diamonds you
wear is a rusty chain, if you could see it in the light
of truth; and its name is obligation to man. Nearly
all of your jewelry, your bracelets and your rings,
are but glittering reminiscences of ancient bondage.
And in what lies the only hope of your emancipation?
Not in the discharge of your duty, not in the love
you may bear your children, but in that love which
must be enkindled to light the heavens and the earth
—the love between you and—not your master, but
your companion—a man.

"He will talk to me that way, won't he?" she said,
and out of the depths of an ache, which I thought was
an honorable heart, I answered, "Oh, yes, when the
time comes. There's the bell."

She dropped the lines and clapped her hands to
her ears. "I don't hear it," she said. "Has it
stopped?"

I nodded. She took her hands from her ears and
gathered up the lines. I told her that we must turn
back. "Oh, not yet," she pleaded with her lips and

with her eyes turned full upon me. ''We haven't got any dew-berries yet—not a single one, and they oughtn't to expect us to come back now. Mr. Mahone will tell them.''

''But he can only tell them that we haven't come back,'' I laughed, making no effort to turn the horse about.

''And that's all they need to know.''

We came to a brook. She said that old Tom, the horse, wanted a drink, and without halting him she walked out upon the shaft, holding on, laughing, pretending that she was about to fall, and unhooked the check rein. She patted him on the back as he drank, beads of water trickling from a corner of his mouth, and told him how good it was of him not to turn around when he heard that miserable old bell. When she hooked the check rein and came back to her seat beside me, she seemed so free and so happy that I had not the heart to do my dúty, to insist upon her returning to the school house; and so we drove along through the cool woods, charmed with everything we saw, a brown thrush with a proud spread of tail, a wavy gray streak of squirrel drawn across the sward.

''This is the way Cousin Wilbur and I will drive to church, one of these days,'' she said, and to myself I mused, ''Oh, velvet kitten, how sharp can be thy claws.''

We had not come within sight of the fence where the dew-berries were, so I said to her:

''Nettie, we must go back. If we don't your cousin will have good cause to scold us both.''

Without a word she turned old Tom about, and with the lines tapped him into a trot. ''And I do hate to have him scold me,'' she said.

"Because it seems to hurt him so?" I inquired.

"No, because it seems to do him so much good, but after a while when I am older I will scold him. After she is married a woman can beat a man scolding, all to pieces, my Uncle James used to say. Poor Uncle James, he went away to fight the Indians and they killed him. Nearly all my men kinfolks have been killed. A girl that came to visit at Aunt 'Riah's house—that's Cousin Wilbur's mother—said that in New York State where she lived they didn't kill people at all. She said not one of her kinfolks had been killed, and I said to her, 'why how funny you must feel.' She looked at me as if she thought I was crazy. How many people there are that don't know when you are joking with them. Well, yonder's that hateful old school. It's not much trouble for me to learn, and I suppose I'll have to after a while, but somehow I've always wanted to put it off as long as possible. Do you want me to learn?"

"Yes; and when I have learned, too, you and I shall have something in common aside from—"

"Aside from merely liking each other," she broke in, with a laugh. "Then I will learn—I will begin today and I'll study hard, but you must let me be natural and talk like I want to for a long time yet. You know they told me what a student you were—but I shouldn't have guessed it, for with you I always feel so free and easy. There's Mr. Mahone, walking up and down the lane, worrying fit to kill himself. I can't help it. I didn't hear the bell."

Refusing to let Mahone help her down, she jumped out of the buggy, climbed the fence and ran into the house. The Irishman got in, his face beaming. He was silent until we had driven half way back to the main road. Then he blurted:

"She loves you Richard. Don't protest with me, for I am one that knows. She doesn't know it yet, and it may be some time before she finds it out, but the time will come and before the day set for her marriage with that—that pale spalpeen. Ah, how much better they must be when you catch them young —children; how much better than to let them become widows before you land them, for then you may have them not. You're silent my boy, and it becomes you. Nor was it your talk that won the child. Them that's won by talk are sometimes lost by the same. What did win her for you? Yourself and the fact that you were wounded and needed tenderness; and when a girl sees a likely youth in that same fix, her heart melts and runs down to the tips of her fingers, and then it is that she wants to touch his lips or his brow, and then it was that this child slipped into the room and put the hair back out of your eyes. Yes, but it means trouble, Richard. That fellow won't give her up without a struggle. He is pale, and the average pale man will shoot you if the occasion arrives—and he doesn't always wait till you have chosen your second."

"Dan," said I, "taking for granted that there is truth in all that you say, what am I to do?"

"Arrah, well put. You will do what Fate tells you —you will wait. You can't run away from that girl. A saint himself couldn't do that. You can't do any-thing to cause her to think ill of you. That would shock the devil himself. Ah, it's always my luck to see trouble coming. But for the first bud of a love like that, I'd let myself be filled so full of lead that they might beat me out flat and cover the roof of a church with me. Education might make an Englishman of any son of Adam, but the sight of a young girl like that would make him Irish all over. Well, so far as you are now concerned, Richard, the drive is over and we might as well go to the house."

I assented, and from the lane we turned toward the Hermitage. Not far in front of us was a buggy, and in it were a man and a woman.

"We will give them a taste of our speed," said Mahone "Old Tom is a famous trotter. Look out for us."

The woman looked around. Mahone seized my arm. "Arabella!" he gasped.

CHAPTER XVIII.

THE buggy halted at our gate and Harvey was helping his wife to alight as we drove up. "Oh, I am so glad to see you out and looking so well," she cried, running toward me. "And how are you, Mr. Mahone?" she added, halting at the wheel. She seized me by the hand. "Dear old Richard," she said. During this time Mahone was sputtering, making no effort to get out.

"I—I—am as well, Madam—beg your pardon, Miss. As well as the circumstances of the occasion will permit. With your permission, I will alight." He jumped out, striking the ground like a log, end first. "Beautiful weather, Mrs. Crenshaw that was— Mrs. Harvey. We were going to have rain last night, but didn't. Ah, and there is your husband."

Having tied his horse, Harvey came forward. He took my hand rather cordially for him, and then shook hands with Mahone as unconcernedly as if nothing had ever chanced, and asked him if he were well. The Irishman swore that he had never been so well in his entire life, and Arabella cried, "Oh isn't that nice!"

"Don't try to get out," Mahone cautioned me. "I'll get the negroes to help you into the house."

"Give me your hand and I'll need no other help," said I. "Thank you, Mrs. Harvey." She was assisting me; and with her on one side of me and Mahone on the other I walked easily. There was something in my heart that made me light.

155

Harvey walked behind us, commenting upon the shaded beauty of the place. "Oh," his wife laughed, "and is it possible that you have discovered it? You know, Richard, he rarely ever sees anything but a price mark."

"I saw a pretty high one on you, my lady," he answered.

"Indeed you did," she replied. "And the market value hasn't stopped going up yet, I tell you. Oh, Richard, *who* is that beautiful girl, out there? Why don't you answer me? Is it possible you don't know that—that magnificent witch? Here she comes. Look out, you are stumbling."

"She is—Miss Blakemore," I answered; "One of the army of the adopted."

Nettie came running, the dogs following her. I waited for Mahone to introduce her, which he did with many marks upon the path; and when the girl had acknowledged the introduction, which she did with laughter and the shaking of her marvelous head, to throw the hair back from her eyes, she playfully ordered Mahone to get away. "I am going to help take him into the house," she said. She took hold of my arm, peeping at Arabella.

"Do they send you to search for the black tulip?" Arabella asked, smiling at her.

"No, they put a black book in my hand and send me to school. And I steal away sometimes and look at the old whale that swallowed Jonah."

"Jonah," cried Arabella.

"Well, Mr. Jonah, then. Come on into the house now, and then we'll all see whether we are glad you came or not. There is my cousin Wilbur standing in the door. See," she cried, "I am helping to bring him."

The young doctor stepped down gracefully, to meet the visitors, but to me it seemed to concern him but little whether I was brought in or turned out upon the road. He gave me a look that I didn't like, but I was still resolved not to hate him. Harvey glanced at his "price mark," and mechanically took his hand, but Arabella gushed over him, and Mahone whispered to me: "Do you mind that, now!"

With her ever present air of motherly dignity Mrs. Jackson met us in the parlor. Arabella, who really loved her, I believe, kissed her rapturously, and again the Irishman whispered to me, "Wasted." The General was out on the estate somewhere, but soon came in. Arabella ran to him and tip-toeing, put her arms about his neck; and as it seemed to be my time to whisper I inquired of Mahone if that were wasted. "Begorry, I am not so sure about that," he said. "But I know one thing—he can stand a good deal of it."

The General requested us to come out upon the gallery, where it was cooler, and then he sent for his pipe. I had noticed that always immediately after lighting it some philosophical utterance followed, and I often caught myself speculating as to what it might be, politics, trade or religion. "I was talking to Preacher Ball today," he began, "and was informed by him that the world attained its highest civilization away back in the days of Babylon, and that it could never again reach that point. 'Then,' said I, 'ever since Babylon, God has been a failure.'" Mrs. Jackson looked up in surprise. "I mean no irreverence, my dear. I simply said it to stump that old fogy. Ha, ladies and gentlemen, the fact is that civilization has not as yet much more than sprouted."

"But do you think the world is as good as it used

to be?" Arabella inquired, not that she had ever thought on the subject and surely not that she cared, but simply to ask a question.

"It is many fold better, madam," he answered.

"And with wars going on all the time, too?"

"Madam, the world advances after every war. The days of bigotry and intolerance follow long periods of peace. War is the thunder storm—the lightning that clears the atmosphere. It stimulates patriotism, the noblest quality in man—for when one man arises that is willing to die for his country, there follow ten men worthy to live for it. But understand me: war should never be waged except in the interest of human freedom—of body and mind. The coward does not deserve to be free or to think. I have heard of timid men that were highly honorable, but I don't think I ever had dealings with one."

"But don't you think," said Harvey, "that commerce has had a great deal to do with the advancement of the world?"

"Undoubtedly, sir, for trade has followed war."

The dinner bell rang. At the Hermitage there was always enough for company. The house was open. At meal time any man was privileged to come in off the road and to take a seat at the table. If the guest were a man, and if he bore the appearance of being a "person of affairs," his name might be asked, as a compliment to him.

This was the first time that I had entered the dining-room. It was large and plain, a room designed for comfort, for air; and I observed that there had been no disposition to over-furnish it—an ostentation which even at this early day had begun to be apparent in the neighborhood.

The talk now became chatty. I sat to the left of

Arabella, with the elf and her cousin opposite. Mahone was between his "former Fate" and her husband. She gave me that old look and cooed: "I came out purposely to see you—I couldn't wait any longer."

Confound her, could she never be honest? Mahone was talking to Harvey. He did not know that she was "syruping" me. "I was so glad when I heard that you had escaped death at the hands of that awful man," she said. "He was my cousin—in a way, but I was afraid of him. He would have ruined me if he had lived—would have wrung money—my home out of me. And—and—" now she whispered—"he swore that if I married Mr. Mahone he would shoot him down like a dog."

"Is that the reason you didn't marry him?" I asked, low of tone for the Irishman and the merchant had ceased to talk.

"Oh, I won't say that—ought not to say it; but he would have shot the Professor. Tell me, did he take it hard? Oh, I hope not, but did he?"

Mahone and Harvey were talking. The General was telling Page about some of the numerous surgeons that chance had summoned to him. Arabella cooed in my ear, "Oh, I hope not."

"You trod upon a noble heart," I said.

"Yes, I am afraid so. But Mr. Harvey—do you know that—"

"Do I know what?"

"That he was so persuasive, and at the time when Cousin Calvin threatened so terribly. I just didn't know which way to turn."

"It seems that you did."

"Well, I happened to turn the right way, for Mr.

Harvey is *so* kind and thoughtful. Of course he's not romantic, but—''

"But he's got the goods," Mahone exclaimed. "I mean, General, that old law proof fellow."

I knew that this was a ready turn-off of his loud blurt; and the General accepted it as genuine, but Arabella comprehended, as he had intended that she should.

I looked across the table. Nettie was gazing at me, and her eyes seemed to have brought away pictures of the lights and the shades we had looked upon in the woods. Page was talking to her. He was good humored. Evidently he had not heard of our truant drive.

"And so you don't like school," said Arabella.

"Hate it," Nettie answered. "But after this I am going to study hard. I promised somebody, and I will."

"Ah, and have you at last promised me?" Page spoke up. "Well, now, see that you don't let that promise slip out of your mind."

She looked at me, a mischievous smile playing about her mouth, hiding in the corners, coming out again; and I knew that Page, in the conceit of his authority had deceived himself.

Arabella inquired of Mrs. Jackson if there were much sickness in the neighborhood. She knew how to touch about to find the live nerve of interest. Mrs. Jackson answered that there was considerable shaking with chills up and down the river, with only here and there a case of fever that might not recover. Not a great ways off a number of very poor people had just moved in from North Carolina, having been told that all they had to do to attain riches was merely to reach Tennessee. During all the day before she had kept two negroes and a wagon busy hauling provisions to them. She was greatly distressed concerning them. But the Lord surely would provide.

The General bowed to her. This was his method of communicating to her the fact that he was about to say something. "Mrs. Jackson," said he, "the Lord will provide every time *you* discover that any one is in need."

"Hear, hear," cried Harvey. It seems that before beginning business he had visited London, to study the methods of trade in that city, and that while there, had looked in upon a debating society known as the "Free Parliament."

Arabella began again to coo into my ear. "That young man just across from us is so interesting, don't you think?"

"I do not," I answered.

"Why, how can you say so?"

Confound her, she had discovered a new nerve and was picking at it. "He is to be a doctor, too," she went on. "And that witch in the sunrise is his cousin." There was a lull in the general talk about the board, and she hushed, but when the chatter was resumed, she continued: "She is mortgaged to him by some family shortsightedness, of course. I can see it in the authority by which he *thinks* he holds her. But she will walk the plank they have thrown out for her. Isn't it sad that a woman is always so ready to sacrifice herself?"

"And others," shouted Mahone—"old Bill Others, General. I don't suppose you ever heard of him, but he talked loud against your appointment as major-general of militia, in the tavern one night, and I led him out by the nose."

"And you acted rightly, sir," the General did not

hesitate to declare. Convinced of his own fitness for any position whatsoever, it was, in his opinion, outrageous to oppose him. To be his friend was to be right. To share his political views was to partake of the wisdom of statesmanship. Never to be wrong is narrow, of course; but always to be right is strength, even though it be error. I am convinced that Jackson believed himself appointed by the Almighty to achieve certain purposes. With no religious bigotry, except as to unswerving faith in his own divine appointment—more impetuous, with more of the easily observed frailties of human nature, he was a Cromwell in the backwoods. The Lord had repented that He made Adam, but not that He made Andrew.

After dinner, the General withdrew to his room for a nap, and his wife, as was her usual custom, excused herself that she might sit near him until he should fall asleep, reading to him the heroic measures of the Bible, the one hundred and ninth psalm, wherein David curses his enemies.

The rest of us, with the exception of Nettie sat beneath the trees in the yard. The girl, hoping to escape notice, hid about in the shrubbery; but Page detected her. She was not far from me and I heard him say to her, "No, you must go to school."

"Let me stay just a little while. These visitors will think it strange if I run away and leave them."

"No they won't. Remember, you promised me."

"I didn't promise you anything."

"What, have you forgotten already? There, now, run along, and when you come back we'll hitch up old Tom for a drive over into the woods."

"I don't like to drive—I hate the woods. I just want to sit down and rest."

"Well, then," he persisted, "run along and when

you come home from school you and I will sit down together, and you may rest while I talk to you."

"But Cousin Wilbur, you don't seem to understand that when I put it off so long rest don't do me any good. What is the use of being a doctor if you don't know any more about people than that?"

He would not yield. We do not have to go very far back into the past to discover how complete was man's mastership over woman—how complete he thought it was, when in him was vested a little authority. "You must go," he said. "It is your duty—to me."

Without another word she went, walking briskly, nor did she look back at us as we sat beneath the trees. About this time Harvey, half asleep, nodded out some word about business, and then it was that the Irishman chanced to remember that he had left the store open with no one to look after it.

"Oh, must you really go?" said Arabella, and I could have pulled her ears, for in her tone and her eyes there was a strong appeal against his going. He had jumped out of his chair, but now he halted.

"I ought to," he mumbled feebly.

"Yes, you ought," spoke up the doctor, man of duty.

"For your quick readiness to decide," replied the Irishman, bowing to him, "I thank you most—most heartily. But, sir, I hope that in the future I shall not be called upon to answer for your patients when you render decision after so little meditation."

Arabella laughed and Harvey awoke to a mild grin. But the young doctor was neither enlivened by mirth nor ruffled in resentment. "Oh," said he, "my patients will take care of themselves."

"Let us trust that they may be granted that privilege," Mahone replied. He bowed himself off; and

Arabella turning to me, asked me to go with her into the garden to look at the roses.

"Now don't speak of the heat of the day," she said to her husband. "You know I don't mind heat. Come on, Richard. It is only a few steps and I will help you to walk."

"I am not his physician, but if I were I should forbid his going," said the doctor.

"Of course you would," she replied. "Come on, Richard."

She took my arm and slowly led me into the garden. "I just wanted to talk to you," she said. "You knew that, didn't you?"

I knew it well enough. "Let us go into the summer-house and sit down, Richard." And when we had seated ourselves beneath the lattice work and the clambering vines she said: "It is so delightful to be here—alone."

"Mrs. Harvey," I began, but she stopped me with an "oh." Then, as I looked at her, into her eyes, she said: "But of course I shouldn't expect you to call me Arabella—now. What were you going to say?"

"I was going to ask you when you intended to stop flirting."

"What—I—flirting? You astonish me. Can't I be friendly—and with you?"

"Yes, and it is not very dangerous—"

"For the reason that the child-witch has put a real spell upon you," she broke in, laughing. "But then, why should you reprove me, or rather censure yourself through me?"

"I was not thinking of myself, but of Mahone. Why do you make eyes at him?"

"Do I? Honestly now, I didn't intend to. Richard, if I were to say something would you think me the most contemptible woman in the world? Yes, you would, and therefore I won't say it."

"Which means that I must urge you."

"No, it doesn't."

"You can't be honest."

"Not in your opinion when you are determined to set yourself against me."

"I admit your conquest. Say what was in your mind."

"It was about love."

"That's a fair start."

"About the only man I ever loved."

"Married twice and—you are not going to confess that you love your husband, or that you loved the one whose ancestors flew the hawks."

"No, to my shame."

"You mean to the interest of your confession. His name?"

"Mahone," she answered. "It is true, and I confess myself a—a weak fool, but I am determined to tell you the truth. But there is this one feature of redemption: I didn't know how much I loved him until I married Mr. Harvey."

"I suppose that is the usual way a woman discovers her love for some one else."

"Wiseacre, what do you know about women? Read this."

From her sleeve, which was now not short, she took a bit of folded paper, a note.

"Do you recognize the writing?"

"Yes. I once received a communication traced by the same pen. Lismukes."

"Yes, read it."

It ran: "Listen to me. If you marry that Irishman I will shoot him down like a dog. You refused to marry me, and my right to kill him lies in the privilege of the rejected lover, not recognized by the law, but by one's own conscience. But why should I speak to you about conscience, something you have never been known to possess! Of course it has not entered your head to marry that young prig, Staggs. You can wind him about your finger like a rag, and his poverty would mean nothing but rags. The Irishman has no prospects, it is true, but I think you love him and love, as I have found out, is a fool. I have begged the loan of money from you and you have refused. You said that you would have to sell your home. Now, you marry Harvey and all will be well. I'll never mention the loan to *you* again. It is the right course for you to take, for marriage is a business contract. If not it is a romantic failure. There are many things I am and a few things I am not, and prominent among the things I'm not is that I am not a liar. Marry Mahone and you murder him.''

I folded the paper and handed it back to her. ''I want you to keep it,'' she said. ''And one of these days, years from now when Mahone has forgotten me, I want you to give it to him. Perhaps it is asking a great deal of you, to believe me honest. You have always said I wasn't; but I am not bad, in a way you think I am. And I acknowledge that is wasn't Cousin Calvin's threat that wholly influenced my action, though it had much weight. I was fool enough to believe that by a marriage with prosperity I could adjust myself to happiness; but it was impossible. We do not quarrel, but I am the most wretched woman alive. He is far from stupid, but I have a contempt for his petty soul. You are the only one to whom I would confide this, and you must keep it until you think the time has come, and then—you may tell him. Will you do this, for me?"

She had spoken with more than frankness, not alone with her lips but with her manner, her eyes. No matter what she might have said or what proof she might have been able to offer I should still have been suspicious of her, and yet I could not but believe that there was much of truth in her "confession." Into my pocket I put the note, before uttering a word in answer to her appeal, and she sat looking at me, with what I could not help regarding as a half treacherous sadness in her eyes.

"I will keep the note and some day I will give it to him," I said. "But if I wait until he has forgotten you, his hand will never touch it. He is full of fancies and is unconsciously humorous. Such qualities may drive away many a care, but from his heart they cannot banish you."

"Gracious me, when do you study up all those set speeches? But do you think so, really? Oh, I hope he won't, and yet I ought to wish for his sake that he will cease to think of me. Now do you think I'm contemptible?"

"No. Was ever a handsome woman contemptible?"

"To hear you say that more than atones for all the humiliation of my confession."

"It was not a humiliation but a pleasure," I replied.

Upon returning to the yard we found Page and Harvey warm in a discussion over free trade, the merchant swearing that there ought to be no custom houses while the doctor swore that it was the tariff that developed the genius of home production.

"My dear," said Arabella, speaking to her husband, "I am ready to go as soon as you are," but I noticed that she gazed wistfully up the road, toward the store where the Irishman must have been agonizing in loneliness.

"I am ready now," Harvey answered, always willing to return to his counter.

A negro was ordered to harness their horse; and when it was announced that the vehicle was ready, I walked with Arabella out to the gate. "Coming here has done me a great deal of good," she said. "I don't feel that I'm half the criminal I was. I wonder if he'll come to tell me good-bye when he sees I'm going." We were now at the gate, and she stood, gazing up the road, her hand upon my arm.

"Are you making your hand tremble?" I asked in a low tone, and she whispered: "Richard, can't you have just a little faith in me? I am not all shallowness and deceit. He is not coming," she added, still gazing up the road, while her husband stood apart from us, to clinch a final point with Page. "He has forgotten me already. No, he is coming."

As Mahone came, pretending to be interested in something far down the road, she stood, silent, with her hand trembling on my arm. I had never seen an actress of any great power, but at this moment I felt that she was one.

"So glad you didn't let me—us go without saying good-bye, Professor," she said; and the Irishman answered: "Madam, I couldn't see you take your departure unnoticed by me."

"Oh, delightful. My dear—" this was aimed at Harvey, but it pierced Mahone like a dart—"how can you so completely ignore me? Professor, will you please assist me into the buggy?"

They drove off, the doctor popping at the merchant the final lash of his argument. Then Page remarked to us: "Devilish handsome woman; and I don't think it was his argument that caught her—must have been his calico."

"You do her wrong," Mahone answered. "She could never have been caught with calico. It was with silk, sir—fifteen bolts fresh from France by way of Stephen Girard, Philadelphia."

"Thank you for your information. By the way, how far is it to the school-house? I believe I'll go over and walk home with Nettie."

"If it is not too far for her I should think you could stand the walk," Mahone answered.

"I have thanked you for your information, and now I am indebted to you for your logic," said the doctor. "But let me add that no matter what the distance may be, the young lady has demanded the privilege of walking. She could ride if she wanted to."

He strode away. Mahone said to me: "He bows under the weight of his conceit; but ah, hah, me ladibuck, it will take more than silk on your part to hold the elf."

CHAPTER XIX.

GREW LIGHTER AT THE WINDOW.

FEELING that I had exerted myself too much, I went to my room, lay down, fell asleep, and when I awoke it was dark. I heard some one calling Nettie, and instantly the window was lighter. Had she been standing there, on the veranda? Going into the sitting-room, I found Mrs. Jackson searching the Bible for fighting passages with which to soothe her husband at bed time.

"I would not let them call you for supper because I thought you needed sleep," she said. "The General and Mr. Peter Cartwright, the preacher, are still at the table. Just walk out and see to it that you are served, Richard. Don't let their discussion blind you to your own interest."

They called Peter Cartwright old, but he was still in the prime of life. He was a most impressive man, not only a soldier of the Lord, as he termed himself, but in many respects a statesman of the Lord. With him, when religion was not humility, it was warfare. With him the sublimation of the spiritual atmosphere of the Book was the sling of David and the sword with which Peter smote off the servant's ear. Physically, he was not tall, not heavy, but his appearance suggested condensed power. When I was presented to him by the General, he arose, took my hand and looking with piercing steadiness into my eye, asked me if I were a saved man.

"I hope so, sir," I answered.

"You hope so. That is not enough—you must *feel*. Have you ever felt the outpouring of grace? Speak up, sir. Don't hang your head."

"Sir," said I, "it is quite possible that my belief may differ from yours and at the same time be just as honestly held."

"Satan's inspired quibble," he exclaimed. "He is after your soul. Have you ever heard me preach?"

"No, sir, I have never had that opportunity."

"Then see that the opportunity is not lacking in the future." With a jesture he dismissed me and addressed himself to the General. Jackson was ready for almost anything, but not for a religious argument. He did not dispute, preferring to let every man believe as he himself might elect; and although he was a strong believer in God, yet concerning formulated creeds of all sorts, he was skeptical. Once in a while as we sat in the dining-room, he would ask old Peter a question, mainly, I thought, to keep from answering one.

As soon as I could escape, I did so—went out upon the veranda, and there I sat, looking across to the distant hill where the sickle moon was hanging. Suddenly there came a footstep, light and thrilling, and I knew that Nettie was near. I arose to give her my chair.

"No," she said, "I haven't time to sit down. I am in my room, studying my lessons. Have you heard what they are going to do with me? I'll tell you. They gave me my choice, to go to Aunt 'Riah's and attend school from there, or to go to the boarding-school in Nashville. And I am not going to Aunt 'Riah's. It is always so pleasant not to go there. From Nashville I can come out here every Saturday night, and then you can help me with my studies, if it's not too much trouble. Cousin Wilbur hasn't found out that we drove over into the woods. I thought it was my duty to tell him."

"But you didn't, did you?"

"No, but I may after a while. Duties keep a long time, you know. As Cousin Wilbur was coming along from school with me, he gave me a lecture. He said I was almost a grown woman and ought to be more careful how I talk. It was all true, but I knew it before he said it. Isn't it strange how much people tell us that we already know? I told him that the time for seriousness would come soon enough. He said it was already here—said his mother was married at sixteen; and then I answered, 'oh, that *was* serious, wasn't it?' And he didn't seem to like it very much. Well, I must go now and make like I'm studying whether I am or not. But I am going to study, Richard; I'm going to get me some big words, and use them as soon as I put on a longer dress. Did I say good-night before? If I didn't I say it now."

The General and Cartwright sat long at their discussion, and when the preacher had taken his leave, which he did after many "final" words, I heard Mrs. Jackson giving her husband his "night cap," a passage from Scripture, dealing with the sacking of Jericho.

About the time I was preparing for bed, Mahone came to my room. "Richard," he said, sitting down with a sigh, "I have been wondering whether or not it would be proper for me to send a copy of Tom Moore, modestly inscribed, to Arabella."

"I should think it would largely depend upon the inscription," I answered.

"Socratic wisdom," he murmured. "You know

I had thought of that myself, and I ruined three copies, getting at the proper dedication.''

''Why didn't you write it first on a separate sheet of paper and then transcribe it to the book?''

''Begorry, Richard, that's where my own wisdom failed me. I didn't think of it. But wisdom must fail somewhere, you know. If it didn't it would encroach upon Divine preserves. But I can stimulate trade by selling the damaged copies at half price. Richard, she gave me a look that started new blood to circulating. And I have thought that even if she did marry him she must have had cause.''

''It would seem so.''

''A very profound observation, Richard. But of course I have kept all suggestion of that look out of the inscription, otherwise it would not be fair to the husband. Here is what I have written.'' He took a package from beneath his arm, where he had held it skillfully concealed, unwrapped it, took out a book, cleared his throat and read: ''To Arabella Harvey, with the most Platonic regard, and with memories of eyes and lips that can never perish from the mind of one who is silent.''

''Is that plain enough now?'' he asked. ''Does it set forth the purposes of its own intention? What are you smiling at?''

I explained, as guardedly as I could, that it would hardly be looked upon as appropriate. ''Then you may write it yourself, sir,'' he said, as if I had engaged him to perform the delicate task.

''Don't misunderstand me, Dan,'' I replied. ''It would be wholly appropriate for her and I know she would like it, but you know we must consider Harvey, too. He might look upon it as too strong a draft on— well, on the near past.''

"You are right, Richard. He is entitled to some consideration, under the law, and we will give it to him. I will be elegant by being more than simple. How would this do: 'For Mr. and Mrs. Harvey, with compliments to the latter?' "

"That's just a little awkward, isn't it?"

"It is if you think so, and it seems that you are determined in that direction. Ah, I have it," he cried, his countenance brightening. "I will sleep over it, and to-morrow morning I may decide not to send the book at all. That will be the best plan, and I wonder that I didn't think of it before. Tell me, in her talk with you did she touch upon the somewhat delicate subject of your killing her relative? But perhaps he was not near enough kin to render the subject delicate. But did she mention it?"

"Yes, but not reproachfully."

"A generous woman, Richard; yes, sir, notwithstanding her selfishness. By the way, the young doctor was over at the store just before supper time, and he was most glib about his prospects. After his marriage he is going to settle down over in the town of Gallatin, not far from here. Somehow he had heard of my affair with the widow—that was—and he said I didn't know how to manage her. I told him, begorry, that he was right. He said that man inherited authority over woman, and that when he showed the least sign of mismanagement, she began to slip away from him. In dealing with a woman a man must never permit his love to weaken him into a lack of firmness. She might for a while pout at his decisions, but soon she would come to respect them; that an ounce of genuine respect was better than a pound of emotional love. He called my attention to the excellent training he was giving the elf. I had my sleeves rolled up at the time, having been lifting some boxes, but I rolled down one of them and laughed into it. If she doesn't love him now, Richard, she never can, but here arises that same trouble that comes upon so many women—she will think she must of necessity love him after marriage. And the trouble with the elf is that at heart she is—I might say—oppressed with a sense of duty. I don't say this, though, to discourage you, for the Lord knows you don't need any discouragement. And if she should pull away from what she regards as her duty to him, then the trouble will begin sure enough. He thinks he needs her and he won't give her up. Then I hinted in the most skillful way.

" 'But suppose,' said I, 'that some fellow wins her love, what then?'

" 'You are supposing that she is to be created anew,' he answered. And when I said I was not so sure about that, he replied: 'When a man knows what it means, he will not be so likely to attempt to win her love. She was born for me, was given to me by her mother, and I will see to it that there shall be no transfer.'

" 'Of property,' I delicately suggested, and he said,

" 'Well, yes, if you desire to put it that way.' "

"But Dan, do you consider the fact that I shall not try to take her away from him?"

"You've done so already, without consideration—and that is why I see trouble coming, but I won't oppress you with it, although it will be the sweetest trouble a man ever engaged in. Good-night. I cannot leave you in pleasanter company than with yourself."

CHAPTER XX.

AFTER sleeping over his "idea" Mahone sent to Arabella a copy of Moore, inscribed, "With the compliments of an unknown friend." The negro who bore this precious gift was instructed that under no circumstances was he to let it be known that he had been sent from the Hermitage, and that if she seemed to suspect it he must declare himself a "free negro, acting without authority." The darky had just passed from sight when the Irishman began to speculate as to the contents of the note Arabella might send back by him; and when in the afternoon he returned with no message, Mahone said to him: "It's the last time I'll ever send you anywhere. Mind that, now."

He waited all day for a special messenger from town—waited during three days, and then he charged Arabella with ingratitude. "I have taken no snap judgment in this matter," he remarked to me, sitting in my room. "I have given her plenty of time and ample opportunity to redeem herself, and she stubbornly refuses. Now, sir, I shall permit her to take her own course."

I was now well enough to enjoy thoroughly the humor of his distress and I did not care to reason with him. But when with repetitions he had ceased to be amusing, I said: "Dan, perhaps she hasn't been able to guess who sent the book. Does she know your handwriting?"

"Begorry, she's had time enough now to become acquainted with it. I sent her the book three days ago."

"But did she ever see any of your writing before?"

"Well, in sentiment if not in form. I am the author of an epitaph cut on a tomb-stone in the graveyard, and it was myself that had the pleasure to stand near by one Sunday afternoon and hear her read it. The lines were descriptive of the virtues of one Dennis Gorman, the same that imported the first Irish whisky into the town, and who lost his life while patriotically trying to roll out a barrel of it when his place of business was burning down. I made bold to take off my hat and to tell her that I was the author of the sentiments chiseled in the stone, and the smile of her approval compensated me for the fact that poor Dennis was no more. Richard, I have a piece of news for you. Just before I came into the room I heard the young doctor say to Mrs. Jackson that he intends to take his departure early to-morrow morning, the same time that the elf drives in to her new school. What do you say to that, now?"

"Well, it ought not to concern me very much but I'm glad he is going."

"Spoken with absolute sincerity. By the way, Cartwright preaches to-night in a church about half way between here and town. I heard the young doctor say he was going to take the elf. Wouldn't you like to go along with me? But why do I ask? I know you would. And Richard, we'll start early enough so we can drive into town and out again—we'll drive around by Arabella's house and note the many changes that have taken place since the notable events hap-

pened. You haven't been back there and neither
have I, and it's been long enough now so that a storm
won't be raised over our appearance. Arrah, that
was an inspiration.''

When the time came to go, and it came early, Mahone closed the store, remarking that as business had
been rather active of late, the place as well as himself
was in need of rest.

The town was busy, and as we drove through the
streets, no one seemed to take note of me. My "little
affair" had blown over. We did not go near Harvey's store, Mahone declaring that he did not wish
to look upon anything that might remind him of business, but drove around by our old home. We did
not hear Arabella singing, but as we drew near we
saw her sitting on the veranda, reading a book. Ap-
pearances did not demand that we should give an excuse for halting, but the Irishman was ready with
one.

"Hah, pleasant time of day to you, Mrs. Harvey.
We have stopped to deliver two fine chickens sent by
Mrs. Jackson, thoughtful and generous body that she
is—but confound that negro, he has forgotten to put
them into the buggy. Mind that, Richard; and I'd
hate to stand in his shoes, the negligent scoundrel.
I am very sorry, Madam; and as we have been
thwarted of the object of our mission we might as
well drive on, as we are in a bit of a hurry."

"Oh, I'm so sorry you forgot the chickens," she
said, holding up her book and coquettishly peeping at
us over the top of it.

"It was not ourselves that forgot them, madam,
but the negligent negro. We saw them after they had
been caught and tied, and Richard remarked of one

of them that he was as fine a specimen as he had ever
seen. But as we are in a bit of a hurry—''

''Won't you get out and come in just for a few
moments?'' she cut him off.

''Oh, well, Madam, since you have so kindly insisted, we might.''

She brought out chairs and we sat down. Mahone
spoke of the genial warmth of the day—it was almost
hot enough to singe a cat—and then remarked: ''It
appears to be a beautiful book you are reading,
Madam. Would you mind letting me look at it?''
She handed it to him. ''Ah, Tom Moore,'' he exclaimed with enthusiasm. ''Now, where did you
come across this precious volume?''

''Read the inscription,'' she said, with a sly look
at me.

''Ah, it is a fine bit of sentiment,'' he declared.
'' 'From an unknown friend.' Judging from the handwriting I should think that the friend is a lady.''
Mahone's quill had been used for price-marking, and
the writing looked as if it had been done with a split
shingle nail. ''It was Hamlet, Madam, who says that
the hand of least employment hath the daintier
touch. You may therefore observe that this hand is
not a slave to writing.''

''Mr. Harvey thought it must have come from a
man,'' she said, with a slight cough.

''Did he, Madam? Surely he must be a man of
great discernment to hit upon such a conclusion.
However, on closer inspection I admit that it might
possibly have been done by a man. But we are in a
great rush, and I hope you will pardon what might
seem undue haste.''

As we were driving away the Irishman said to me:

"Why the devil didn't you knock me down? Couldn't you see I didn't want to go? Didn't I hobble to the gate like a ham-strung horse? And you sat there and let me deny having sent her the book. Now she never will write me a note telling me how charmed she was to receive it. But Richard," and he gripped my arm. "I'll tell you what I can do—and I will. Do you hear me now? I will buy a couple of chickens and take them back to her with their feet tied, and tell her that we found them by the roadside, where they had fluttered out. What an inspiration that is, now!"

It was a measure so full of humor for me that I offered no word against it. And so, he bought two chickens, pawning his word for them, swearing as we drove back toward Arabella's house, that it was the saints themselves that had enabled him to obtain credit with the poulterer, a stranger. Arabella was on the veranda with her book. "We found the chickens not far from here, Madam," Mahone cried as we drew up at the gate. "Yes, Madam, a little boy saw them as they fluttered out of the buggy and kept them for us and here they are."

He came forward, carrying the squawking hens by the feet, and with a bow presented them to her with the compliments of Mrs. Jackson.

"Oh, I am so much indebted," she replied, taking the chickens and then calling a negress to convey them to the place of future execution. "Oh, thank you so much for all your trouble, Mr. Mahone. And this very day, I will write a note of thanks to Mrs. Jackson and send it by a special messenger."

Mahone's jaw fell. "Oh, I don't think she desires you to feel under such obligations, Madam. I'm quite sure she does not. And now I remember her

saying that she hoped you wouldn't take the trouble
to write. She is one of the most charming of women,
Madam, but she is peculiar that way. Richard heard
her when she said you really must not write.''

"Oh, it will be a pleasure rather than a trouble,"
Arabella replied.

"Oh, no, Madam. You may think so, but I assure
you, as a man of more experience than yourself that
it will not.''

"But I know her better than you do, Professor,"
Arabella insisted. "Once she sent me five pounds
of butter with explicit instructions that I must not
write my acknowledgments, and because I didn't she
seemed hurt the next time I met her.''

Mahone was an easy if not always a graceful shifter
of positions. "Perhaps you are right," he admitted.
"Write, and confer upon me the honor of bearing
the note.''

Arabella shook her head. Was this woman acquainted with every trick that man could devise?
"That would look too much like a business receipt,"
she declared.

"Ha, Madam," Mahone cried, "you may not know
it, but Mrs. Jackson, gentle and affectionate as she
is, loves business. She insists upon writing all the
General's receipts. And I think she would like your
acknowledgments much better in the form of a receipt.''

"Well, perhaps I'd better not write at all," she
finally decided, and Mahone drew a long breath as if
he had just reached the last step of a long flight of
stairs.

"Richard," Arabella said to me, "have you set
out determinedly to cultivate the habit of silence? Or

has the midnight-eyed little witch stolen your tongue
as well as your heart?"

"Whenever there are hearts to be stolen you demand that they shall be left for you to steal," I answered, with good humor and with such she accepted
it, replying that when a woman ceased to lay modest
claim upon hearts it soon followed that she lost not
only the esteem of men but even the commonplace
regard of her own sex.

"Begorry—begging your pardon for the expression—" Mahone began, "but the hearts of men are
like wild cattle; they belong to those who catch them
and brand them. But sometimes the branding is
done with an iron that has been heated to white heat,
and then—then the devil's to pay—I beg pardon,
Madam. But we are still in a great hurry, Mrs. Harvey, and must go, thanking you for your kindness."

She did not say a word that might detain him;
she hoped that he would come again, some Sunday
when there was no business to keep her husband at
the store, and she shook hands with him, her lip
trembling, I thought, now that her almost unconquer-
able spirit of mischief had subsided.

Mahone did not speak until we had driven some
distance and then he remarked: "Are you a Biblical
scholar, Richard?"

"Not to boast of. Why?"

"I want to know what the Book says about man,
born of woman."

"Says that he is of few days and full of trouble."

"But are you sure it doesn't say he's an arrant
fool, a few days and full of trouble? If it doesn't,
it implies as much. If I hadn't waved that branding
iron we might now be sitting there in her presence,

receiving grace from a mere look of her eye. But I
had to be a fool; I had to proclaim that my heart had
been branded—burnt to the core. Then self-respect
insisted that I should no longer remain in her presence. But do you think she knows who sent her the
book, Richard?''

''Just as well as you do.''

''Then there's something to be thankful for. But
wasn't that chicken trick a shrewd one? In that de-
vice we have her completely deceived.''

''It was as plain to her, Dan, as your writing in
the book.''

''What, do you think so now? Surely not, Richard.''

''Just as plain as your writing was to yourself,''
I insisted; and leaning back with a sigh he swore that
never for a single moment did the devil lose track of
him. ''And you sat there, Richard, and saw me make
a fool of myself.''

''We had both made fools of ourselves before we
got there.''

''It is most charitable of you to include yourself.
Hah,'' he cried, ''but if she has at last discovered
who sent the book, she will write her grateful
acknowledgments and I can press the precious docu-
ment to my lips.''

His mood was so enlivened that I had not the heart
to rob him of a happiness which with him was so
easily snatched from the atmosphere and so easily
turned loose, to fly away like a bird; and as we drove
along, out toward the church, we were silent for the
most part, Mahone falling occasionally into deep
meditation.

The keeper of a way-side tavern, not far from the church, requested us to halt and to have supper with him, which we were more than willing to do; and when the negro waiter had brought a roasted chicken and placed it before Mahone, to be carved, the Irishman said to me: "Even the fowls of the barnyard remind us of our folly. Did you notice, Richard, that those two chickens, the last in the coop, were about the oldest in creation?"

"If you noticed it why did you take them?" I asked.

"Because I didn't notice it at the time, but now, with my memory; and that is the trouble with me— I notice too much from recollection. In that lies the difference between a man of judgment and a man of regret."

Then he proceeded to explain to the inn-keeper and his wife that he had bought from a poulterer named Mason, two hens that must have escaped the famine at Jamestown, during the earlier days of that settlement, and the inn-keeper and his thrifty better half broke out in loud laughter. "We let Mason have them a week ago for three yards of calico," said the man, "and early this morning when I was in town he said he hadn't been able to get rid of them. We had three, all of the same family, and tried to eat one of them, the youngest, I believe, and she held her own with two preachers a whole day, and when a hen can do that you may know she came out of the ark."

"Richard, mind that now," said Mahone. "What am I to do about it?"

"Go back and tell her that they were not intended for the table but for the nest," I answered.

He looked at me quizzically. "Do you mean that now? It would bring about an awkward situation, and you know that is something I cannot abide. No, sir, I'll let those hens take their own chances."

The inn-keeper said that the chances were all in their favor, whereupon his wife remarked: "They oughtn't to be put in with other chickens for they are inflicted with mites, the littlest insects you ever saw, and if they get on you they are the most annoying things you ever did see, that is, if you could see them, but you can't and that's where the trouble comes in."

It was now nearly sunset, and as services were to begin at early candle-lighting, we drove over to the church. Those were surely the days of intense religious fervor. As an organization, the Methodist church was comparatively young. Very old men who had heard Wesley and Whitefield in Georgia were still living, and dated the real reformation from that time. The circuit rider was more than a preacher—more than a path-finder; he was a path-maker. If in the cane brake you heard two sticks snap, one was broken by a bear, the other by an itinerant preacher of the Methodist church. One of the requisites of a minister of this faith was absolute fearlessness.

From every direction the people were coming, through the dusk, many of them singing hymns. During more than a week a revival had been in progress, but it was Peter Cartwright's first night in this, a new church. The house was soon filled to overflowing, the women and girls all sitting on one side of the aisle, the men and boys on the other. All was quiet before Cartwright arose, and when he did arise there fell a silence, a pulsating hush that was pain-

ful. The healing wound in my side throbbed. It
seemed that I could hear it.

We know that all great orators are great actors.
Cartwright had doubtless never seen the inside of a
theatre, but he was a wonderful actor. And at times,
every gesture was a climax. Not with the pen, not
with spoken words themselves could an adequate idea
of the range, the modulation and the power of his
voice be conveyed. In speaking of the greatest of all
emotional preachers, the copied master of Cartwright,
of Lorenzo Dow and of thousands of others who have
followed—in speaking of Whitefield, David Garrick
is said to have remarked: "He can pronounce the
word 'Mesopotamia' in such a way as to move an
audience to tears."

In the light of day, in print, Cartwright's words to
any reasoning mind would have been, not even rhetoric of the most flamboyant order, but bombast of
most ridiculous degree—coarse, not to say at times in-
decent; but spoken in the candle light, now in trem-
ulous melody, now in a bugle call, their effect was
miraculous. Sometimes he sobbed, and in one sob
was a torrent of words. The house no longer held an
audience, but an emotional mob. Women fell upon
the floor, shrieking; and an old man sitting near me
sprang to his feet and cried out: "If the devil is
present, let him step forward and I will meet him
face to face—I will fight him."

"Sit down, deluded brother," the preacher exclaimed. "Know ye all that the only way the devil
can be fought is with fire, not with his own fire, but
with fiery zeal for the Lord. But there is one among
you—" and at this moment his eye pierced me—"one
among you, if no more, who defies the power, who

sets himself up as his own criterion. Oh, young man,
put aside your vanity, come forward and kneel with
us at this altar. Because you narrowly escaped the
devil once, do not persuade yourself that you can do
so all the time. Pride and a fine horse will drag you
down.''

It was a long time since I had heard of my horse.
Other things having arisen to occupy my mind I had
forgotten him, except when I chanced to meet him in
the pasture and even then not making much over him,
not being particularly enamored of horse flesh.

''When you think you are well mounted and safest,
young man, you may find yourself floundering in the
muck and the mire of perdition. Come while it is yet
time. Think of the promises you may have made to
some young girl or to your mother. Don't let Satan
shout 'coward' in your ear. He is stubborn,'' and he
shook his finger at me, a fiery lash. ''But let him go
his way, Satan's way. The dews of death may lie
cold upon his countenance, frozen in the agony of
despair. Let him go, not that his soul is not precious
in our sight, but that his fate may serve as an example. Shall he perish?''

''No,'' shouted a man, seizing me by the arm. ''No,
we will drag him to the altar.''

How I escaped from him and got out of the house I
am unable to tell. I remember, however, that the
man clung to me until the preacher cried: ''Let him
go his way. Those that we must force to come are so
full of the devil's commandments that they would
pollute this altar. Let him go his way.''

I thought that I had been offered up as a spectacle
to the whole congregation, but found afterward that
it was an incident too common to be recalled. Out-

side in the grove, wives were searching for their husbands, mothers for their sons, shouting for them to come out of the darkness into the fold before the gates were closed forever. One woman seized me by mistake, and even as I was trying to explain that I was not her son, she strove to drag me back into the house.

I found Mahone sitting in the buggy. "How did you escape?" I inquired.

"Begorry," he answered, "I soon found that it was no place for an Irishman, and I got out about the time I went in. Did you see the elf?"

"No. Is she there?"

"Ah, is she? A beautiful flower in the midst of the wind; and although the tears were streaming down her face, yet I could see that she is not of this— this exorbitant faith. Get in, and if the sinners that have taken refuge in the darkness haven't cut our traces we'll drive out of this. Did you see the young doctor? He was there, and I looked through the window at him, and his countenance was as smooth as a silk handkerchief folded and ironed out. At the beginning of the discourse when the preacher touched upon Christian duty, the doctor looked over, caught the eye of the elf and smiled, turning it all to his own account."

Shortly after we reached home, and while I was walking alone beneath the trees, the doctor and Nettie drove up to the gate. I stood apart in the shadow to let them pass me on their way to the house. Together they entered the front door, but a few moments later the girl came out, alone, walking slowly down the path, towards me. "Richard," she softly

called, but when I stepped out into the pathway she
seemed frightened.

"Why, I really didn't know you were here," she
said. "I didn't see any one at all. And I called because I was thinking about you—how they treated
you over at the church. But I am sure they didn't
mean any harm by it. I could have told them that
you had been baptized in the Episcopal church. How
did I know? I was talking to Aunt Rachel about you
and she told me. Cousin Wilbur said it was a good
joke, the way they treated you, but it made me feel
awfully bad."

She took my arm and we walked out toward the
gate. "I am glad I found you," she said. "Twice
I've called you out in the dark, and you were not
there. I wanted so much to see you to-night because I
am going to town to school to-morrow, and can't
come out here again for nearly a week, but ofter that
I will come out every Saturday night. Are you cold
this hot night? You shake like you had a chill."

I told her that I was not cold, declared that I was
not shaking, spoke a hundred meaningless words;
and, hanging lightly on my arm, she laughed at me.
"Are you glad I'm going to stay here instead of going over to Aunt 'Riah's?" she asked, and I could
but answer in commonplace assurance that I was
"very glad indeed."

"Now we must walk right straight back again,"
she declared when we had reached the gate. "For
the first thing I know, Grandpa Cousin Wilbur will
wake up and think it his duty to find out where I
am. And it is, too, I suppose. Come on."

She swung me about, and with increasing slow-
ness, as Mahone would have said, we walked toward

the house. At the door we halted, neither of us knowing what for, and on the step above me she stood, just within the fan light. Nothing is too vague for the fancy of youth—and I imagined that from her hair perfumed shadows were falling. "Good-night," she said. and nothing but shadows remained.

CHAPTER XXI.

I did not see Nettie before she was driven into town on the following morning, but I had what I had long looked for, the opportunity to bid Wilbur Page good-bye. He said that he would like to speak with me alone, and together we walked out toward the barn. I felt that something was coming and it made me nervous. It could not, thus early, be the trouble that Mahone predicted, but I knew that it could not be a pleasure; and with him I walked in dread of what was coming.

"Fine day," he began, with natural skirmish, leading up to the engagement of all his forces, and I agreed that it was.

"Mr. Staggs, there is something I wanted to talk to you about."

"I presumed as much, sir, and I hope that you will proceed at once."

We had halted at the fence. From a rail he ripped a sliver and with his knife began to whittle upon it. I knew what it was to be shot, but I didn't want to know what it was to be stabbed, so I kept a sharp eye on him.

"I know, sir, that you are strongly attached to—"

"Only in a most honorable way, sir," I broke in.

"Yes," he said, plying his knife, "attached to your horse, but—"

"To my horse?"

191

"Yes, and very naturally so."

"Is it my horse you want to talk about? Then go ahead without any embarrassment."

"Oh, no embarrassment, I assure you—except—well, the truth is, he is the very animal I shall need in my practice, and while I do not desire you to mention it to the General, or to any one else, for that matter, yet I should like to buy him and give you my note."

I was almost grateful enough to have given him the horse, but I answered: "Your note is perfectly good, no doubt, but I don't care to sell him even for cash."

"I hope you'll think better of it, sir."

"That is the best I can think of it."

"Well, then, I'm sorry—don't mention it—good-bye."

While I was standing there, Mahone came along, taking a short cut from the store, never taking one toward it. I told him the outcome of my dreaded talk with Page, and he roared, and when he could speak without laughing, he said: "Why, he thinks his authority over her is so well established that—that he doesn't need to warn you."

"But you mistake me, Dan. I shall never attempt to—to swerve her from her duty to him. We ought not to love where we have no right."

"Oh, the moralist. If Mr. Addison were not dead, I would write to him. I would ask him to compose an essay on the moral obligation of a duelist. Love is like a new country—it is a matter of conquest; and when a woman, either consciously or unconsciously gives a man an opportunity to take her love and he doesn't—why she always holds it against him afterward. I am a man of vast experience—"

"How many love affairs have you had, Dan?"

"Only one, but in that one the experience was vast. And let me tell you: A man that would speak of a horse as this fellow did when he had good cause to speak of a girl, and one of the handsomest in the world, at that, deserves to be robbed—it would be a Christian duty to rob him."

The moral duty of a duelist! I thought of it many times during the day, while walking about, while trying to read; and I must confess that there were moments when my obligation to moral duty did not seem strong.

That night when the General returned from town rather late, he sent word to my room that he desired to see me in his library, on important business. Dressing as hastily as I could, I went to his "library," a room where on the walls there were a few books, many pistols, swords and the tails of foxes. He was sitting in his arm chair, but as I entered he arose as if I had been a man of importance, and bowed to me. "Sit down," he said, and when I had done so, wondering what was to come out of this late meeting, he inquired: "How long has it been since you had any direct information relative to your estate in Virginia?"

"Not since I came to Tennessee. There was such a tangle—"

"Not so much of a tangle as you may have been led to believe," he interrupted. "To-day there arrived a lawyer named Beal. Have you ever had any correspondence with him?"

"If I remember rightly, he wrote to my guardian, some time ago."

"Well, he has come out here to see you, is at the

Nashville inn now and will be at the Hermitage early
to-morrow morning. The matter of your interest has
come up for final adjustment and it will be necessary
for you to go to Virginia at once. Are you able?"

"Yes, sir, I feel strong, and my wound doesn't
pain me any."

"Have you any idea as to what you may be worth,
when you return?"

"None whatever, sir."

"Yet you intend to practice law, which is statesmanship as well as business. You ought to be worth
at least a hundred and fifty thousand dollars. And,
sir," and here his voice wavered, "I have learned by
accident that you made me heir to this estate, in the
event of your death at the hand of Lismukes."

"The amount involved made no difference, General. It would have been the same if I had thought
it was worth a million."

"Yes, I understand that. But it moves me deeply.
I know how you felt on that morning, walking to
meet a sure shot—almost certain death. Of course
you have heard of my trouble with Dickinson." He
glanced up at two pistols, crossed on the wall just
above his head. "The one with the butt toward you
killed him—has a slight notch, cut in the stock on that
morning. His aim was known as certain death. He
could stand off ten steps, and upon the word, put as
many bullets as he chose to fire in a space not bigger
than a half dollar."

"I have read numerous accounts of your meeting
with him," I answered—"all thrilling; but I should
esteem it a great favor if you would tell me the story
yourself You never speak of it, I know, and I have
heard that many attempts have been made to induce

y●u to express yourself, to tell how you felt and how
you still feel—'' I strove to put it in other words
but heard myself say—''toward that unhappy oc-
currence.''

''Unhappy indeed,'' the General replied. ''I had
resolved, Richard, never to speak of it to any one,
but I owe you, my son—owe you more than any man
could pay; but ·mind you, I shall not do so as a discharge in part of my great obligation, but as a confession of the close kinship that lies ʻbetween us.''

He arose and began slowly to walk up and down
the room, having with a gesture enjoined silence upon
me, not wishing me to thank him.

He began: ''Charles Dickinson, a young man, had
come here from Virginia, was, as we understood,
from an excellent family, and in consequence was
highly respected. To say that he was not always
sober would be the truth, but the same could be said
not only then but now, concerning nearly every
prominent man in the State. I had done him no in-
jury, had uttered no word against him, and I am unable to find a cause for the violent dislike he formed
against me. The byways leading to the main issue
were many and wearisome, but one day, word was
brought me that he had spoken of Mrs. Jackson. By
the Eternal! He had uttered the hell-invented false-
hood that the scoundrel Lismukes afterward repeated
in your hearing, and which, as you know, could not
help but have cost him his life. Well, I sought Dickinson, found him—and in the most quiet manner
asked him if the report regarding what he had said
were true. He answered without hesitation that he
may have spoken to that effect but that he was drinking at the time and therefore he was not responsible.

I pardoned him and went my way. This ought to have ended it, but did not. He took occasion to denounce me, and, sir, to repeat his slander. And now it was clear that his intention was to force a challenge.

"One day General Thomas Overton rode out to my place with a piece of decisive information—that Dickinson had written an infamous attack about me and had submitted it to the editor of the Impartial Review, for publication. 'General Overton' said I, 'go back to town as quickly as you can, ask to see the article and return here with your mind made up as to what I must do.' He did so, galloping away, and I waited, mortal hour after mortal hour.

"When Overton returned he said: 'You must challenge him.' I knew that it was an affair—of death, and I answered that I must see the article myself. And so, I mounted my horse and rode to town. Mr. Eastin, the editor, did not hesitate to show it to me. It has been published and you know that a more scurrilous lie could not have been written. A moment after looking at it I had made up my mind, and within an hour later I handed my answer to Overton —a challenge. Then, when the thing was done there came a sort of relief. The trouble had been long drawn out—after one of his denunciations of me, Dickinson had gone on a long voyage down the river and had just returned; and, sir, I had heard that during the whole of the time of his absence he had practiced with his pistol to render his deadly aim more deadly. On the same day my challenge was sent, Overton received from Dr. Catlet, Dickinson's second, an acceptance. Both seconds conferred and drew up articles, agreeing that we, the principals, should meet on a Friday the thirtieth instant at Harrison Mills, in Logan county, Kentucky, but when the paper was submitted to me, I objected to waiting a week. Catlet had urged delay on the ground that his principal had no dueling pistols and that it would take time to procure them.

" 'He shall have choice of mine,' said I. This was on Saturday, May 24th, and it was finally settled that the meeting was to take place on the following Friday. What an age can be held within the bounds of so short a time! I had to keep it from Mrs. Jackson; had to seem that nothing of unusual moment was on my mind; and at night I sat, listening to her as she read the Bible. Thus the days crawled along. Often I detected myself wondering, 'what shall I know this time next week? Shall all the hidden mysteries that religion has sought to fathom, be plain to me?'

"One night—two nights before the meeting, Mrs. Jackson, after having read from the Bible, which I preferred to the New Testament, put the book aside and requested me to let her read the story of the conversion of Paul. I consented, of course, and for a long time I reflected over that great man. For all churches I have respect, but my own views were Calvanistic. I believed that if I had been created to be saved, nothing could destroy my soul. But my body! Overton, who knew Dickinson well, and who had seen him fire at a mark, could give me no encouragement, other than that I might also kill him—and with all of my speculations over Paul, this was the sweetest hope he could have given.

"Thursday came. The place of meeting was a day's ride. With my party, whom I met in Nashville, I was

on the road before sunrise, but Dickinson and his
friends had preceded us. This was brought to my notice in a most significant manner. It is true, as has
been printed in the several newspaper accounts, that
while riding along, Dickinson engaged the attention
of his friends with fine shooting, and that at a public
house, having with his bullet cut a string that hung
from a tree, he told the landlord to call my attention
to the feat. The landlord did so, remarking in his
rough way that if he had a negro with no better hold
on his life he would sell him cheap on credit. I needed nothing to make me more serious. The sad faces
of my friends were enough, but Overton was inclined
now to be hopeful, not however that escape on my
part was possible, but that I might be only wounded.
In the fine shooting of Dickinson along the road he
read signs of over confidence.

"The method which had been decided on was far
out of the ordinary. We were to stand with pistols
down until the word was given to fire. There was to
be no counting, no word of warning. At the command
each was to fire as soon as possible or to wait, at discretion, just as he thought best. There was a bare pos-
sibility that by firing first I might hit him, but Overton stood against this notion. He declared that Dickinson being quicker was sure to fire first. After some
discussion of the chances of being wholly disabled, I
agreed to take his fire. Late in the afternoon we arrived at an inn not far from the shores of the Red
River. Here we put up for the night. Dickinson and his
party found accommodations at a tavern not far
away. I am passing over many details because they
must already be familiar to you. After supper, and
I had been hungry, my spirits rose, and I felt livelier

than for more than a week past. Occasionally, the
picture of my home would arise before me, but with
an effort I would blur it and join in with my friends,
telling stories.

Overton had been an old Revolutionary soldier,
and I never grew weary of hearing him tell of the
hardships he endured, of the battles in which he had
been engaged. It was late when we went to bed, but
we were up early, and before breakfast rode down the
river to the place appointed for the meeting. When
we had dismounted and were approaching the field,
one of my party whose countenance was anything but
encouraging, asked me how I felt about the situation.
I told him that I felt well and had perfect control
over myself, 'and I shall bring him down,' I added,
but I saw by the expression of his countenance that
he did not believe it. The other party had arrived.
There had lately been rain, and the country was fresh
and beautiful. I recall a red bird flying, like a bit of
flame, across the small open space. Down near the
river bank, where a field fence ran, a quail was calling.

"Dr. Catlet won choice of positions for Dickinson, but to Overton fell the office of giving the command to fire. There was no unnecessary deliberation. We were placed in position, and Overton inquired of us individually if we were ready; and
upon receiving the assurance that we were, Dickinson speaking last, my second cried—'Fire.'

"Instantly I felt a terrible shock, and a moment
later a feeling of great exultation came over me. I
was hit, but not mortally—and through my mind
there shot the thought, like the flight of the red bird,

like a flame: 'The vengeance of justice shall cut down the slanderer.'

"Overton was gazing at me—had, as he afterward said, seen a puff of dust from the left breast of my coat, saw me raise my left arm, stared in dread of my falling; and then drew a long breath of relief. It had been Dickinson's aim to shoot me through the heart, and his aim had been almost perfect, but the buttoning of the lower button of my coat, puffing the upper part, had deceived him as to the size of my body, though this being my habit I had not thought to deceive him.

"Ha, I remember his wild look of terror when he realized that I was not to fall. 'Great God!' he cried, 'have I missed him?' And Overton, with his pistol raised, thundered: 'Back to the mark, sir.' Dickinson had fallen back, but instantly he stepped forward and stood resigned. He knew that his time had come, and I knew it, for as I was reported to have said, I should have remained standing long enough to kill him if he had shot me through the brains."

The General paused and took down the pistols, the one with the notch cut in the stock. The candle was burning low. Shadows flew about the walls, red birds, black birds.

"Yes, by the Eternal God, his time had come. In my heart there was no more of forgiveness than there is in the heart of nature when man has outraged her. I raised my pistol, this pistol, and took steady aim. I felt my blood flowing, but my nerves were steel. I pulled the trigger. The hammer stopped at half-cock. Enemies said that I had done this to prolong the agony, but I had not. My agony was to see him still alive, the slanderer of—of her." **He** pointed toward the room where his wife was sleeping. "I recocked the pistol, took another aim, as steady as before, and fired. Dickinson staggered. His friends ran forward and caught him and eased him to the ground. Overton walked up, looked at him, as they were stripping off his clothes, came back and said to me: 'He doesn't need anything more from you, General.' Then he discovered that I was bleeding. I assured him that my wound was not serious. But to the main point, the expression that so many have sought to extract from me. I deplore the necessity, but I do not regret the act. There can never come a time when I shall not believe it was a righteous decree—his death at my hand.''

He stood, a grim statue; and then, darkness. The candle was out.

CHAPTER XXII.

MRS. HILLIARD AND HER ACADEMY.

ATTORNEY BEAL came out early on the following day. He first went to the pastures to look at the stock, and then was kind enough to mention to me the nature of his important business. It was soon decided that on the next day we were to set out, horse-back, for Virginia. Then he went over to another pasture to look at the cattle. In the afternoon I sat with Mahone, beneath the trees, in front of the store. With the thought of my leaving him he was greatly depressed. But soon he brightened.

"Richard," said he, "I've been thinking of a great scheme for us both. In the event that the lawsuit is settled in your favor you will want to invest some of your fortune. To a man of my industrious habits it would seem a crime to let it lie idle. So now I have a plan. I have shrewdly observed that all up and down this river there are fine sites for stores. Build one and put me in charge of it as your active partner. I might suggest larger operations, in Nashville, but it would look too much as if we had designs on Harvey, to rob him of his trade because he had robbed me of the widow that was. What do you think of it?"

"I think we'd better postpone any definite arrangements until we settle up the estate."

"Perhaps you are right. Yes, that was well thought out. How long do you suppose it will take?"

"Well, you know what courts are."

"I do, sir; my father's brother had a small case in court, and it wore along till the court itself was finally abolished and no one ever knew what became of the suit. My father said it must have fallen out of the wagon as they were hauling off the ancient furniture. But tell me: Will you see the elf before you take your long journey?"

"I'll ride into town this evening to see her."

"Arrah, I applaud your decision. But mind you, don't leave her without saying something. Sometimes, you know, a man beats about the bush till there is nothing left but bushes to beat. Mind that."

I did mind it as I rode along toward town, but with the tongue shut in the hard stocks of duty, what can one say?

The school building was not pretentious. It was constructed of logs, "frame," and with a new addition of brick. A brass plate on the front door informed me that it was "Mrs. Hilliard's Academy for Young Ladies." I lifted an enormous bronze knocker, head of a lion, let it fall, and the whole neighborhood was reverberant with noises, a great sound shattered, the fragments meeting one another at corners, in the garden, to blend and then to split, to fly off into the distance and to fall down upon the hills. If no one had come I should not have knocked again. I would not have run another risk of fracturing the community. Fortunately, some one came, a negress, who asked me if I wished to see any one, and upon receiving unqualified assurance that I did, she invited me into the parlor, where there were pictures that looked like the portraits of governors. In a corner stood a harp, and as I was looking at it, won-

dering how many hands had swept its strings, in
came a woman stately enough to have aroused the
envy of Martha Washington. And as I bowed lower
and lower, I thought of something said of the elder
Pitt, by Chesterfield, I believe, that in the presence
of royalty you could stand behind this great de-
fender of the Americans and see his hook nose down
between the calves of his legs.

She said that she was Mrs. Hilliard, which I would
not have doubted for the world, and then she asked
if she might be so bold as to inquire as to the object
of my visit. I believe that at this moment, had the
window been raised a little higher, I should have
leaped through it and run away after the shattered
noises, to fall down with them upon the distant hills,
but as there was no way of escape open I bowed again
and mumbled, "Miss Nettie Blakemore."

"Ah, a relative?"

It would have been hazardous to declare myself
her cousin. Cousins were as dangerous then as now;
and I feared to proclaim myself her uncle. I hesitated.

"A relative, sir?"

I thought of Mrs. Jackson's host of "distant con-
nections." "Yes, madam, her—her adopted—she is
my adopted sister. I adopted her with the consent
of—of all parties concerned." Again I bowed.
Straightening up I saw that she was looking at me
fixedly.

"Will you please state your business with her?"

"I would most willingly; yes, madam, but the fact
is I have no business, except to tell her good-bye.
My name, begging your pardon for not having introduced myself—but the fact is, if I must acknowledge

it, that with your unexpected grace you have overwhelmed me." It was time for another bow, and when I looked up she was smiling. "Madam, I am Richard Staggs, from the Hermitage."

"Ah, why didn't you tell me where you were from?" That seemed to make more difference than who I was. "I will send Miss Blakemore down at once. Be seated."

She floated out of the room, and without seeming to employ her feet, ascended the hall stairway. I stood with my back toward the door, looking at a portrait —and then my blood rippled. Nettie was in the room, laughing.

"Let us sit over here on the sofa, where none of the girls can peep at us down the stairs. Oh, but it's good to see some one from home, for it seems like a year since I left there. And you are looking so well. Your face isn't half so pale as it was. Did Cousin Wilbur tell you good-bye?"

"Yes, he led me over toward the barn and—"

"And said something about me. I know he did, although he promised not to. What did he say?"

"Not a word about you."

"He didn't—not a word? The—the stingy thing."

"What did you expect him to say?"

"Oh, I thought he might tell you how much he thought of me."

"No, that isn't it. As Mahone would say, you are beating about the bush. Tell me, didn't he lecture—"

"Oh, he always does that. He can't talk without lecturing. He is the lecturingest man in the world. How is Mr. Mahone? Oh, Mrs. Harvey was over here last night, and she walked about in the yard with me and talked about him all the time; and I wondered why she didn't marry him, but I suppose it was her duty to marry Mr. Harvey—she must have promised she would, and Aunt 'Riah and the preacher that comes there, say that promises of that sort are almost as sacred as marriages, and I suppose they are, don't you?''

''No, I don't—I mean I don't know. But Nettie, I do know—''

''Know what, Mr. Wise?''

''I know that marriage without love is a great crime.''

I was looking into her eyes, and she opened them wider—that was all. Her countenance did not change. ''But when people marry there must be love, of course. Why, they are married then.''

''But, Nettie, marriage does not always mean love.''

''I thought it did. But don't let us talk about it. Do I look as if I'd been studying hard? I have—as hard as ever I can; and pretty soon when you come to see me I can talk just like Mrs. Hilliard—and walk like her, too. She tries to teach all the girls to walk that way, and it gets so funny that I have to slip off somewhere and laugh. But I'm not giving you a chance to say a word, and they won't let you stay very long after the negro woman lights the candles. Here she comes now.''

The candles were lighted. I heard some one coughing slightly, at the head of the stairs, and I knew that Mrs. Hilliard had sounded the first alarm. When the negress had gone out, I said:

''Nettie, I have come to tell you good-bye.''

''Why don't you put it, come to say howdy?''

"I mean that I am to be gone for a long time, in Virginia, to settle an estate that has been in the courts many years. A lawyer has come for me, and I am to go back with him to-morrow morning."

She sat perfectly still. She did not utter a word. I took her hand, but it lay limp, but warm, like a bird just shot dead. "But I shall be back long before you are—are eighteen." The bird fluttered to life, flew away.

"Oh, I am awfully sorry," she said, and now her face was pale. "And I do hope you will come back before—before then."

"If I should be gone a very.long time, I hope you won't forget—the ride we had in the woods."

"The old whale that swallowed Jonah," she said, smiling faintly. "No, I can't forget that—can't forget anything."

The cough was coming down the stairs. I arose and took her hand—both hands. Gently I drew her toward me, nearer—and our lips met.

The cough had formed itself into a loud "ahem," at the door.

CHAPTER XXIII.

JUST WAITING.

BY sunrise the next morning, Mr. Beal and I were under way to Virginia. Mahone had arisen before day, to ride with me the first few miles of the long journey. Beal's horse trotted along in advance of us. The day was cloudy, as were my spirits, and yet within my heart a happiness came, to throb, to die away and then to come again. It was a memory sweeter than the honey of the poplar bloom. Her lips had come gladly to meet mine. There had been no beating about the bush, and I told Mahone so, as we rode along.

"Arrah, you are getting a little sense in your old age," he said. "And if you want her, I don't see how the devil himself can take her away from you. I blame myself for being so conscientious with the widow. Conscience is all well enough between man and man, but when it comes to woman, you've got to use your judgment, and the sharpest judgment you have. And the more time you give her to think, the less she thinks of you. Of course, you'll write to her. But don't write in care of that school. That Mrs. Hellion, or whatever her name happens to be at the time, would read it publicly and then order it burnt by the hangman. Richard, an inspiration. Send it in my care and I will take it to Arabella, and she will take it to the elf. I wouldn't take a thousand dollars and a pair of mules for this mind of mine.''

"I don't think I'd better write to her, Dan.''

"Of course you don't. I could have told you that. And you'll think that way up to the time you take your pen in hand. By the way, as old Falstaff would speak it, there is villainous news abroad. Did you see the paper yesterday? It says that a gentleman whose word cannot be questioned has arrived from Washington with the information that war will soon be declared with England. And if it should be, where will you find Daniel Mahone? In the front rank, where he belongs. I'm getting tired of this mercantile life. I was not cut out for these costermonger times. And if the war should come, hurry back as soon as you can and we will go in together.''

"I'll give you my hand on that, Dan.''

We drew up and solemnly shook hands. "This is a good time to leave you,'' said he. "How few men know when they have reached the proper climax. Take care of yourself, and the Lord bless you.''

I overtook Mr. Beal, and as I was now full of a subject which I had heard the General discuss, which had been talked about for a long time before the gentleman whose word could not be questioned had arrived from Washington—the war, I spoke of it to my companion. He shook his head gravely and answered that he feared there would be trouble. This angered me somewhat, believing as I did that every patriot ought with enthusiasm to welcome the event of war. He admitted as a truth, that England insulted us on the sea, and everywhere, for that matter; he acknowledged that the great Mississippi valley would become stagnant unless we owned without question the mouth of the river, "and yet," he declared, again gravely shaking his head, "I hope that there will be no war. It would ruin our commerce and—"

"Sir," I exclaimed, "a people that are afraid of losing their commerce—who place their shipping above everything else, do not deserve liberty."

"Tut, tut," he said, "you are a boy in a debating society. You stand ready to declaim, 'I come not here to talk. You know too well the story of our thraldom. We are slaves.' Now my father was a soldier during the Revolution, and I know something about war."

"On which side was your father, sir?" I demanded.

"Tut, tut. 'On the Grampian hills,' and so forth. If this war comes up, a decision in your case might hang fire for years."

"I don't give a snap for the estate as compared with the honor of the country," I shouted, and boy like, meant it, too.

"Pish, tish, 'an honest man, my neighbor, there he stands'—but we know all about it."

I sulked behind and did not join him again until evening, when we halted at an inn for the night. Then I found that he was simply having fun with me, and as soon as I discovered his humor, our relationship became pleasant enough; and so, by the time we reached the little town of Ashport, the end of our journey, we were friends.

The town was old and shabby, and exceedingly aristocratic, though the long-drawn lawsuit, but more especially my horse, got me into good society. I had no ready money, but the tavern-keeper was willing to

trust—my horse. Every day or so I would go to the
courthouse to see what progress my affairs were making, and each time was told that they were moving
with all the swiftness that circumstances would al-
low. I could not see why my presence was required.
Nothing was referred to me. I asked Beal why he
came for me, and he answered that I might be needed
at any moment to sign important documents.

There was a round-about mail between Ashport
and Nashville, and I wrote to Nettie—every night
during the first three weeks, but did not send one
of the letters. But I sent a letter to Mahone, and in
due time received an answer.

"As you doubtless know," he said, "the war talk
is still kept up. For the life of me, I can't see why
they want to be so slow. Deliberation is a fine thing,
Richard, but too much of it has lost many a battle.
On last Sunday who should drive out but Arabella,
and that 'yardstick' which the law forced upon her.
And now something is coming. At the dinner table
Arabella says to Mrs. Jackson: 'Aunt Rachel, I
want to thank you for the beautiful hens you sent
me some time ago.'

" 'Hens,' says Mrs. Jackson, in great surprise, 'my
dear, I didn't send you any hens.'

"Arabella looked at me with a smile that could have
been stirred off into sugar; and then it was time for
me to explain, which I did immediately. 'Oh, yes,
madam, you did send them,' I said to Mrs. Jackson.
'You may not think so, but surely you did.' And
then, adroitly, I changed the subject—I says, 'Come
now, let us talk of something else.' But Mrs. Jackson
wanted to talk about those damned chickens, till at
last a happy inspiration saved me. I put it all on

you, Richard. I said it was a joke you played on
Mrs. Harvey. 'In the toughness of the fowls lay the
fun of it,' I says. Wasn't that a shrewd way to get
out of it? There is an important piece of news which
I have neglected to set forth in the foregoing remarks. It is this: The plantation store at the Hermitage has been disposed of, and I am no longer an
active force in the great American world of barter.
And thus you see, as I predicted, all the copies of
my Tom Moore investment have been sold. The new
owner, a man named Quincey is not, in my opinion
the author of the Junius letters. While we were
taking stock I called his attention to the beautiful
books, and with the characteristic comment that business has for literature he said: 'Damn the books.
Count them hams.' Will he succeed? He will. Why?
Because he does not deserve to. I am not, however,
to be out of employment long. Soon, I am to take
charge of the school, now historic in your affections,
held in the unpretentious house beside the lane. It
is said that some of the youngsters are real students,
and if this be true, it will necessitate a little brushing
up on my part, for about me there is so little of the
pedant that I forget my learning almost as soon as
I have turned my back upon it. If you decide to
enter with me into the commercial life, I can give up
the school very easily. All I'll have to do is to turn
it loose, and it affords me an opportunity to tell
truth in saying that this will undoubtedly be a great
pleasure. It is always a relief to do something else,
no matter what you may have been doing previously.
It is thus that we inculcate diversity and make the
world move; but I am becoming philosophical, and
this should be avoided.

"The General bristles with the spirit of the coming war. His hair is on end. The other day, after having engaged in the social amenities of the town, he came home with his collar bone broken, but two of his enemies, when they come out again, will appear on crutches. He could lend them a few sets, including the long one that the boy Andrew still rides about the house. In case of war the General, as commander of the Tennessee militia, will offer himself and twenty-five hundred men. It is now understood that Tecumseh, the famous chief, has again visited the Indian tribes in Alabama, urging them to unite with the British against the Americans. If the Indians should heed him, and they undoubtedly will, as he is a great organizer, the country may expect more trouble from the savages than from the English."

The months dragged by. A decision was rendered in my favor, which gave me great pleasure until there came a frown from Beal—the information that an appeal had been taken. "But now we are getting down to it in earnest," said he. I thought so myself. Then I asked him how long it might take, and he seemed hurt. "How long indeed!" he murmured, untying a bundle of papers and tying it up again. "You must know that law is deliberative, not to say solemn." I told him that I thought it solemn, whereupon he seemed hurt again.

Winter came, and the inn-keeper began to grow suspicious—of my horse. But as my case was now rushing, having almost reached the front door of the court above, I succeeded in borrowing a thousand dollars, paid my bill, and received a gracious smile. Spring came, and with it hot wind from the blast furnace of war. Early summer, and war was declared. I decided to return at once to Tennessee and to offer my services to General Jackson.

Reaching Nashville in the evening, I found the "city" in the throes of great excitement. The journey had been long and wearisome, but there was an especial cause to keep me out of bed—General Jackson was making a speech on the public square. In the glare of bonfires and torches he stood upon a hogshead of tobacco, haranguing a great and enthusiastic throng of citizens. The government had accepted the offer of his services, and he was now calling for volunteers. Amid the clamor I heard the distant shout of "Arrah, arrah!" and peering through the crowd I saw Mahone standing with one hand resting on the orator's persuasive "pulpit,"—a pulpit indeed, whence came thundering forth the doctrine of Patriotism. It required some time and not a little force, but finally "edging" myself within reach of the Irishman, I touched him on the shoulder. He looked around and then with a louder "Arrah," he seized me. Then the General's eye fell upon me, and, reaching down, with a pause in his fervid appeal, he grasped my up-raised hand. As soon as we could, Mahone and I "wormed" our way out to the edge of the crowd. For a long time we spoke but little and in low words, giving our attention to the General's speech, but when the orator had closed, Mahone broke forth:

"By the faith of me, I expected you, and this very night, too. I don't know why, but I did. Come, let us go on over to the inn and be near the General. Each word he utters has peculiar significance for me now—he is my commander, and yours."

As we proceeded toward the inn, I asked the one

question nearest my heart. It was vacation time and
I inquired if Nettie were at the Hermitage. "The
news I have for you is bad, but I will break it gently, not to say adroitly. Therefore, we will talk
about something else, leading up to it. The—"

"Confound it, tell me, man."

"I will, then. She was there until yesterday after
the school turned out, and then she was dragged
away on a visit to her Aunt 'Riah, the young doctor
having come after her. She had been talking to me
about your coming, and a happier creature I never
saw, but along had to come that spalpeen. She put
as bright a face on it as she could, but I saw her cry-
ing behind the currant bushes. Go ahead, Richard, I
don't blame you for cursing the luck; I did it for you
before you got here."

"Have you any idea as to how long they are going
to compel her to stay?"

"Until school begins in September, and by that
time we'll be far into the war, if not well into
eternity. Don't grieve, for it is a sure shot that she
loves you, and when a man is assured of a woman's
love, he oughtn't to care so much then what becomes
of her."

Out of this "logic" I drew but little consolation.
Love, loving is never assured of love—in youth, in
absence. It was a trick of that infernal doctor's.
He knew that the beating of the drum would call me
home.

At the tavern there was much clamor, much drinking. In the bar-room two men sat at a table taking
down the names of volunteers. Mahone and I were
soon enrolled. The General was so busily employed
here and there that I had but small chance to talk to

him, but he requested me to ride out home with him,
saying that he would take his leave about midnight.

"I reckon that young fellow will fight," said an
old man, pointing to me, and the General answered:
"Sir, I would stake my existence on his bravery."

This made me feel as proud as if I had captured
a British battery. Numerous men came forward to
shake me by the hand, as if I had really done something, and for a time I was a hero, so great do we
weak mortals regard one who stands in the light of
authority's favor.

It was past midnight when we set out for home.
Absence and imagination had rendered objects along
the road familiar to me, and I looked for them. Here‐
and there by the wayside, bonfires were burning, and
in front of the tavern where Mahone and I had eaten
supper just before going to hear Cartwright preach,
a man was beating a war drum. The General in high
spirits, said: "I am a stranger to the powers in
Washington, or if known at all, better known through
my enemies than my friends, and the government's
ready acceptance of my services was a surprise to me.
I did not support Mr. Madison for the Presidency,
and my friendship for Aaron Burr stood against me.
Mahone, to-morrow morning you start out and do
what you can toward raising a company, and you
shall have a commission as captain of infantry."

"Arrah!" cried Mahone, "I'll start with the first
peep of day, and it is not for me to boast, General,
but I will merit the confidence and the commission.
No one can love this country more than an Irishman,
sir—and no one is more ready to shed his blood for
any cause—whether he thinks it's right or not. Infantry! I like to walk, and you would see me walk-

ing now, but for the fact that I couldn't keep up
with more than one of you at a time. Something will
rouse the early bird from her nest in the morning,
and it will be no other than myself.''

The General waited patiently until Mahone was
done, and then he said to me: ''And, Richard, there'll
be need of you, close to me. You shall be on my staff,
with the rank of captain. Governor Blount will
make out the commissions at my request, to-morrow.''

My much-praised horse had never seemed so high
before. On him I was trotted, just beneath the stars.
I do not know what extravagant words of gratitude
I uttered, in the emotion-blindness that had fallen
into my eyes, there in the darkness.

The next morning Mahone aroused me before daylight. ''I hope I find you well, Captain,'' he said
when I had lighted a candle. ''Begorry, it was little
I slept, but it makes a great deal of difference in a
man's feelings when he hasn't slept much and gets
up before day, what he gets up for. No matter how
well he might have slept he wouldn't feel well, getting up to be hanged, but you and I get up for great
purposes, Richard, and the lark in the dew is no
fresher than I.''

The General was astir early, too, and we ate breakfast by candlelight. Mrs. Jackson made no pretense
of deploring the coming of war; she was pleased because her husband was delighted. At the table he
beamed upon us, like one inspired with a great mission, and surely it was his conviction that he had
been appointed by a higher power than the government at Washington. On his long crutch the boy
Andrew rode to the table, now no longer a mere

race horse but a war steed. Outside the roosters were crowing war, and the birds, when the day grew lighter, twittered their call to arms.

History proves that republics are rarely prepared for war. Where there is much liberty there is also much blind faith in the justice of the cause. Equipment decides battles, and the justice of the unfortunate cause is afterward pointed out by the statesman as a warning. But Tennessee was better prepared than almost any other state, not because she had an organized militia, but because nearly every man was a sharpshooter. The farmer that shot a squirrel in the body rather than in the head was accounted a poor marksman. But with all the drum beating and the rapid enrollment of the men, real progress was slow; not from any lack of incentive at home, but due to the sloth at Washington. The Tennessee troops were expected to furnish their own small arms and clothing—their own horses, in fact—but the government was negligent in providing artillery, ammunition and tents. Hull had disgraced his country with his cowardice, the shameful surrender at Detroit, and throughout the North there was the deepest melancholy. In the South the great Indian tribes, the Cherokees and the Creeks, stood ready to murder the whites, by this time persuaded by Tecumseh and his brother, the Prophet, to espouse England. Europe was shaking with Napoleonic ague. The world was groaning, and little thought was given by the Northern press to the ambitions of a backwoods General of raw militia, clamoring for a sight of the enemy. Jackson had succeeded in enrolling more than two thousand men, a great army considering the thinness of the settlements lying among the hills re-

mote from the river. At last encouraging word came
from the Secretary of War, and an order was issued
for a "massing" of the troops in Nashville, early in
December.

Mahone's activity had not surprised me; I had an-
ticipated it, but I was astonished at his executive
force. He not only raised one hundred men, but soon
fashioned them into the best-drilled company in the
regiment. Colonel Coffee, of the cavalry, who had
taken to wife one of the numerous nieces of Mrs.
Jackson, remarked one day to the General: "It
doesn't seem possible that your Irish captain is the
same man that used to sit about the store. Why,
this fellow has genius."

"Ah," the General replied, "genius deprived of all
opportunity is like a candle, unlighted; and there
are times when it can no more make opportunity
than a candle can furnish its own fire."

Mahone's commission and mine also had been made
out and signed by the governor. Mrs. Jackson super-
vised the making of our uniforms, and we were two
of the most gorgeous men in the army. The Irishman
loved the parade, the panoply of war, and one afternoon as we were walking about in the yard, casting
glances down the road toward Nashville, longing for
the call to battle, he turned upon a rooster that
thought to outstrut him: "Aroint you fop, or I will
pull out your tail to adorn my hat."

Had he been furnished with a pretext he would
have worn the entire chicken. "When you go in
swimming," said he "take off your clothes, but going
to war, put on gilt and brass. It is a part of the
game. There have been commanders noted for their
slouchiness, but as a general thing the dressiest sol-

dier is the best. I was anxious for Arabella to see
me in my regimentals, but bethought myself that I
ought not to excite her regret. Ah, and with the
women it takes a fast bolt of silk to run a race with
shoulder straps. If the elf could only see you now,
Richard, she would forget her duty to the spalpeen.
Have you written to her since you came back?"

"No, it wouldn't be wise."

"Wise is it? In love with a girl and expect to be
wise! You can't be both at the same time."

"Why, the doctor or her Aunt 'Riah would be sure
to see the letter, intercept it, no doubt, and that
would make it unpleasant for her."

"You are right. A man cannot be wise and in
love, but sometimes he may love and be right. The
weather is turning cold, do you notice? And to-
morrow we meet in grand review. I wish the enemy
were in front of us and it was an order to fire."

That night there came the heaviest fall of snow
that had been known since the settlement of the country. Shelter could not be furnished for the troops
in the town, and so, poorly provided as they were,
they camped on the common. A thousand cords of
wood were burnt to keep them from freezing. The
General set the example and the officers remained
with the men. Among these hardy pioneers there
was no complaint, except that there was no enemy to
be encountered. On the morning after this desperate
night, the General entered the inn where a number
of "civilians" were sitting about the fire. One of
them, a red-faced drover, was expressing his opinion
at the time, and evidently he did not know Jackson by
sight.

"What a shame it is," he said, "that those poor fel-

lows had to suffer in the cold out there all night while
the officers were tucked up in bed.''

''You infernal scoundrel,'' the General exclaimed,
''let me hear another word out of you and I'll teach
you what it is to be warm. I'll ram that red-hot and-
iron down your throat.''

Every one waited, but the drover was silent.

A number of flat boats had been constructed, and
before noon, the troops were embarked for Natchez,
by water eight hundred or a thousand miles distant.
Colonel Coffee with his cavalry proceeded by land.

''The luck of him,'' Mahone remarked. ''He'll be
sure to get into a fight, while we can do nothing but
float safely down the river.''

Jackson was a patriot, as the world knows, but he
was also a man—a human being. It was his determination, in the absence of explicit orders, to disembark
at Natchez rather than to proceed to New Orleans.
General Wilkinson was commander of the forces oc-
cupying the Crescent City, and he and Jackson were
not friends. Reporting to him would have chilled old
Andrew's soul, besides, no enemy had been seen on
the southern coast. It was our hope to encounter the
Indians and the English somewhere in Mississippi.

Our quarters at Natchez were comfortable enough,
but as the impatient General remarked, as we waited
for orders to march into the interior, we were comfortable at home. One day he wrote to the War Department, almost demanding service, submitting a
plan for leading his men against the Canadians. How
anxiously he waited for an answer! I well recall
the morning it came. I never saw him more excited
than when he received the paper. He ripped it open,
and then I had to turn my face away. I could not

endure that suffering countenance. The order was, in short, that the troops were not needed, that they should be disbanded immediately, and that the munitions should be turned over to General Wilkinson. It was soon known throughout the camp that the news was bad; and it was soon understood, too, that the peremptory order was not to be obeyed, except in part.

"Disband my men here and let them wander home like sheep! In Washington, they must take me for an idiot. Turn my guns over to Wilkinson! By the Eternal! he shall not have one of them."

But it required money to move even this little army. We had floated down, but we couldn't float up, and the boats were therefore useless. The men were, many of them, in need of shoes, and for the sick transportation was required. To the merchants of the town Jackson pawned his own word for shoes and clothing, in the event that the government refused to pay; and so, one morning we broke camp and sadly marched toward home, five hundred miles distant by land. The horses were needed for the sick. The General walked, striding in advance, and it was at this time that to him was given the nickname of Old Hickory, the latter because he was so tough, and "old" because the men looked upon him as their father, facts set forth in history, and the "lives" written of this remarkable man.

On the way we met a modification of the peremptory order to disband, but nothing was said about expenses or the payment of the soldiers, who for their services and their hardships had not received a penny.

Mahone was crushed. "It is a death blow to all

hope,'' he said to me one night as I sat with him in
his improvised tent. ''The President and all the
secretaries at Washington are a lot of kittens with
their eyes not open. The idea that such men as these
not being needed at a time of war! What is war
getting to be? A 'good morning to you,' the drinking of a glass of skimmed milk, and the yawning and
stretching and gaping of one wasted day into another? I am now fully convinced that I was intended
for a soldier, but along comes Fate and befuddles her
own design.''

In such lamenting was shown the spirit of every
man, in bivouac by night and in weary march by
day. It seemed an army returning from defeat; and
when at last we marched into Nashville, the cheering
of the people fell as taunting mockeries. Drawn up
in order, we were compelled to listen to welcoming
addresses, to hear such empty, such humiliating
words as ''our gallant volunteers—our brave sons.''
The ladies had made for us a silken banner, pictured
with scenes of victory; and we accepted it, the flag,
the lies tapestried upon it, and hung our heads.
There was now nothing to do but to go home, and so,
we were disbanded.

Together, Mahone and I rode out toward the Hermitage, and now I did not care to look upon objects that absence and imagination had rendered
dear and familiar to my dreams. ''The world may
stagger along a few days more,'' said Mahone, ''but
I doubt it. It's wheezing for breath. A flag was it
they gave us? Why didn't they bring us out a rusty
chain forged in Birmingham? And I am now to
throw off this cocked hat, and set in its place the dull
and dusty cap of the schoolman. I am to prate to

the children about patriotism when the government hasn't any more than could flounce about in plenty of room on the point of a pin. Ah, Arabella, you were wise in marrying a man of the times. And if he sells a few more bolts of silk this year, I have no doubt they will make him Secretary of War the next."

Upon arriving at the Hermitage I found a letter, calling me back to Virginia.

CHAPTER XXIV.

NEWS THAT WAS NOT GOOD.

MY cause had progressed. It had been taken to a higher court, had actually succeeded in obtaining recognition. The judges did not know, of course, that it had arrived, but the lawyers were aware of the fact. This higher court sat in Richmond, and to that city I took my way, and, upon arriving, plunged into dissipation—went to a theater. The play was Macbeth, and although there was some prejudice against it, having been written by an Englishman, yet the ill feeling largely subsided when a man came before the curtain and stated, on behalf of the management, that the author, though a Britisher, had died long before there arose any trouble between England and America.

"He was a Monarchist," some one shouted.

It was admitted, on the part of the management, that this might be true. "But," the speaker proceeded, "in his plays he made kings kill one another, and this was about as good a service as he could have rendered America."

The interrupter withdrew his objections, the candles were snuffed and the play proceeded. Lawyer Beal, who sat beside me, wanted to talk about my affairs. But I was living in another world; a world that will be real when many a hard reality of this world shall have passed away, when the conqueror's cannon, in the distant future, shall have been blown away—dust; when knowledge, a proper understanding among men, shall forever do away with war.

Along toward the end of the drama a man who sat next to Beal became much excited. "They can't whip old Macbeth," said he. "He's as mean as the devil, but, like the devil, he will come out on top."

"McDuff kills him," Beal answered.

"Bet you ten dollars he don't," bristled the man. "He can't—he hasn't got the force. Why, Macbeth is twice as strong."

"But my friend," Beal laughed, "it is written that McDuff must kill him in the end."

"I don't care how it's written—I'm looking at the men, and I want to tell you that I know men when I see them."

When the final scene came, with McDuff bearing the head of the tyrant, Beal's neighbor cried out: "Jugglery, sir. That's some other fellow's head."

That night, in bed, I thought of the play more than of my own affairs, and I was still musing over it the next morning at breakfast, when Beal came to drive me about the city. The lawyer assured me that my case would be rushed. The docket was about clear and there was no cause for delay. Had I been wiser, I could have told him that causes for delay made no difference since delay without cause was a privilege inherited from the first bench set up by man.

One morning I was pleased to receive a bulky letter from Mahone. He addressed me as "Dear Captain." But his news was not pleasant. "The General is in his normal condition," said he, "in bed and shot full of holes. Business being dull, he had a little difficulty with his friends, Thomas H. Benton and brother. I say friends because they had been such.

If it hadn't been for Benton's persistent activity, the General would have had to pay for those supplies in Natchez, and all of the expenses of bringing the army home, but that made no difference—the time was in bloom for fight and it had to come. The General and Colonel Coffee, and he has a keen relish for a row, too, let me tell you, met the Bentons at the inn, and as the affair had been properly led up to, the engagement opened with derringers, pistols of more polite and smaller caliber, suitable for spring wear, and with dirks intended for hot summer weather. Everybody was down at one time or another, and if it hadn't been for the failure of a pistol to fire now and then the undertaker would have been kept busy. When the smoke cleared away, it was found that among the other calamities the General was badly wounded, left shoulder broken among other visitations of cuts and bruises. Those Bentons can shoot hard. And so the General is in bed, and Mrs. Jackson is reading to him about Joshua, commanding his men, if they were willing to fight, to get down and lap like dogs. She wanted to read something about Lazarus, but he declared that he hadn't time for that, just at present. It struck me, however, that he had about all the time he could use. His disability comes inopportunely. The Creek Indians are more restless than ever, and more than likely we shall be ordered out again very soon. But what will it avail you and me if the General is not able to take command? I spoke to him about it, and he said, 'By the Eternal, sir, I'll be there. Don't you fret. Let them put it off for a month and I will ask no other odds.' I asked him how long it usually took him to get well. Before he answered, Mrs. Jackson came in to blow the ram's horns about the walls of Jericho for him, and so I got out, having heard those horns till I could recognize them if blown at night with a pack of hounds following. Now, my advice to you is this: Get back here as soon as you can, for, unless all signs fail, something is going to happen.''

After reading this letter, I asked Beal if he thought that my remaining would have any influence toward hastening the proceedings of the court, and failing to see the point of my shrewd joke, he answered: "Why, sir, the presence of the Governor himself could have no such influence.''

"In that event I shall return at once to Tennessee,'' said I. "And in the years to come, when gray-haired and toothless, I hobble back here on crutches, you may be able to tell me something definite.''

He argued against my leaving; he said that while my remaining could have no possible bearing on the court, yet it might weigh upon the general atmosphere of the cause. In the absence of any possible reason, this might have been a good thing to say, since more than half of what we utter in this life is meaningless, but it could not restrain me from my purpose. I know now what my nearness to the scene of the decision meant to him, that he would earlier get his share of the "clean up.''

Again I was on the road. In every little news center along the highways men discussed the desperate state of our affairs, and in a village one night I was enraged to hear a public speaker declare: "This sand rope known as the United States has about had its day. Nearly all its days have been dark, but a darker one is soon to come. The great men who brought about the Revolution have nearly all of them

passed away, leaving us weaklings to revert to the
King of England, our original owner." Such was
the melancholy opinion held in some parts of the
South and largely throughout the North. Disaster
after disaster would naturally weaken a people's
spirit, but in the North it was not disaster that
aroused a loud clamor against the war; it was the
loss of commerce. A convention at Hartford prayed
for peace at any price; but committees lying remote
from the sea did not beg for peace. About the time
the Hartford convention was supplicating the loudest, the Tennessee Legislature was passing an act for
the appropriation of money to equip Andrew Jackson's army.

I found the General sitting up, with that active
cavalryman, the boy, riding about him on his crutch
horse. The bullet-shattered man arose to greet me,
and then dropped back in his chair. I remarked,
with all the enthusiasm I could draw from a reservoir
not well supplied, that I was surprised to see him so
nearly recovered, and grimly smiling he answered:
"Captain, I shall be ready when the troops are. This
time, by the Eternal, this time, it is not to be a meaningless march, and the presentation of an unearned
banner; this time it means blood, for I shall march
into the enemy's country. We no longer lack an incentive. Look at the massacres by the Creeks. Get
into your uniform, sir."

Into my uniform! Brave words, in few accents a
promise of fame.

Mrs. Jackson came in to tell the General that he
must not sit up too long. Upon my arrival she had
greeted me as a mother greeting a son, with tender-

ness; and as I turned toward Jackson's room she had cautioned me not to say anything to "stir him."

"Why, my dear," he said, "the longer I sit up the stronger I feel. A man gathers most strength when his determination is exerted the most. Lying down, in the position of the vanquished, we cannot feel very determined."

"But it is bed time, Mr. Jackson," she gently persisted. To her he was never a soldier; he was always "Mr. Jackson," her loving husband.

"Mrs. Jackson, my dear," he tenderly—fought, for he could not plead—"it should not be bedtime for those who are not sleepy." But at that moment he caught sight of her Bible, and he therefore knew that his hour had come. I wondered as to whether his sleeping potion was to be the ram's horn or the sling of David, and as he bade me stay, I waited, assisting him to bed. But he asked for neither the horn nor the sling. His mind was dwelling, no doubt, upon some tardy official in Washington, and he therefore requested the hanging of Haman. He listened to the reading as a child listens to a fairy story, thrilled by every detail. "Ah," he said when his wife had ceased to read, "in another book scarcely less immortal there is this warning: 'Heat not a furnace for a foe so hot that it do scorch yourself.' I can sleep now."

A moment later he was asleep, and we tip-toed out into the sitting-room. Knowing that Mrs. Hilliard's Academy for Young Ladies had again called to books, to an attempt to walk "like the president," I asked Mrs. Jackson if Nettie came out every Saturday night.

"Why," she answered, "they have sent her to some

high-sounding school somewhere in Kentucky. I had a letter from her not long ago, and she seemed to be very much dissatisfied. She wanted to come back here—said she had never been so happy in her life as she was at our house. When she came here I thought she was to make this her home, until the time for her marriage. Why, she is my adopted niece, but, of course, 'Riah, as Wilbur's mother, has more of a claim on her. Nettie told me to say to you that she never could forget you—you had been so kind to her. She said, too, that she would come here on a visit just as soon as possible."

"They will not let it be possible," I answered bitterly.

Mrs. Jackson did not pretend that she misunderstood me. With motherly tenderness she looked at me. "It is very unfortunate," she said. "I told the child—I could not keep from telling her that obedience to the will of others instead of to the demands of her own heart would ruin her life. I told her that with my first husband—a duty marriage—I had been worse than wretched; and the poor child begged me not to tell her any more. Of course, promises to a dying mother ought to be kept sacredly, so far as possible; but from the deathbed even mothers cannot always look forward and see what is best for their children. It is deplorable, but when the time comes Nettie will sacrifice herself."

"I cannot believe it," I answered. "It is not in human nature. She—"

Slowly shaking her head, Mrs. Jackson shut me off. "Yes, it is in human nature, my son; it always has been and doubtless always will be. And, the more character a woman has, the more sacrifice. Nettie believes, as most girls do, I suppose—and as I believe—that love must surely follow marriage. It is not impossible, is true very often—but—I think I heard Mr. Jackson calling me."

She hastened from the room, and I went to my bed, to dream of Mrs. Hilliard's door knocker, of a cough at the head of the stairs, of willing lips coming to meet mine.

CHAPTER XXV.

A TASTE OF FIRE.

NEXT day, I found Mahone in camp, chaffing because he was not on the march. "We are waiting till the Creeks show they are in earnest by scalping the Governor. This ought to be written down in history as the tortoise war. Richard—Captain, begging your pardon, come off here with me. I have something of import to say to you."

He led me to a tree, and beneath it we sat down. With his cocked hat he fanned himself, and I noticed that to complete his military adornment he had not yet robbed the rooster of his tail. "Captain," he began, but I cut in upon him. "Don't Captain me. Be your own self."

"Surely, Richard, and glad of the opportunity. And now this leads me up to what I was going to say. You know Harvey—but of course you do. Well, for some time his lungs haven't been acting up to regulations, and so the doctor told him that what he needed to keep off death was an outdoor life. And then what does Harvey do? What indeed! He joins the army as a quartermaster with the rank of major, and, begorry, he wears a uniform that makes mine look like a set of cast-offs. Isn't that luck for you?"

"But what difference does it make? Why should you care how fine is his uniform?"

"Why should I care? Begorry, he'll keep on till he wins that woman's love. And do you know what

I'm going to do? I'm going to consult the authorities
as to what is the regulation uniform for a quartermaster, and if he has overdressed the part, I am
going to make him come out of it. Mind you, it is
not patriotism on his account; it is only a make-shift
to preserve his bellowses. But it gives Arabella a
grand opportunity—to stand in the store as the chief
head and supreme reference of the establishment,
and nothing could please her more than that, for,
Richard, when a woman has once been a widow, no
matter whatever else she may be, she is business. I
went around to the store to buy something—so it
would seem—and there she was issuing orders like
the commander of a division. She appeared to be
glad to see me, and thus appealed to, I said 'Madam,
I will be frank with you. I have no right to be here.'
But did she blush? She did not. She simply answered, with a long bit of ribbon in her mouth, 'Oh,
this is a public place and any one has the right to
come in, under the constitution of the country,' she
says, and then I answered, 'Oh, and if that is the
case, Madam, I bid you good day.' And I did; for I
wish to say right now that no woman can throw the
constitution at me with impunity.''

I could never tell by Mahone's manner, by the
tone of his voice, whether he were in earnest or playing me on his humorous line, like a bass; I never
knew when he was in real distress—but not even his
sorrows could be dark, for upon them a whimsical
light was sure to fall.

"Have you seen Atcherson?" he inquired, and instantly he added: "If you haven't you will very
soon. Is he a full-fledged preacher now? He is.
And is he more than that? By that same token he is

—yes, a chaplain in the army, and the first thing you
know he'll be around to pray with you. He came
around to see me—said he was glad I was in the army,
and begging his pardon in advance, I says, 'And
where the devil did you expect to find me?'

" 'Not at church,' says he, scoring one. Richard,
I suppose you have seen the order for the grand rally
of the troops, at Fayetteville, six days from now. It
is more than eighty miles away, and how the General
is to ride horseback that far when it is as much as he
can do to sit in a rocking-chair, is beyond me."

"When the time comes, you will find him at the
head of the troops," said I.

"That may be," he admitted, "but it will take
some pretty strong doses poured out of the ram's
horn, I arise the same to remark. In the meantime
let us hope, and pray—in case Atcherson gives us the
opportunity."

That night I called at Arabella's house, and there
she was, handsomer than ever, I thought. Major
Harvey, her husband, thinking that there was plenty
of time for the fresh air cure, continued to remain at
the house. Out of his bright uniform there came a
slight cough; and I looked at Arabella, but she did
not appear to have noticed it. The major said that
he longed to be on the march. There was nothing
particularly the matter with him, he declared. As to
his lungs—they were perfectly sound; he had been
confined too closely, that was all. I did not see anything in his condition to excite alarm, nor did his
wife, for though very gentle with him, she joked
him on his bearing as a soldier. Pretty soon he began
to fret over his business, and then, becoming serious,

Arabella assured him that his affairs had never been more prosperous, and that under her management they would continue to improve. After a time he went up to his room, and I heard him coughing after he had gone to bed.

"The doctor assures me that all he needs is a few months of open air life," said Arabella. "We—we have been getting along better of late," she added, recalling, of course, what she had said to me in the garden at the Hermitage. "Oh, we never did quarrel, you understand, but he seems to know me better than he did. I had a letter from the elf. You may draw your own conclusions as to why she wrote to me. We were not so well acquainted, you know." She looked at me with her old-time smile. Then she spoke of the General, of Mrs. Jackson, of Atcherson —of every one but Mahone, nor did I mention his name. When I returned to the camp the Captain asked me, knowing in what direction my visit lay, if she had inquired concerning him, and when I answered that she had not, he remarked:

"His failing health and that uniform have won her, two most potent factors, Richard. A woman is nearly always congenial with the man she nurses— for then she's got him helpless in her hands. Well, out in the field, I'll do all I can for him to cheer him up. I'll tell him that after he's gone I'll not try to marry her."

"No, Dan, you must never do that," said I, knowing that it was like him to "console" Harvey in that way.

"And why not? Am I not that generous? I will show you."

At this moment, the flap of the tent was put aside,

and Captain Atcherson entered. Some preachers so
subdue themselves that you can never tell whether
they are really glad to see you or whether their
smiles and tempered handshakes are given to all men
in common. But Atcherson appeared pleased to see
me again. Nor was it long before he inquired as to
the condition of my Virginia estate. General Jackson had spoken of the amount involved, and with
that sum of money a great deal of good could be ac-
complished toward the betterment of man's condition
in the Western country. There were many com-
munities where churches were needed.

"And schoolhouses, too, remember, as you go
along," said Mahone.

Atcherson sighed and admitted that no doubt at
least a few more schoolhouses ought to be built. Then
he asked me as to the condition of my soul, whether
or not I was ready—

"To meet the Creeks?" Mahone blurted. "Begorry, yes, and we are only waiting for the word to
march. And now, Brother Atcherson, don't worry
over our souls. Or, if you do, worry over the army
in a lump and let the individuals alone. We know
you are sincere, now, so don't fret about that; and
we know, also, being men of emancipated understanding, that no man can save the soul of another man—
and, wait a moment, we know, too, that if one man
tries to save souls to make his own shine brighter—
why, it is a sort of soul fame, a selfishness. Forgive
these few remarks, and join us in a bite to eat."

My duty was not at the camp, but at the General's
headquarters—his bedside; and as the slow days
dragged along, it seemed that for some time to come
the sick room would continue to comprise the scope

of his military activity. The regiment to which Mahone belonged was ordered to "mobilize" with the
army at Fayetteville, and a few days later the General and his staff set out.

Up to the very hour of his departure, I did not see
how it was possible for him to go, except in an am-
bulance; but he arose and dressed himself when his
horse had been led around to the steps of the veranda.
It was only with the utmost difficulty that he could
walk out of the bedroom; but when we had helped
him on his horse he seemed suddenly to gain strength.
Still he looked a sorry conqueror, with his left arm
in a sling and a bandage about his head. He rode,
though, like a warrior, erect and grim; but with all
his determination he could not reach Fayetteville at
the appointed time, so he wrote an address to the
troops and sent it forward by Major John Reid and
myself to be read to them. Like the Romans, Old
Hickory believed in haranguing his men, and not in-
frequently, he seemed to forecast the possibilities of
success by the force which had shown in his "docu-
ment," as the soldiers termed his military effusions.

Major Reid "addressed" the troops, and there was
much cheering. Reports had already been received,
announcing that a large body of Creek warriors and
renegade whites were marching upon us, and this put
the men in high spirits. Coffee, now a General, commanding the cavalry, had already captured and de-
stroyed an Indian village, killing in the operation, a
number of warriors; and Mahone, still morbidly impatient said to me: "Ah, the luck of that man.
Didn't lose but a few men, and each of them that was
killed stood a chance of killing an Indian! I was
talking to Quartermaster Harvey to-day, and he gave

me the unwelcome assurance that there is going to
be trouble about supplies. And it would be just my
luck to starve to death. Poor Harvey, he'll never be
able to starve. His cough's getting worse all the
time. But I haven't said anything to him about my
generous resolve. He thinks he's getting better. May
the Lord help him—and at the same time give him
the needed assistance toward getting supplies for
the army."

There was great cheering when the General arrived, for additional information had come assuring us that the Creeks in full force were marching
rapidly to give us battle. The old Indian fighters
smiled. Their Indian was not the red man of romance,
but of the real woods, the sneak and the slaughterer.
They know, however, that of all the Indians of the
South, the Creeks were the most to be dreaded, being
the shrewdest to find advantage and the most merci-
less afterward. The "alarming news" pleased the
General. "Ah," he said, "the enemy having heard of
my physical condition has most kindly consented to
assist me in cutting short the distance between us."

But a forced march of many miles failed to bring us
within sight of the enemy. The accounts of his disposition to accommodate the General had been over-
drawn. So we crossed the Tennessee River, went into
camp and waited for supplies. No matter what we
might be doing, the next thing was to wait for something to eat.

There was now, however, no doubt of the fact that
all the Indians of the Southern border, having listened
to the appeal of Tecumseh, were the allies of Great
Britain. The old Indian fighters knew that there
would soon be work enough for us to do; nor was the

first task of that work long deferred. But I have not essayed to write the annals of this or any other campaign. The Creek war, historical by many pens, is on many a shelf; and the Tennessee Historical Society possesses a thousand letters written from its battle-fields. My only object is to give a bit of character here and there, to recall to myself those blusterous days; to dream i quiet over them.

Our first taste of fire was the battle of Talladega. We had been waiting for reinforcements, and for supplies, of course. Neither had come. We did not care so much for reinforcements as for refreshments. The General resolved to strike while yet he had some little strength. Shrewd white men among the Indians knew the weakness of his meager army; they were counseling an attack upon him, in his camp, and could not imagine the desperation of his attack upon a superior and well-fed force. And when he did hurl himself upon them, there was no other conclusion than that he had suddenly received large reinforcements. But the Creeks made a brave stand.

It was not a great battle, it is true, but to me it was a thrilling sight. I saw Mahone, with his sword, cut down Black Paw, a chief. I saw Atcherson among the men, exhorting them—saw him seize a dead man's musket and turn it upon the enemy. I was near him —I spoke to him and he blushed as if I had detected him in some worldly sport.

One body of our men, mistaking an order, began to fall back. In a moment the General's ire was up. He had his own way of issuing an order or of speaking a command. "Head those damned sheep!" he yelled to me. They were easily "headed." They turned back and did good work. Soon the battle became a chase and then a hunt in the hills. "Improvident devils," said the General, "why couldn't they have been better provisioned? Why, they have devoured their corn down to the last peck."

Harvey was active in his search for supplies, so much so, it afterward developed, that he forged beyond the line of discretion. Three warriors, springing from ambush, seized him. His gorgeous uniform spoke great words to them. England would pay big for his scalp. He must be Jackson himself. Tecumseh had told them that the King of Britain wanted scalps rather than prisoners. Here was one of greatest value. The king-chief would wear it in his belt at council. There was no time to waste. They would kill the prisoner and then dispute as to who should bear off the trophy, his scalp. At this moment Mahone came clambering over the rocks. In a second he saw it all. He rushed upon them. With his pistols he shot two of the Indians. The other one, with tomahawk, turning sullenly upon him, threw his weapon. The Irishman dodged it, and, as the Indian was scrambling to scale a rock, sabered him. Harvey was almost dead, they had so roughly handled him. Atcherson, who had been striving to lend his aid, and who now came up, reported to me what had passed.

"Major Harvey, I hope I find your health improving, sir," said Mahone.

"Captain Mahone, you have most desperately risked your life to save mine."

"Major Harvey, have you found any cold roast beef among the remains of the enemy? I wouldn't mind eating a snack."

"Captain, I don't know how to thank you."

"Say grace over some potatoes," said the Irishman.

We had slaughtered the enemy, but our own loss had been light. Great, though, was our disappointment in not obtaining provisions. After the battle the General issued an address.

"Echo of the ram's horn," said Mahone to me, as a staff officer began to read the address. And then he began to wince under the mention of his own name for conspicuous bravery. He was recommended for promotion, and that night, when the General had sent for him he entered the tent like an embarrassed boy.

"Captain Mahone," said the General, "your commission as Colonel will soon be on the road to meet you."

"Begorry, I thank you, sir. And it is fine weather we are having."

"Your rescue of Major Harvey, to say nothing of your other acts of gallantry, was most brilliant, sir."

"The major and I are old friends, sir—we used to board at a place where we had more to eat than we have now, not only when there was company, but on wash days as well."

"Captain, I hear of mutinous mutterings among the men—particularly among those whose term of enlistment has about expired. What have you to report?"

"This, sir, that the first one of my men that turns his back on you will find a sword in front, cutting at his throat."

"I mean, have you heard any complaints or the expression of any determination to march off in a body? Mind you, there is no fear of individual desertion."

"If there has been such talk among the men, General, it has been kept from me. I remember now hearing a sergeant say that no man ought to be expected to stay after the expiration of his three months' term

of enlistment. I did not pretend to cope with this
man in logic—he having made a specialty of that
branch of learning. I always try to avoid an argument
with a man in his own particular field. I remember
a professor of chemistry who—''

''But what did you say to the sergeant, sir?''

''Oh, the sergeant. Why, I made some casual remark, sir, to the effect that if he continued to spread
such talk as that I'd have him shot. He saw that I did
not care for a polemical discussion, and he took it in
good part—said, as inoffensively as he could, that he'd
go home as soon as he got ready; and not to be outdone
in good humor, I assured him that the home to which
he referred might be the one that man stayed away
from as long as possible. And with that we parted
never to meet again on this earth, for shortly afterward he was drowned in the Tennessee River, sir, and
I am now reporting his death to you.''

Mutterings among the troops arose in loud threats.
Hunger was their complaint. They had come out to
fight and not to starve. The officers assured them that
if they remained, the General would furnish them with
fighting enough.

For the man who was destined to become the hero
of the Nation these were desperate days. To the Governor of Tennessee he wrote most piteous letters, begging for provisions. I can see him now as he stood on
a mountain top, gazing toward the land whence might
come a wagon train; but the days slowly limped away
and no provisions came. But one day there arrived a
letter from Governor Blount. He was a good corre-
spondent. He knew that letter writing was an art,
and he had cultivated it. He was a man of varied
accomplishments, but the knack of raising immediate

supplies was not one of them. In this letter he said
that he was sorry. He knew what it meant when a
number of men were hungry. He knew what he would
do; if food were not sent to him he would repair to
some place where it might be had. Then he advised
the General to disband the army, for unless the volunteers were accepted as soldiers in the pay of the general government, the expense would soon ruin the
State of Tennessee. Disband his troops! The General
refused to take this advice. He would have refused
a peremptory order. He wrote again, one of the most
pathetic appeals ever sent from one man to another.
In the meantime trouble broke out. The militiamen
swore that they would march home in a body. Their
time had expired, and besides, the weather was not
pleasant. The General appealed to the sentiment of
the volunteers.

In an address delivered by himself and in a manner
that would have made the fortune of an actor, he appealed to their sentiment. He reminded them that
when the Secretary of War, of the nation itself, had
ordered him to disband them at Natchez he had, at
the risk of his own eternal ruin, refused to obey the
command, and had led them home. Would they desert
him now? The volunteers swore that they would not.
They cheered the address. So, on the following day
when the militia formed in marching order they found
the volunteers drawn up to oppose them. And there
was the General with his address. He called them
brave men, and they were; he said he knew they were
hungry, but, by the Eternal, he would shoot down
the first and the last man who attempted to cross the
dead line, a mark not visible but well understood. Yes,
the militia were brave enough, but they did not de-

sire to die in such a cause, so they returned to their
duty. This was most encouraging. But two nights
later, Mahone came to the General's tent with the dis-
tressful news that the volunteers had decided to march
home on the following day. The commander roared
that the last one of them should be shot down. Mahone admitted that this would be just. "But, General," said he, "who is going to shoot them?"

"The militia, sir," the General thundered.

Then he rushed forth to address the militia. He
told them that the volunteers had kept them from
going home Now it was their turn to compel the
volunteers to remain. The militia cheered. And on
the following day when the volunteers formed to
march off, there in front of them arose the militia
with their guns cocked. Thus order was again re-
stored. But only for a brief time. The men were
almost starving, and hunger is a restless rebel.

One morning there came another letter from Governor Blount. It was courteous and graceful, but it
was something more. It contained information. The
general government had accepted Tennessee's offices,
and in due time would pay the expenses of the campaign. Therefore he had ordered supplies to be for-
warded with all possible expedition. When this news
was communicated to the men they cheered, but
rather faintly. Nearly every man and many of the
officers had resolved to return home at once. Their
time had expired. They were not strong enough nu-
merically to march into the enemy's country, and
soon they would be unable to defend their own position. This could not be denied. One man swore that
he would lead the way.

"Then you will lead the way to hell," Old Hickory exclaimed. He seized a musket and resting it on a horse, leveled it at him. The rebel, being a quick thinker, thought better of it and sat down.

"Now," said the General, "I have a proposition to make. Wait two days longer and if supplies do not arrive, I will lead you home."

Then there was cheering.

Before sunrise on the following day the General was on the hill-top, gazing across the country. The sun set, and the supplies had not arrived. That was an anxious night for Old Hickory, tough as he was. Up and down he walked, in front of his tent. The moon was shining. Mahone and I sat on a rock not far off. From a tent near by there came an occasional cough.

"Who is in that tent?" Mahone inquired, inclining his head.

"Harvey," I answered.

"Ah. He ought to be at home. Why doesn't he go?"

"I heard the General tell him that he must go tomorrow."

"Begorry, there'll be a lot of them that will go, then, too. Richard, I hate a monarchy, and yet in time of war republics are failures—till they are almost whipped. They won't fight—don't know how to get at it until they have both cheeks smacked. Look at that restless, almost deserted old hero out there, walking up and down, a lion with a rusty chain about him."

"Dan, I was thinking what a change your character has undergone since I first met you, a professor."

"My character has not changed, Richard. You

were simply unable to read it rightly. As a teacher, I was always struggling to hold myself down; and you must know that an Irishman under restraint is a cripple. Hah, hear that poor fellow cough! The Lord knows that I would do anything for him that lies within my power."

"And he knows it, too, Dan."

"Yes, I believe he does. The other night he came over to my tent, took my hand and wept like a child. And he said things to me that I can't repeat even to myself. He spoke of the great wrong he had done me. Then I began to bat my own eyes, I tell you, but I couldn't see where he had done me a wrong. To be sure, he had married the woman I loved, and I told him that was his right, that I would have done the same thing myself. But he insisted that he hadn't done so altogether in a fair way; intimated that he told her that with me she would have a very hard time of it, over the wash-tub probably, when I had squandered her little home, but that he would put silks on her, and says I to him, with the candle light blurring, 'begorry, you have done that same.' Then he told me that whomever she may have loved, she didn't love him. He had put laces on her shoulders, but he couldn't tie a ribbon about her heart. Men can get very close to one another in a tent, in the light of a candle, Richard. They can and no mistake; and he said things to me that I shall not repeat —but not the one thing that I longed to hear, that she had confessed to him that she ever loved me. Surely she did not; and when he has passed away I shall not renew my suit, for she will be a rich woman then, and the judges and the great men will be reaching after her.''

In the pocket of my coat was buttoned up the letter that Lismukes had written to Arabella. But the time had not come, and it remained buttoned up. I heard the dying man cough.

CHAPTER XXVI.

HAD BECOME SOLDIERS.

THE General walked late, but he was on the hilltop at sunrise. The hours melted slowly away. Noon, and no provision train within sight. The men had their fires built, their pots and pans ready; and then began to make ready with something else— their knapsacks. When the sun had set, the General issued orders for the march to begin early on the following day. There was some growling but no threat of mutiny. That night there was hunger in the camp, but the men were cheerful, and sitting about the fires they sang home songs. Hearing continuous roars of laughter from a group gathered about a burning stump, I joined the circle, and not long was it before I discovered the cause of the merriment. A tall, graceful backwoodsman, the picture of strength and agility, humorous with every expression of countenance, entertaining every moment, was telling stories, the quaintest I had ever heard. Of some one near me I inquired the name of this unique entertainer, this great character, for such I instantly knew him to be.

"Davy Crockett, the scout," I was informed, and though at that time I had not heard of him, yet I requested an introduction, and felt, as I took his hand, that I was gripped by a man destined to grasp the great affairs of this life. I shall not attempt to re-

249

produce his dialect. Indeed, it was not a dialect so much as an accent, soft and musical.

"Yes, boys," he said, "I'll go home if the rest of you do, though it don't make much difference to me where I am—at home anywhere I find a bear track, and keeping house if I find the bear himself. Not long ago my boy wanted a cub bear for a pet, and I told him he'd better take up with something that wouldn't keep him quite so busy—that wouldn't make him sweat so much during the hot weather—but he was hungry for bear, and when a fellow feels that way, why, nothing else will satisfy him. So, I promised him a cub bear, and I always try to keep my promises, even to my wife and children—except when I'm in politics. On my hunts I kept a sharp lookout for a bear's nest, and one day I found one, in the hollow of a big red oak. I looked in, delicate like, for I wasn't acquainted there, and discovered that old Miz Bear wan't at home. This suited my purpose just as well, fer I don't like to kill a bear that's engaged in keeping house. There was only one cub, a mighty likely little fellow; and so I climbed up and got down into the house, woke him up and told him I had come for him. He didn't appear to mind it much —sorter boxed at me with his paw and wanted to go to sleep again, but I told him I reckoned not. So I gathered him and climbed up, and just as I stuck my head out of the hole, I saw old Miz Bear on the ground, looking up at me. I had left my gun outside, and while I am right sociable with a knife, I don't like to use it, especially when a bear has taken it into her head that her duty to her family demands that she shall squeeze me to death before I can use it. It was she bears, you may have heard your mothers

and wives read about, that the old prophet 'Ligy or
'Lisha—I always get 'em mixed—called on to help
him with the children that made fun of his bald
head. He knew what sort of bears he was calling on,
for he was a wise man and was possessed of a good
deal of experience. Well, I looked at old Miz Bear
and she looked at me, but neither on my part nor on
hern was there a sign of recognition. It was clear to
be seen that we had never met before. I said to her,
'Madam, if you'll give me the opportunity I'll bid
you good day.' But she just kept on looking at me.
About this time something hit the ground on the inside of the hollow. It was a cub bear, and I didn't
think he was intended for my son, either. About the
time he hit the ground he bawled; and then I wanted
to see my home worse than some of you men do this
minute. Here she came. There wasn't any way for
me to compromise matters. I couldn't use my knife
hanging there, so I dropped back into the hollow,
fell against the side and busted a hole through the
rotten shell. Just happen to hit it in the right place.
But I reached back, grabbed up the cub and away I
went—wanted to keep my word with my boy, you
know; but pretty soon I says to myself, 'Now, mebbe,
old Miz Bear is more attached to this cub than my
son is. And as betwixt me and the cub there ain't no
kin at all.' And I dropped him.''

Just at this moment an orderly came up and informed Crockett that General Jackson desired to see
him. Shortly afterward I entered Old Hickory's
tent.

"But, General, you have given them your word,"
Crockett was saying. "You must not break it. The
men all love you, but the powers at home ain't treat-

ing them right. There's too much self-interest and
politics behind us. Somehow, we didn't get our best
foot down first, and if we ain't barkin' up the wrong
tree, we're barkin' mighty weak.''

''There is weight, sir, in what you say. You are a
sort of independent here, but Captain Crockett, will
you remain at all hazards?''

''General, I am a whig and this is a sort of a democrat war, but show me an Indian that ought to be
dead and I'll stay till he's shot. But my neighbors
are determined to go home. They have more than
served their time out; they are tired of this thing
and want to do something else. You can't accuse
them of cowardice.''

''Nothing is farther from my thoughts, sir. But I
tell you we must stand our ground. Not only that,
we must advance. Our southern coast is practically
defenseless—what little of it we can really call ours—
and the first thing the government knows the British
and Indians will be swarming across the state line of
Tennessee herself, sir.''

''The first thing the government knows! Why, of
course. The most impossible may happen before the
government knows anything. Is that all you wanted
with me, General?''

''All! By the Eternal, isn't that enough?''

''Well, yes, I reckon it is—nearly. But these men
feel that they have done their duty. And it now remains for duty to be done in another quarter. There
ain't nothing fairer than turn about. Good night.''

I expected to hear the General denounce Crockett
but he did not. ''There is a man that will do great
things,'' said he, ''but his time is not yet ripe. Well,
Captain Staggs, to-morrow morning we begin our

ignominious march; and it was for that that I tore myself in agony out of my bed. Yes, I will keep my word with them. Orderly!''

A soldier stepped forward and touched his hat. ''Has everything been done to render the transportation of Major Harvey as comfortable as possible?''

''Yes, General—everything.''

''Very well. Captain Staggs, will you look after him on the way?''

''Yes, General, that is, if I go.''

''What do you mean, sir?''

''I mean that something might possibly turn up— reinforcements; and in that event I shall ask permission to remain here.''

''Ah, and do you still hope? Give me your hand, sir. Come in Colonel Mahone.''

''A sweet sound that would have for me—Colonel —in the presence of the enemy; but I fear now that it is empty. I just met Atcherson, and I told him to pray for us—while he had nothing else to do. He had preached obedience to the men until they left him standing alone.''

· The General made no answer. He strode out into the dark, and we heard him walking up and down, and we knew that his mighty spirit was still battling. ''I wonder,'' said Mahone, ''how many military geniuses have been snuffed out in that manner. Cromwell could have died a brewer's horse; Washington as a surveyor could in obscurity have dragged his chain through the woods; Bonaparte could have remained an unheard-of leftenant of artillery, and the great Frederic himself could have rested under no other reputation than that his father snatched a flute out of his hand and broke it over his head. Think of how many generals have died in the cradle, and, for the matter of that, how many that never lived at all. Doubtless just as great men failed to be born as were born. Mind that now."

I told him that he could not long be serious. "Serious is it?" he replied. "I am the very soul of seriousness itself. But at the same time I am a speculator; and, to casual observation, speculation never appears serious. Well, the morning will tell a sad story, I am afraid; am afraid, it will snuff out more than one military genius—not meaning mine, of course, but leaving Fate to draw her own inferences."

When the drums beat the next morning, the men more than exhibited their willingness to march. To those of us who desired to remain, it seemed a shameful enthusiasm. The General was yellow with suppressed rage. He did not issue an address. He was silent. There was no breakfast to be prepared, no kettles to be washed, but rusting from lack of use they were thrown upon the wagons. At the first step forward some home-sick youth lifted his weak voice in song. The General heard him. "Stop that!" he demanded. "Sing your puny lays when you have reached your effeminate fireside."

Ah, but we had not marched more than two hours when a thrilling sight burst into view—a drove of cattle coming over the hills to meet us. Steers were never more welcomed. Cheering, the men rushed forward to meet them. Then there followed a wolfish feast. How narrow the channel that separates civilized man from the savage! And that channel is not literature; it is the belly, upon which Frederick the Great said, an army moved like a snake.

When the gluttons had gorged themselves, the Gen

eral issued an address. He declared that as they now
had provisions they must return to their duty. But
the leaders among them swore that their duties were
at home. Their time of service had expired. They
were beyond command, and so the General called for
volunteers. He swore to them that the State had
called for a new army, which was true, and that they
would soon be honorably relieved; but a large majority of them, declaring that as they were now
private citizens, they were going home—and they did.

With a few hundred men Jackson returned to his
former position. Out of a company of ninety-six,
Mahone reclaimed thirty-four, a good showing the
commander assured him, and he answered as we
marched along: "Pitiful blackguards, and I shall
hold the rest of them personally responsible. And it
is a good thing that I hadn't completed the organization of my regiment in furtherance of my commission as Colonel. I would have had my hands full
of personal responsibility, for Richard," he said to
me, "some day I expect to thrash each one of those
fellows individually."

The new army was soon formed, too weak for an
invasion of the enemy's country, it was true, but with
old Jackson that made no particular difference. Fort
Strother was established as a basis of scant supplies.
No regular army officer would have counseled the invasion. The Creeks were savages, but they were more
accustomed to war, better disciplined, indeed, than
the militiamen from the plow and the cross-roads
store. The few hundred of our men who had been
under fire were regarded as seasoned veterans; but
the majority of the fifteen hundred, or fewer, of the
new levy were ignorant of the word of command.

They had joined the army for a three months' lark, and had engaged to serve no longer. This was agreed upon and at the expiration of the term they were free to go home. Thus it was that our army was constantly forming and as constantly disintegrating. Jackson was determined that the "three months men" should see service, that they should eat powder and breathe smoke. The first battle was not long in coming. The Creeks were more than willing to meet us. Some of the friendly Indians had gone to them, laughing derisively at our appearance. One morning we were attacked by a vastly superior force. Almost instantly the rawest of our militia were thrown into confusion. They not only began a retreat but ran over one another, but Jackson met them with his sword flashing in the sun. He presented an aspect more terrible than a Creek; he was Vengeance on horseback. "You scoundrel!" he cried, halting a big plowboy at the point of his sword, "why are you running away?"

"Me! Am I running? I'll be danged if I knowed it. Just show me which way you want me to go, and I'll travel in that direction. Come on back, boys, and let's look into this thing a leetle."

The flying men rallied and redeemed themselves. "Fightin' is all well enough," I heard one of them say, "but it seems to me that this thing needn't to have been so blamed sudden."

The Creeks had never fought with greater energy, and with what was worse, more tact. Here and there the effect of British training plainly could be discerned, but nothing could stand against the determination with which Jackson inspired his men; and, as I flew about the field, delivering his orders here and there, it seemed to me as it must have seemed to many others, that a word of commendation from him was worth the risk of a life.

The Indians were defeated but not in a manner to please Old Hickory. To see them run away meant nothing to him so long as he thought that they might rally again; he demanded that they should lie bleeding on the ground. On this occasion, one of the officers sought to congratulate him. I had learned better. "Please, keep your fair words until I deserve them," said he.

Soon afterward there came a hotter fight, and another wing of "three months men" turned about to fly. But Jackson was among them with his sword, and, what was more terrible, with his oaths. It seemed that when he swore the grass began to turn yellow and the leaves to wither on the trees. The troops "recovered their shame," or at least, the commander compelled them to recover it by plunging for it among the savages. Again the Creeks were defeated and with considerable loss; but Jackson was sullen, complimenting a few, but looking upon the majority of those raw fellows with contempt. Better preparation, and above all better discipline was necessary; and so, being in need of supplies, of course, the army was led back to Fort Strother.

At last Old Hickory had begun to attract notice in the North. Newspapers opposed to the administration had made little of American victories, magnifying American disaster, until the average reader believed that the country was ruined. But Jackson's fighting qualities offered some few rays of hopeful light; and the general government "observed" him, not merely with a compliment, which to him would have meant nothing, but by sending to his aid a de-

tachment of six hundred regular troops. There was
great rejoicing in camp when these men arrived.
Among them was a young ensign whose appearance
caused me to seek his acquaintance, Sam Houston, he
who was to stand so high in heroic annals. Jackson
had known him, a youthful lawyer, in Tennessee—
knew his metal, and upon meeting him, said: "Sam,
some men look for a chance to run away. See, sir,
that you don't seek for an opportunity to get killed."

"I shall do my duty, General," the young officer
answered; "and if it lies in that direction, so be it."

The General turned to Mahone. "Colonel," said
he, "I desire you to understand, sir, that impetuosity
is not primarily a soldier-like quality. Don't let your
enthusiasm make a horse of your judgment, to ride it
into a bog."

"Begorry, and that's sweet flattery," Mahone answered.

"I mean it as a reprimand," the General replied.

"And, sir," the Irishman retorted, "with no disposition to dispute your authority, let me say you
might take a fair dose of that same medicine yourself, leaving a sip in the glass for our friend Richard,
here."

The General smiled grimly.

Among troops of such individuality, it was almost
impossible to enforce discipline. The commander
repeatedly issued orders, warning the men that some
one might be called upon to suffer, but, despite all
this, there were now and then ugly evidences of mutiny. One day a young soldier, John Woods, whose
name is still remembered when the deeds of heroes
have been forgotten, walked off from his post as
sentinel in camp and proceeded to eat his breakfast

in his tent. An officer came along and seeing a number of beef bones scattered about, ordered Woods to gather them up. Woods answered that this was at present out of the line of his duty, that he was on guard, but had left his post by permission. The officer persisted. Woods became violent. The officer ordered his arrest. Woods seized a musket and attempted to shoot him. Jackson heard the noise and came roaring upon the scene. "The scoundrel shall die," he swore. The young soldier was subdued, put into the guardhouse and in due time court-martialed. The majority of the officers, including Colonel Williams, commander of the regulars, thought that nothing would come of it, other than a sharp reprimand; but I knew better and so did Mahone. We had heard the "old man" swear, "By the Eternal, the time is more than in the harvest and I will make an example of him."

The court-martial found Woods guilty and sentenced him to be shot in "full view of the entire army." And then there arose a loud clamor for clemency. Chaplain Atcherson called on the General to exert his influence on the side of mercy. "General," said he, "I desire to speak to you concerning John Woods."

"Then be brief, sir, unless you desire to speak of the dead."

"General, he is the sole support of an aged father and mother."

"I am sorry for them—they have my sympathy, but war is war. So long as it is play, mere parade, it is a disgrace to one's country. And this war has been prolonged by insubordination—by open mutiny. It has been declared time and again that I did not dare visit severe punishment upon a fellow citizen. Sir, it is to the interest of the country that I command soldiers, not citizens, and if they are not soldiers now, some of them will think better of it before night. Do you hear those drums? Do you know what they mean? They mean that your mission of clemency has been fruitless. I admire your bravery and your zeal, but I wish you good morning."

Woods was shot. Sadness fell upon the camp; but when the sun went down there was about the fires no talk of mutiny. The citizens had become soldiers.

CHAPTER XXVII.

AT HORSESHOE BEND.

THE Creeks were determined upon a final stand at Horseshoe Bend, a peninsula formed by the Tallapoosa River. This place was fortified in a way that showed more than the redman's military training. A fort of enormous logs had been constructed. A great stockade had been built. Hundreds of canoes were in readiness along the shore. They presented the appearance of a primeval navy. Prophets had convinced the Indians that the place was impregnable.

Horseshoe was more than fifty miles from Fort Strother. Between the two points there was a dense forest. Through the trackless thicket a road had to be cut. This required labor and time; but there was no shirking, no mutiny. I heard one man remark to another: "If your time is out why don't you mention it to the General?"

"Oh, I'd rather not," his companion answered. "The old man's watch don't keep very good time, but he doesn't like to be told of it."

It was many days before we arrived within sight of the fort, with our two little spit-fire cannons. Our force numbered about two thousand. The Indians were fewer, but they were the most stalwart of the Creeks, and so advantaged that one man could count against five. General Coffee, who had been wounded, but who was again in command of the cavalry,

crossed the river to attack, if possible, from the other
side. Jackson at once ordered the "artillery" to
open. From the top of a hill, the two little guns began to bark, and the Indians began to shout with
laughter. The balls were embedded in the great logs
and wrought no damage. In the meantime Coffee's
men crossed over to the peninsula, set fire to the
cabins in the rear of the stockade and captured
the canoes, rendering an Indian retreat impossible.
And now silencing the guns, Jackson ordered a
charge upon the fort. The men sprang forward with
a shout. It was difficult to scale the walls, and
through the portholes the soldiers and the Creeks
fought, muzzle to muzzle. Young Ensign Houston
was the first to leap over into the fort. In an instant he was pierced through the thigh with an arrow, and would have been dispatched but for Mahone
and his men, who had followed at his heels.

He requested Mahone to pull out the arrow; and
the Irishman answered: "This is my busy season
and I'm not much of a surgeon, but I'll do the best
I can." He pulled, but the arrow was barbed and
would not come. "Harder," Houston shouted, and
Mahone brought it out, tearing the flesh so badly that
Houston was taken fainting from the fort. They
stretched him upon the ground. Soon he began to
revive. Jackson saw him, and said as he cast a
glance back toward the fort: "Houston, I positively
order you not to go back in there." But shortly afterward, amidst the slaughter in the fort, Jackson
looked up and found Houston at his side, but there
was no reprimand. It was not for such insubordination that Old Hickory censured.

It was known that the Indians would neither give

nor accept quarter, and thus with a complete understanding of the situation, the white men proceeded
with their work of extermination. During all this
time the fire started by Coffee's men was raging. The
shanties were dry and burned rapidly. The walls of
the fort were soon ablaze. Hundreds of Indians were
shot in the river. Some of them killed themselves
when they found that escape was impossible. The
last remnant of them, about two hundred, took position behind a huge pile of logs at the upper end of
the peninsula. The cannon could not make any im-
pression upon their defense. Jackson called for
volunteers to dislodge them by assault. Young Sam
Houston, without waiting to see whether or not he
was to have followers, sprang forward to the attack.
He was called upon to halt, and he did, but not until
he was almost riddled by a volley from the enemy.
Then he was carried away and laid upon the ground
to die. The surgeons said that there was no hope
for him.

The Indians were dislodged, butchered; and then
began a still hunt through the woods. From off amid
the timber came the occasional cry ''Remember Fort
Mims.'' It was here that the war began, the mas-
sacre of hundreds of whites, women and children.
The day and the night of vengeance had come. Jackson would have spared the Indians, would have treated the prisoners kindly, but we could not make the
Creeks understand that there was mercy in our hearts.
Some of the warriors, dying, fired on our men who
were striving to aid them. In the night, out in the
darkness there was the slow, deliberate firing of the
huntsman. Finally all was quiet; but a few of the
Indians had escaped. More than six hundred had

been killed. Our loss in killed and wounded was fewer than a hundred.

Houston lay without attention until past midnight. The surgeons, declaring that he was beyond aid, administered to those who had a fighting chance for life; but they found, along toward the turn of the night, that he was battling for life. They then dressed his desperate wounds. The General came to him.

"Sam, do you know me?"

"Old Hickory," Houston murmured, faintly.

"I begged you—" he did not say commanded now —"I begged you not to go back into the fort." The General was kneeling beside him. How tender he could be! "I begged you, Sam."

"Yes, I know. But don't worry over me. I'm all right."

Jackson's headquarters were beneath a tree. A fire burned. He stood near it, reading some dispatches that had just been brought from Governor Blount. Out in the dark, a rifle popped like a coach whip, and a bullet whizzed between his face and the paper he was reading. "See who that is," he said to an orderly. The orderly went out into the dark, was gone a few moments and, returning, saluted: "An Indian paying his last respects to you, sir," he responded. "He is dead."

The General handed me one page of a letter. "From Mrs. Jackson containing news that will interest you," he said. I read the news and returned the paper to him. Then I went forth to look for Malone. I found him sitting on a log, in the light of a fire, smoking his pipe. "These red devils know what good tobacco is, Richard," said he. "Sit down. I found some of it, and it tastes like a wild rose smells.

Well, how's all over your way? But first let me tell
you, lad, that you did fine work. Begorry, anybody
could tell that your mother was an Irish woman. Ah,
and if the little elf had seen you to-day, she wouldn't
be proud of her cousin, the doctor, I'll tell you that.
What's that paper you've got there?''

''A letter from Lismukes,'' I answered.

''The devil you say!'' he cried, moving farther
away from me. ''And how can you keep up a correspondence with him now that he's been dead so
long?''

''Dan, will you listen to me for a moment?''

''Sure I will, gladly.''

''This letter was written to Arabella on the day
before the duel. Read it.''

He read it over and over again, and then asked:
''How long have you had it?''

''Ever since that day she and her husband drove
out to the Hermitage. When you went over to the
store she and I sat in the summer house, in the garden—and she gave it to me then, and told me to give
it to you—at some time in the future, 'when he has
forgotten me,' she said.''

''But I have not forgotten, Richard—never can,
and why should you give it to me now?''

''Because her husband is dead.''

''Arrah—I mean I'm sorry. What a fool mouth a
man can have. How do you know?''

''I have just seen a letter written by Mrs. Jackson
to the General.''

''Then,'' said he, ''I don't suppose there can be
any mistake about it; couldn't be much of a mistake
anyway for he was nearly dead when he left us.

Well, I tell the truth as nearly as I can when I say I'm sorry.''

"Yes, I believe you. You did everything you could to save him, but disease devoured him and you couldn't save him from that.''

"And my thinking about Arabella at this moment doesn't make his fatal disease any more fatal.''

"She has always loved you, Dan. She told me you were the only man she ever loved.''

"Yes, Richard, but didn't she have a quaint way of showing it? Probably she loved me more after she found out that she loved drygoods less. I ought to tell her to go to the devil, but begorry, I'm afraid she might do it. Now what am I to do? Write her a letter of condolence? That would look as raw as a militia man that wants to go home.''

"You couldn't write her a letter of congratulation.''

"Couldn't I? But I could say I am sorry her husband is dead but glad she's a widow. No, I'll leave it to time, the great healer and adjuster; I'll wait till tomorrow.''

The power of the Creeks was broken. Nothing more was to be done here at the Horseshoe. Jackson took up his line of march to Fort William, at least sixty miles distant. Progress through the wilderness was slow, but finally, and without meeting any hostile Indians, the Fort was reached. Beyond this point, lay the land which the Creeks called Holy Ground. Their prophets had told them that no white man could set foot upon it. They had not measured old 'Andrew's feet. Holy Ground was entered. The war party fled to the swamps of Florida. Chief after chief came in and surrendered. Fort Jackson was

constructed, and it was to this place that the great
chief Billy Weathersford came to give himself up.
He was a splendid looking fellow. His father was a
white man, his mother a Seminole woman. She must
have been handsome. He came into the General's
tent bringing with him a deer that he had shot on the
way. He threw down the deer and said: "General
Jackson I am not afraid of you. They accused me
of murdering the women and children at Fort Mims.
That was a lie. I tried to save them; but I have not
come to beg mercy for myself. You may kill me as
soon as you like. But I do beg mercy for our women
and children. They are starving in the woods, and
unless you feed them, they must die. I did not kill
women and children. I kill strong men."

The General took his hand. "Weathersford, I believe you," said he. "You are a brave man. You
know how to fight. Your women and children shall
not starve. Nor shall you remain here a prisoner.
You are free."

Jackson kept his word. The women and children
did not starve.

It was now time for an address from the General and it came. He thanked his soldiers, called
them brave, and assured them that they should soon
return home. I noticed that Mahone did not frown.

Soon after this, General Pinkney, of the United
States army, arrived and took command. In this
quarter Jackson's work was done for the present.
Pinkney complimented the troops and praised our
commander. A banquet followed, and then our army
was disbanded. The homeward march was swift, and
Mahone kept up with the best of them. As we were
riding along, I asked him if he had written to Ara-

bella. "I have not," he answered. "It was a delicate thing to do. It has been three months since her
husband died, and I suppose she has married some
one else. When a widow gets into the habit of marrying it is a hard matter to stop her. Give my regards to her."

"Why, you'll see her as soon as I do."

He shook his head. "I think not. I am going to
join the regular army and fight my friends, the
British. The General will recommend me for a commission. If I don't get it I'll go in as a private."

But the next day, he told me that he had written to
Arabella. I remarked that he would reach Nashville as soon as his letter, and he answered: "No, I
can halt outside the town while you take it in. I am
going to send it by you. And perhaps I'd better let
you read it. I wish you would. Here it is."

He gave me the letter and this is what I read:
"Honored Madam:—Captain Staggs gave me the Lismukes letter, not because I had forgotten you, but
because there did not seem to be any immediate need
that I should. I could never forget you. In the
songs of the birds lives your voice, and while they
sing I hear your words. I have been thinking a
great deal since I read that letter, and for the matter
of that, I thought a great deal before reading it. I
recall that desperate night, that buggy out in front.
Ah, it was a hearse in which my heart was to be
hauled away. But a heart may be a Lazarus—it may
arise from the dead. It is still too early since your
late bereavement for me to ask you to be my wife, but
it is my secret wish that you will. I can bring you
no fortune, but this ought not to make any difference since you have one of your own. If I had one

ten times as big you should have it. This letter, as
by this time you will have observed, is handed to you
by Captain Staggs. You may tell him what you
think of it, or write to me, just as you yourself elect.
I never had but one letter from you and that was
written by Lismukes, a dead man. I am sorry you
feared him. Had I known it at the time I would have
killed him myself.

"Speaking of your fortune reminds me that I am a
provident man. No man can point to any money I
ever squandered, and assure yourself that your money
will be just as safe with the both of us as with you
alone. I was thinking that you might give it to some
charitable institution, reserving, of course, enough for
yourself, the amount to be determined by your own
judgment. Let me remind you that everything possible was done to prolong the life of the departed one;
but in this life events shape themselves. I am not a
Fatalist, but had it been intended for him to live
longer he would doubtless have done so, regardless of
what might follow. Richard had hinted to me that
you were not happy with him, but this is a point
which it is both premature and too late to discuss.
But neither is it too early nor too late for me to tell
you that I love you. The poets have said that love is
a disease, and if this be true, I am mortally stricken.
If I could have 'unloved' you I would have done so,
but after meeting you the first time it was too late. If
I do not speak plainly enough, you must draw your
own conclusions, and I request you not to be too modest in doing so. In the event that you are not already
married, this is hoping that it may find you well; and
in case you answer this letter, I shall gladly receive
the same.''

"What do you think of it?" he asked as I returned the letter to him.

"Dan, I don't believe I'd send it."

"Ah, and do you know I was thinking of that same
thing myself? I was. A man may be silent and pass
for wise, but put a pen in his hand, and how easy it is
to be foolish. What do you think I ought to do?"

"Leave it all to chance," I answered, and he
winced.

"Begorry, I did that once and you saw what came
of it. Chance has never been my friend, Richard."

"But I think she will be this time."

"You do? But would you mind making chance
masculine instead of feminine? Let me try *him*
rather than *her* this time."

I agreed to make chance masculine, and he brightened.

Swift horsemen had sped the news of our victories.
In the settlements through which we passed there was
great rejoicing, and food in abundance was provided
for us. To the victors belong not only the spoils of
war but the hospitalities of peace. Nashville was
wild with excitement. Troops of gentlemen on horseback rode out to escort us into the city. Dinners were
spread in every passage-way, and at the Bell Tavern
a grand ball was given in honor of the officers.
Everything was in readiness before we entered the
town. Mrs. Jackson did not approve dancing, but
she met her husband at the Tavern. In our worn uniforms we cut but a sorry figure, amid broadcloth and
silk, but our deeds were bright, and a faded shoulder-
strap was glory's dazzling mark. I saw Mahone
dancing with the daughter of the president of the
Cumberland University, formerly our old Davidson

Academy. When the "set" was over the Colonel came to me, drew me aside and said:

"Richard, I don't see the widow that was and is."

"Of course not," I answered. "Did you expect to find her at a ball so soon after her husband's death?"

"Begorry, I never thought of that. It is astonishing how many things I never think of; but do you suppose she will think ill of me for coming so soon after that sad event?"   •

"Of course not. You have nothing to do with it."

"But she might have sent me some word?"

"In answer to the letter you didn't send her?"

"I hadn't thought of that, either. Hold on, the General is going to deliver an address."

The Commander's speech was full of praise for his men. He did not mention mutiny or any of his troubles. A stranger would have supposed that his work had been a willing co-operation with soldiers still more willing. Among those who applauded loudest were former officers who led their men home before the Creeks had been subdued. When we had received what we knew was to come, the address, I asked Mahone if he would join me in a stroll about the town. He looked at me. "Yes," said I, "in the direction of Arabella's house." In a moment his hat was on his head. Out upon the street he began to caution me.

"Now, if we go in, which we must not, don't tell her you gave me the Lismukes letter. Let time work that out."

I promised and we strode on. When we turned a corner and saw that Arabella's house was ablaze with light, he gripped my arm.

"Begorry, it looks like a wake," he said. "I don't think that I've got the courage to go in."

"But I am going to take you, Dan."

"All right. In that event I'll go along peaceably."

Our knock at the door was answered by the negress whom we knew so well. She did not take our names to her mistress, but ushered us at once into the sitting-room. Arabella had arisen and was coming toward the door when she caught sight of us. She hastened forward, took my hand with some murmured word of welcome, some inarticulate emotion, and turning to Mahone, holding forth her hand she said: "And you, too, Captain Mahone."

"Colonel, Madam—or Miss, I beg your pardon," the Irishman answered, taking her hand and bowing low over it. "I hope you are well."

"Very well, I thank you. Ah, you remember our friends, here."

In the room were Judge Black, and his wife whose former husband, it will be remembered, came down the river on a raft. The Judge cried out, "Why bless my soul!" And in turn warmly grabbed each of us. His wife remembered us with a cool smile and a thin hand. We sat down while Arabella seemed to flutter about, looking for something, and the Judge, clearing his throat, preliminary to some important observation, remarked that some time had elapsed since last we met. Arabella's sleeves were short again, and though arrayed in black, she did not seem to have passed through a season of very profound sorrow. She observed that the weather was pleasant, and Mahone blurted that if she said so he would swear to it, and then begged pardon for his impetuosity, declaring that the General had reprimanded him ''for that same.''

Knowing that Arabella had not begun to take boarders again, I wondered as to how long the Judge and his wife might be disposed to inflict us with their uninteresting not to say hampering company. And Mahone, who was sometimes as quick to understand a situation as at other times to misunderstand it, remarked to Arabella that she must pardon us for calling so late. It was politeness for her to protest that it was not late, but nothing demanded that this fool Judge should agree with her. He did, though; he said it was just turning the elbow of the evening. Then he spoke of the great improvement that had taken place in the city since we left.

''And if we had not left and stayed away so long as we did there might not be any city at all here now,'' Mahone spoke up. ''The Creeks would have burnt it down.''

''Oh, perhaps not that bad,'' the Judge replied, yawning. ''They would have found us ready to defend our homes.''

I looked at Mahone to restrain him, but it was too late. ''As soon as you had caught sight of a Creek warrior, your thumping heart would have knocked out the memory of all your possessions except as to your legs, sir,'' the Irishman declared, and Arabella laughed to cover his affront.

''I have never run away from home yet, sir,'' the Judge retorted. ''You will always find me there.''

''I don't doubt that,'' Mahone roared with laughter. ''And there are many of the same sort; but I beg your pardon, Judge. I didn't mean to offend you.''

"In that event, sir, all is smooth between us; but my dear," he added, addressing his wife, "it is time we were going home."

Arabella went with them to the door. She returned laughing. Mahone begged her pardon. She assured him that he had committed no offense. In a rocker she took a seat, between Mahone and me. I wondered what blunder was to come next, on the part of my friend. I did not wait long.

"Death is a sad thing, madam," said he. She did not answer. "I mean outside the army," he explained, and realizing he made a bad start, he looked to me for help. I pretended not to notice his distress. Finally he roared at me: "Richard, why the devil—begging your pardon, Miss—don't you say something?"

"I was waiting for you, Dan."

"But haven't you got better sense than that? And I suppose if I were to get up to go right now you would let me, as you did on a former occasion. Mrs. Harvey, I have much trouble with my friend Richard, but for all that I am under many obligations to him; and that was a fine letter he gave me—that you gave him from Lismukes—"

She did not speak but she looked at him and he was silent, till she held out both hands toward him, and then he gulped and struggled with himself, and said, looking at her hands, reached out to him: "For me, Madam?"

"For you, Dan—always."

I turned away. "I am ready to go now, Richard," he said after a time, and when I looked back, the great big-hearted fellow was wiping his eyes.

CHAPTER XXVIII.

A MESSAGE FROM WASHINGTON.

MAHONE sang his way out to the Hermitage, in the dawn; and I let him sing, knowing that there had never been a heart more truly full of music. We slept till noon, and then I walked past the school-house, into the woods, where the old "whale" lay, covered with moss. As I was coming home, Mahone met me in the road and turned back with me. "Ah, my friend," he said, "happiness is a great thing to be sure. It is worth waiting for; but here arises a trouble. I've got to go back into the army again before we marry. Society demands that her husband shall have been deceased a respectable length of time before she ought to marry again, and I'm not going to sit down and wait on society—I'll tell you that. And besides I am not going to become a peaceable citizen so long as America has a British enemy. Among the letters waiting for the General, he told me just now, is one from the War Department offering him a brigadier's commission in the United States army. But I don't believe he'll accept. And he ought not to. They ought to rate him higher than that, and I believe they will very soon, and when they do, it will mean a chance for you and me."

"But Arabella may object to your going into the army again," said I.

"Do you think that, now? Well, I don't want to dispute with my wife that is to be, but I'm going into the army. It's a man's duty to be a patriot before he is a husband.''

Mrs. Jackson told me that Nettie had visited her once during my absence. "And every day," said this tender, artless woman, "she would walk over into the woods with little Andrew, and would talk about a great whale that they had seen—the very whale that swallowed Jonah, the little fellow said.''

"I wish some whale would swallow a Jonah or two in the War Department" the General spoke, looking up from his papers. "If the news is true that Napoleon has fallen and is to be sent to Elba, and there seems to be now no possible doubt of it, there will fall upon America perhaps the darkest day in her history. England no longer compelled to struggle on the continent, will concentrate her revengeful energies upon us. Our very life as a nation is in danger; and there is not a country in Europe that will help us. Abroad we are accused—and by the Federalists at home—of a sympathetic alliance with Bonaparte against all established order. This will mean at least the moral support of the world against us, in favor of Britain. New England cries that her ships are rotting at the wharves. Our credit is exhausted. Girard and Astor have refused to advance more money. The treasury echoes like a church. The President and the Secretary of State have had to pledge their private estates for the loan of not more than two million dollars. Spain pretends to be friendly, but the Spanish Governor at Pensacola, is harboring the fugitive Creek chiefs and the English will arm them and put them into the field against us. I see the situation in a noon-day sun—and, by the Eternal, they offer me a

SEARCHING FOR THE SOOTHING MUSIC OF A QUIET PSALM.

commission as brigadier-general, to serve under some old incompetent. I will not accept it.''

"Oh, no, you must not accept it,'' his wife declared. "It seems to me, Mr. Jackson, that you have done fighting enough. You are not well anyway, and your wounds are not completely healed. You have need of rest.''

She took down the Bible, turned past the ram's horn and the sling, and I think, was searching for the soothing music of a quiet psalm, when there came a knock at the front door. From town there had come a courier, bearing a special message from the War Department.

"Wait a moment,'' said the General when he had opened the packet and glanced over its contents. And then, seizing his turkey feather he wrote rapidly for a few moments, folded the paper, sealed it, addressed it, and handing it to the courier, dismissed him. Then he walked up and down the room.

"Was it anything very important, Mr. Jackson?'' his wife inquired.

"Yes, Mrs. Jackson, very important. Major-General William Henry Harrison has resigned. The major-generalship, with assignment to duty as commander of the southern division, has been offered to me, and I have accepted it. Richard, this means that you are to retain your position on my staff. I shall apply at once for your commission.''

"I am deeply grateful, sir,'' I answered.

"Grateful because you are a patriot. Where is Colonel Mahone?''

I went out to look for him, called, but received no answer. Then it occurred to me that he must have gone to town, and so I reported to the General.

"Ride in and inform him that I desire his presence here, at once."

I found Mahone in Arabella's sitting-room. I also found her there. As soon as I entered she said: "Richard, tell him he is not going to the war. I just know if he goes he'll never get back alive. I really can't let him go."

Then he blurted: "Begorry, you ought to be used to husbands going by this time—I beg your pardon, sweetheart, I didn't know how that would sound. But really, you must not try to persuade me. I like society very much and have all sorts of faith in its good sense, but I can't sit around here like a village postmaster because it says that Major Harvey hasn't been dead quite long enough—didn't know how that was going to sound, either. Just let me have my way this once and I'll make you the most obedient husband you ever had—ever saw."

She sat smiling at him. Then she appealed again to me. "I can't help you any," I answered. "The fact is that a major-general of the United States army has sent for him."

"Arrah," he cried. "A major-general? And who is he, pray?"

"Andrew Jackson. His appointment came just now and he has accepted it."

"Where is my hat. Sweetheart, you must not hide my hat. Give it to me, please."

She brought his hat and tip-toeing, put it on his head. "You'll come back, Dan, to tell me good-bye, won't you?"

"Yes, gladly—I mean I will."

She put her arms about his neck and kissed him; and when we had mounted our horses at the gate, he said: "Richard, it begins to look as if she really does love me."

"When a wealthy widow marries a penniless man the natural inference is that she loves him," I answered.

"Arrah, there's encouragement in that wise observation."

The hour was late but the General was waiting for us. "Colonel Mahone," he said, "I don't know that I can obtain for you a commission as Colonel in the United States army, but feel assured that I can as Captain of Cavalry. Would you—"

"You delight me, sir."

"That is sufficient. Good night."

Within a few days there came a letter from Beal announcing that the Supreme Court had sustained the numerous decisions of the courts below, and that I was now the undisputed possessor of a handsome estate. Along with this news came a statement of the amount due for attorney fees. Being a careful man it was not likely that Beal would overlook even so minor a point. As it was the General's determination to start for the south within a few weeks, I had not the time to go to Virginia, so I sent Beal a check for the amount due him and in a letter told him that if they should by any possible chance establish a higher court, to keep my affairs out of it until I could get there, which meant until after peace should be established between Great Britain and the United States.

Within one day from the time set for the General's departure our commissions arrived, but Mahone was not sent off somewhere to find a vacancy in the cavalry; he was assigned to duty on the General's staff. Over this good fortune he whooped like a boy.

"Now, sir," he said to me, "Arabella wouldn't want me to stay even if I should make of it a special request. Well, no, I don't want to think that," he corrected himself. "But surely it ought to make her a very proud woman not to be the wife of a militia officer."

Once more, on the night before we took our leave, the sling and the ram's horn were brought out. But the reading, though the hour had grown late, was interrupted by a number of visitors who had come to bid the General good-bye. Among them was Governor Blount himself, a quiet, dignified gentleman, from whom you might expect a well-written letter with very little news in it. He had just issued a call for more troops, and he knew that the brave sons of Tennessee would rush forward to fill the quota. And such afterward proved to be true; indeed, so eager were they that after the quota was filled sums as high as one hundred dollars were paid for the places already held by early applicants.

The general tenor of the news brought by the Governor was bad. He had been shown a letter written by Mr. Albert Gallatin from abroad, which more than confirmed the reports that England, with both hands now free, was going to box the jaws of America.

"And that red-sashed assassin, Spain!" exclaimed the General. "She is secretly aiding England by arming the Creeks that have fled from our just vengeance."

The Governor said that he hoped not, whereupon the General exclaimed: "But I have direct evidence of the fact, sir, and when I know a thing, I know it."

The Governor admitted that when a man knew a thing he knew it. He shook hands with the General, and did not tell him that he would write soon, but I knew that he would.

Nothing can be slower than war, except, perhaps, the formation of a satisfactory treaty with Indians. In the "Holy Ground," during weather hot enough to bake a lizard, week after week, the General was detained. Instructions from Washington assured him that in relation to the Creeks he was treating with a conquered people, but Old Hickory needed no such assurances. He knew it and the Creeks felt it. The government insisted that the Indians should cede land enough to compensate for the expenses of their own defeat, and this staggered them. Week after week the chiefs argued in secret council, and occasionally we heard of one of them running away to receive the shelter of the Spanish governor at Pensacola. But finally everything was "signed up" in a satisfactory manner—to the government, the Indians ceding nearly the entire territory of Alabama.

The General now proceeded to take command of his army, three thin regiments of United States troops; but the Tennessee levy was on the march and soon joined us. It was more of a great hunting party than an army. The youngsters had wandered off from the ranks and shot squirrels by day and had howled their coarse and tuneless songs at night; and now, under actual military restraint, some of them began to talk mutiny. Then there came from headquarters a piece of information: "Young recruits will please remember that they are now in the service of the general government, commanded by a Major-General, not of militia, but of the regular army." After this bit of not vital intelligence followed a paragraph that caused the squirrel hunters to bat their eyes: "Any one stimulating mutiny will be promptly shot."

, Again had "fellow citizens" become soldiers. How orderly they were, under Old Hickory's "kind advice!" Raggedly they marched, of course, for an army's grace must come of long, unconscious acquirement, not of sheer determination, but there was no whooping after squirrels through the woods.

It was delightful, coming out of the timber's stifled air into the cool breezes of the gulf. And there was another stimulus—we were to encounter a civilized foe. The English had effected a landing on the coast. Indeed, Colonel Nichols had, with a force of ex-Britain troops, found entertainment with the Spanish governor at Pensacola, had issued a most insulting proclamation to the people of Louisiana, calling upon them to support the cause of England, applying to the Americans every hard name that ink could spread. Jackson's always ready turkey feather flew to business. He opened up a polite correspondence with the Spaniard, and incidentally inquired why, as agent of a friendly government, he not only gave refuge to murderous savages but harbored an English armament, avowed enemies of America. The Spanish governor answered in great astonishment. He could not understand why his dear friend, General— ah, yes, Jackson, should so accuse him. The Indians! Those whom he had succored were subjects of his majesty, the King of Spain. The English! Why, they were his guests, and in honor of a nation which Spain revered so much, he had hoisted their flag over his fort, along with the colors of his own dear country. Jackson wrote again and came so near calling the Spaniard a liar that the agent of the once mighty peninsula reprimanded him for his American lack of diplomatic procedure. Jackson's turkey feather fluttered. He reminded the governor that the correspondence on his part was no attempt to bring about a love affair. He had not the time for a polite flirtation, and he made one of his natural demands. The British must be instantly expelled. The town and all munitions must be surrendered. For the stores, receipts would be given, and at the proper time everything should be returned to the Spanish owners, together with all necessary explanations. This was outrageous. The governor strutted forth in front of his "palace" and pawed the earth. There was great applause. Sturdy Englishmen clapped their hands and then laughed in their sleeves. Jackson sent an envoy to confer with the Spanird. He was fired on. Still the General hesitated. He sent another pleader for peace and quiet, a Spaniard. The governor sent back words which sounded like "bah, pah; fudge." Then we opened fire on the town, charged, routed out the English, who, blowing up a fort at the entrance of the harbor, sailed away. We captured the Spaniards, those of them who were not killed by grape-shot, with which we raked the streets, and put the governor in the calaboose, feathers and all. And, on the part of our government, with the most statesmanlike pen of an Adams, it took a long time to "explain this little incident."

With all its blustering promises, in the low country the war lagged. The hot weather passed and autumn set in. Every day, though, there was a fresh promise and so we were in no want of encouragement. The General's health was bad. Mahone termed him "a grim epidemic ready to seize upon the vitals of

the enemy." "Ah," the Irishman said to me one
night as we sat where the moon was sparkling through
the pines, "I have a letter from that most charming
of all women. And, Richard, she is afraid that I
have not quite forgiven her for marrying Harvey, as
if that was anything to me—I mean, as if I had any
authority over her at that time. She tells me that
I don't love her as much as she does me. Mind that,
now, as you go along. She wants to have a grand
wedding. I didn't approve of it, but I told her I'd
be there, no matter what sort of a wedding she had.
With your fine estate, Richard, you are not going to
remain in the army after peace is declared, are you?"

"No. It would be insupportably dull. My intention is to buy a tract of land somewhere up the river
from the Hermitage, and live like a gentleman."

"A fine way to live, to be sure."

The General came upon us, in one of his meditative
walks. He halted, and arising we offered him our
log, but he remained standing. "It is now clearly
the intention of the enemy to concentrate his forces
for a blow at New Orleans," said he. "And to-morrow we march in that direction."

Upon his face the moon sprinkled her light, gauzing
his countenance with a silver veil. He stood for a
few moments, in silence, and then he strode off,
amid the black shadows of the pines.

On the following day we took up our line of march.
A ragged array, indeed, to encounter the very flower,
the bloomed rose of the British army. The way was
for the most part worse than rough; it was mire,
and, after marching with all possible haste, we arrived at New Orleans on the first of December. The
city had for some time been in extreme alarm and

now was in great excitement. The legislature was
in session and Governor Claiborne was issuing an occasional address, requesting the people to be quiet.
The legislature passed a joint resolution, declaring
that the British should not enter the city. A copy of
this resolution, when presented to the ladies, ought to
have allayed their fears, but did not. There were
mutterings of sedition in this mixed population; but
this pleased Old Hickory. It gave him the opportunity to declare martial law.

It was now known that on the gulf, near New Orleans, there were fifty English warships. Some of
these vessels commanded by Nelson, had fought in the
Battle of the Nile. The soldiers were of equal re-
nown. They had achieved victory under Wellington. They had captured Washington City. Among
them was the famous Highland regiment whose backs
no enemy had ever seen. This armament comprised
about twenty thousand men. Jackson's army, including regulars and militia, numbered fewer than
three thousand. He knew that reinforcements were
not likely to reach him; that in Europe such odds
would compel retreat, but with his awkward squad,
his long haired riflemen, he felt supreme, and chafed
because the enemy came in such deliberation. But
even in fretful mood he neglected no detail. His
restless eye saw everything—noted it. He could eat
only boiled rice, a few spoonfuls a day, and he did
not sleep more than an hour at a time, on a couch in
his office. Every assailable point was fortified with
earth and logs, and so careful was the General of his
stores, that as Mahone remarked, he would have
picked up a grain of powder had he found it in the
street.

The days passed with "alarms and excursions,"
and with an occasional letter from Governor Blount.
December was more than half gone, and still no enemy
had shown himself within the vicinity of New Orleans.
The legislature continued its session. One thoughtful member declared: "As we are under martial law
we might as well quit." But another member, equal-
ly thoughtful, thus answered him: "No, we ought
not to adjourn until we have passed a few more laws
for the next general assembly to appeal."

The French part of the city was exceedingly gay.
It was not intended that war should interfere with
sociability. Paris did not grant such a right to a
siege, and here was Paris in the swamps of America.

"Ah," said Mahone, "if the British can shoot as
straight with their muskets as these creole women can
with their eyes, not one of us will be left alive after
the battle."

From time to time, came information that the British forces had effected a landing, to be disproved by
later more careful scouts. Finally, on the twenty-
third of December, there came positive news, brought
by Major Villere, a creole planter who had been captured by the enemy and who had escaped. Having
approached as near to the city as they could by
water, the river being too shallow for the great ships,
the English had landed at Bayou Bienvenue, in the
delta, not more than ten miles from Jackson's headquarters. They were now camped on Villere's plantation.

"By the Eternal," the General exclaimed, "they
shall not sleep there undisturbed. We must attack
them to-night."

It was now nearly two o'clock in the morning.

Jackson had not lain down during two days, and a
moment before receiving the news he looked yellow
and feeble; but now he appeared strong—an avenger.
Orders were at once issued for a forward movement;
but to deliver these orders required time. There were
so many points to be defended that the small bodies
of troops were widely separated; but by daylight our
men, having been commanded to march first to New
Orleans, were pouring into the city. The ''navy''
consisted of one ship, light of draft, and now at
anchor off the levee. Astride his horse, in the square
in front of the old Spanish Cathedral, the commander reviewed his army: regulars—Tennesseeans,
Kentuckians, Mississippians, creoles, Chocktaw Indians and a company of free negroes—a motley array
to any military eye. Many of the men were ragged
and without shoes. How different the scene among
the British we could easily imagine—rich young men
seeking reputation; veterans who had achieved it;
Major-General John Keane, known for his valor and
his skill on many a field; and Sir E. Packenham,
commander-in-chief, favorite at court.

When our troops had all passed, the ship Carolina
weighed anchor and sailed slowly down the river.
Jackson spurred his way to the head of the column.
The march was of necessity a cautious, feeling-for-
ward move, and it was nearly dark before we discovered a red coat, a line of pickets. The General was
eager but restrained himself. There was no opportunity to issue an address, and this must have weighed
upon him. In order not to expose to British view his
meager force, he resolved to wait for darkness. A
night attack is a desperate thing. All rules of warfare are then forgotten. In the west there was still a

glow. We waited. Among the men deep silence lay. The British were led to believe that the Americans never attacked. Nothing but the actual fact could have convinced them that "one Andrew Jackson Esquire," as he had been named in a proclamation, would rush upon them in the night. There was no moon. The cypress woods were black.

Mahone whispered to me. "Begorry, she may be a widow again before she marries me. Ah, there's a good many of us that will not come out of that woods alive."

Suddenly there came a boom from the river. The ship Carolina had opened with her guns. "Forward," was the word of command. I can never recall that night without a shudder of horror. A British officer, writing of it long afterward, declared it to be one of the most desperate memories of history. In the darkness and among so many obstacles, nothing like order could be maintained. Officers and men were jumbled together or scattered wide apart. Jackson and his staff were on foot. We could discern no enemy; did not know where he was till a sudden flash of musketry revealed for a second his red coat. The bullets whistled above us. Then came the order to charge. It was individual man leaping forward. Now it was a hand to hand fight, friend and foe almost unable to distinguish each other. There was no time to reload after the first fire. The underbrush and dry grass ignited, blazed; and in the glare there was many a fearful sight, men with their brains dashed out with musket butts—throats cut with hunting knives. I saw two men locked together, one dead of a knife stab, the other of a bayonet thrust. At times I lost all track of the General, till I heard his voice above

the murderous cries. Twice I was captured, once re-
taken by Coffee's men and once escaped by seizing a
momentary advantage—by knocking down my guard,
with a leap out into the dark.

Only a few groups of our men were engaged in
this fight. The most of them were scattered through
the woods, and unable to distinguish friend from
enemy, were afraid to fire. The knotted battle—this
murder in the dark, lasted about an hour and a half,
and while we could not claim victory to any great
sense of advantage, yet our army bivouaced closer to
the enemy's headquarters that night than had we not
attacked him. This, however, was but a brief statement of our case. The argument was to follow.

CHAPTER XXIX.

TWENTY-FIVE MINUTES.

I SHALL give from recollection, rather than from notes, only a brief account of a battle so well known to the school boy—only a few glimpses mainly to catch sight of Jackson's character, here and there, as he flashed its different aspects.

In the morning, Jackson began to fortify his position. Some Frenchman suggested cotton bales. Accepted in a moment. A ship near by was unloaded and the bales of cotton erected into a wall. An easy rampart to build. The enemy used hogsheads of sugar. Both schemes totally failed. But cotton was not accepted as a complete defense. Earth works were thrown up—mud works, for the soil was soft. Jackson was here, there, everywhere up and down the one mile of his battle-front. He said to me:

"Here is where I forfeit my life if I do not succeed. Defeat, and that trench is to be my grave. Fail! By the Eternal, we cannot fail. It is impossible, sir."

Doubtless a world-educated soldier would have regarded failure as lying somewhere within the broad domain of chance. With what reinforcements had come up our force was still below three thousand, and to Napoleon or Wellington it might have seemed at least barely possible for an army of more than three times our number—the best disciplined soldiers

290

in the world—seemed this side the miraculous that they might overcome these backwoodsmen.

In the night attack I had lost sight of Mahone, as I did of every one and everything else, and I was anxious concerning him, till I found him the next morning sitting on a log. "Ah, and it is you, is it Richard," he cried. "A fine lad to give me such a scare about yourself. I didn't know what had become of you. I should know better than to stray off that way. There is going to be some business transacted here very soon. Before I forget it let me say that I've just had a letter from Arabella; and for the purposes of modest display she wants to know something about my ancestral roof. Begorry, I remember once, when we couldn't pay the rent, the landlord had the roof taken off so that it would rain in on us; and I have sent her that gratifying intelligence. Well, lad, either one way or another this will soon be over."

Along toward noon, a number of dispatches were brought to the General. He considered them briefly, put them aside as soon as he could, and long and lovingly held in his hand a letter from his wife. "She sends her love to you, Richard," he said. "Noblest creature on the earth," he mused aloud. "God was kind to the world when your tender soul was created."

It has always been a wonder to me that the British permitted us, unmolested, to construct our long line of works. Undoubtedly, they were totally ignorant of our strength, and were waiting for reinforcements and heavier cannon from the ships. Keane may have been a brilliant soldier, as Europe had proclaimed him, but on this day he was blind.

What a hearse of time, even active war! The days
dragged. On the twenty-seventh, three days after the
battle of the night, Jackson had not slept a moment.
His longest pause from activity, it seemed to me, was
while he held his wife's letter in his hand. It has
been asserted, and it is true, that not during four
nights did he lie down to sleep, this gaunt man; nor
did he sit down to a meal. But he appeared more
vigorous as the time of trial drew near. He was
more cheerful than I had ever known him; exchanged
pleasantries with the men as he rode up and down the
line, calling many of them by name. "See that you
keep your flint well picked, old Bill Brown. You've
shot many a squirrel's eye out. See that you give it
to that old fox squirrel, Red Coat, between his two
eyes. Glad to see you, Parson Atcherson. In case
you forget your calling and grab a musket, grab a
good one."

The little Carolina did great work, continuously
raking the enemy, and this is no doubt the reason why
Jackson's work on his line of defense was allowed
to proceed without molestation. Now it was obvious
that all attention would be concentrated against our
"navy," strengthened by the Louisiana, a still smaller
vessel, which was anchored several miles further up
the river. Large guns and furnaces for heating shot
were brought from the ships during the night of the
twenty-sixth, and planted on the levee. This meant
that it was all over with the brave little craft. She
was blown so nearly out of the water with the first
few discharges from the enemy, and was set on fire
in so many places, that she was abandoned.

A loud cheer in the British ranks told us that the
court favorite, Sir Edward Packenham, had arrived

to assume command. Through a battered telescope
Jackson observed it all. Sir Edward soon decided to
"feel" of us, and it cost him the lives of fifty of his
men. Then he withdrew and spent the time in con-
sultation with his officers. Although his advance had
been met with such opposition, and although, as one
of his officers afterward wrote, he was given an exhi-
bition of the finest artillery work he had ever seen,
yet he and his advisers continued to hold the Americans in contempt, believing that they were only waiting for an opportunity to run home.

Jackson continued to strengthen the weak places
along his line; continued to cheer his men. Had Sir
Edward met this "Andrew Jackson Esquire" he
would have smiled. The General's boots were rusty,
his cloak almost thread-bare, his general appearance,
to the eye that does not search for the soul, anything
but "victorious." But we who knew him could see
victory in his countenance.

Headquarters were in a mansion house about two
hundred yards from the breastwork, and here at the
window the General would stand, with the battered
telescope, viewing the enemy. New Year's day. We
had eaten breakfast. The General was at the window.
Suddenly there came a bombardment and a crash.
Two batteries had opened on the mansion, and within a few moments it was almost a mass of ruins. Our
escape was miraculous.

The long season of silence between the army was
to end. "It will be a cock-fighting from now on,"
said Mahone, looking out over the plain lying between the two armies. "And in my opinion we're as
well heeled as we'll ever be."

We had ten guns in position to rake this "review

ground." The artillery men were ready, with matches lighted. The hair-triggers of the riflemen were set. The enemy's batteries, thirty heavy guns, opened fire. It was instantly returned. Our cotton bales were tumbled about and many of them set on fire. The smoke was blinding.

The thunder was so great it seemed that the river was to be shaken out of its banks. We could not, on account of the smoke, observe the effect of our work; but we knew that the artillerymen fired a cannon with the precision of a squirrel rifle. · Along toward noon the enemy's fire began to slacken, then ceased. The first sight of the result of our splendid work caused a shout from every American throat. The British batteries had been demolished. The sailors were fleeing to the rear. Old Hickory smiled. "Everything is going well," he said. We waited for a renewal of the attack—waited four days. On the second day we were reinforced by two thousand Kentuckians, ragged, barefooted, and for the most part, unarmed. A little later the British were strengthened by sixteen hundred soldiers fresh from victory in Europe. Then fell another lull. The quiet was so suspicious that we feared a new design upon the city, a counter movement. But reconnoissance proved this anxiety to be groundless. The enemy was resting, still in the enjoyment of his contempt. It was now known that Packenham would storm the works.

Eighth of January. At one o'clock Old Hickory left his couch, and strode up and down the lines. "They will be upon us soon," he said as cheerfully as if he looked forward to the visit of a friend. Daylight lagged in mist. Up into the slowly yellowing air a rocket sped. It was the Britains signal for the storm. The mist flew like a cloud, the sun came out; and then I stood in wrapt astonishment—at the magnificent demonstration on the plain. I had never before seen a real army, ''accoutered with dazzle'' and moving like the perfection of some great mathematical design. The gallant General Gibbs was in the van of this majestic tread, he and his men all too confident, contempt within their hearts. The guns opened fire, the small arms were held in reserve. Was there ever such needless slaughter! A great gun doubly charged and crammed to the muzzle with musket balls belched forth its tide of death, and mowed them down like grass. But re-forming, still they came, until within the rifle's reach and then they reeled, and those who had not fallen, turned and fled. Their commander strove in vain to rally them; stormed, begged, hacked at them with his sword, there within full view and easy shot of us. But bravery threw its spell and no sharp-eyed rifleman drew a bead on him.

Then came the praying Highlanders, dreaded ninety-third, with bagpipes that had urged them on to many a victory. Old coon-skin cap, old homespun from the woods sighted long, and then upon the word let fly his lead. Five hundred of the Scotchmen fell; the others, halting, stood a glittering mark, received another fire, and then the remnant broke and in panic flew. Up dashed Sir Edward, shouting brave words—and fell to shout no more. It had been just twenty-five minutes since the first fire, and the British army was riddled. A thousand insults, the burning of Washington had been avenged. Old Jackson looked out over the scene, at the flying enemy, at the ground covered with the slain. His hat was off and on his head I saw a scar, the saber cut of so many years ago. England had paid for it with her best blood.

CHAPTER XXX.

CONCLUSION.

I HAVE no disposition to linger over the scenes that followed; the exultation, the wild joy in New Orleans. The war was done, the treaty had been signed—which we did not know—and Jackson was to be an idol not only in his own state but of the nation. A new world-man had arrived. We were to linger for some time in this delivered city, long enough for the General to issue an address or two, engage in a personal encounter and to play Cromwell with the legislature. Mahone requested leave to depart for home in advance, assuring the General that he had some rather important business to transact, and permission was granted him.

"Richard," said he, "I should like very much for you to be at the only wedding I've ever had, and we will wait, but if you halt for old hero there's no telling when you'll be back."

I accompanied him on his way an hour's ride and returned to the city, now the gayest place on the continent; but this life, this constant flattery meant nothing to me. I longed to buy an estate on the Cumberland river; to build a house after my own notion, and—that was as far as I could see. Time had been dragging while we were in the Creek War, while we were under arms facing the British, but it had been flying, too. Since first I came across the hills of East Tennessee the years had passed.

It was a great pleasure when the General announced his intention to visit his home. The journey was too triumphal a progress to be expeditious. Man had a new hero and demanded the right not only to look upon him but to take him by the hand. Negroes fought one another for the privilege of leading his horse.

Nashville was more than wild; it was mad with enthusiasm. But the General did not halt to receive or to deliver addresses; his desire now was to reach his home and there to await orders from the War Department, for he was still of the army. When we came within sight of the Hermitage and looked upon the dark mass of people gathered there, he remarked to me:

"I now feel, sir, that I am entitled to a few days of rest and of quiet; but I do not see that either is waiting for me."

Neither could I see it. I knew, as he must have known, that the sun of his fame was just now fairly ablaze, over the hill; that the voice of the Nation would call him.

The weather was pleasant for the time of year, and a great dinner was served on the lawn. I looked about for Mahone, but did not find him until rather late in the afternoon. Then, with Arabella beside him in a buggy, he drove up to the gate. "Arrah," he cried, "it is yourself, is it? And you were smart enough to give us the slip. Arabella, my dear, jump out like the feather you are." He caught her in his arms as she sprang from the buggy. "Kiss her," he said to me—"kiss her that was and is—Mrs. Daniel Mahone. Yes, we were married a month ago, and a happier pair I have never seen. You may kiss her again if she don't object, and I know she won't."

There was no conjecture now as to the state of Arabella's mind. For the first time her every look, tone, word, seemed genuine. "Oh, I thank you so much for sending him back to me," she said.

"But I didn't send him," I answered. "He wanted to come and the General granted him leave."

"Still the same old bush-beating Richard," she replied. "Wretch, don't you remember having saved this life in the night attack?"

"I do not. But I did a good deal of running on that occasion, and I might have run over some one that was close after him."

"Listen to the vain boaster, will you!" cried Mahone. "But come, let us get inside. Since taking up my abode amid luxuries, I don't like the edge of this cutting wind."

It was a long time that night before we were permitted to sit in quiet about the fire-side; and when at last this boon was granted us—the General, his wife and me—it was good to see the warrior rest, in his easy rocking chair. The cool wind whistling about the house, the comfort within, the fire muttering, exerted their soothing influence, and the soldier slept.

"This is the first opportunity to tell you the news," said Mrs. Jackson, speaking in a low tone. "Nettie will be here tomorrow." I started up, but the sadness of her look restrained me from uttering a word. I waited.

"Day after to-morrow she will be eighteen. How time does fly! And on that night, here in our house, she is to be married. She has yielded every point to Wilbur and his mother, save one—her determination to be married beneath our roof. 'Riah urged her own physical inability to make the journey, which in fact is not far, but Nettie would not yield. Richard, I have prayed—''

"Don't shoot till you see the whites of their eyes," the General muttered, then awoke. "Ah," he said, "I was back there on the field at New Orleans. Mrs. Jackson, my dear, I believe I will go to bed."

"I think it would be well, Mr. Jackson, for you must be very tired," she answered. Her Bible was ever handy and in a moment she had it in her hand; and the book-mark, hanging down from between the leaves showed to my accustomed eye that the "potion" was to be neither the "sling" nor "ram's horn." And conjecture was right, for shortly afterward I heard the voice of the gentle woman, calling him down beside the "still waters."

I did not wait for her to come back. She had told me enough.

It was about ten o'clock in the forenoon of the following day when Nettie and Wilbur Page drove up to the gate. I did not go forth to meet them; I went to my room, and remained there until Mrs. Jackson sent for me to come into the parlor.

In the young woman every promise of the girl had been kept. She was radiantly beautiful. Wilbur came forward and shook hands with me, and then I took her hand, looked into her eyes, and had we been alone, I should have drawn her toward me, her lips to meet mine as they once met; and over me came the feeling that she would not resist. By the young fellow's air I could see that in his belief his "authority" was settled into "divine right," and that on her part there could be no resistance. Still, he kept a sharp

lookout for me, I thought, sometimes finishing a sen-
tence for me when I addressed myself to her. The
General said that he was going out to look at the colts,
and inquired of Wilbur, and most innocently, too, if
he cared to go along; but he answered that he believed
not. Nor during the entire afternoon did he budge.
But my mind toward the girl was made up. I would
save her from him if I could, presuming, of course,
that she desired to be saved. However, I did not
wholly like her humor; there was not enough of sadness in it, so great a sacrifice on her part being near,
and I wondered if she had finally learned to love him.
Night came and still I had not spoken for her ears
alone—bed-time, and there he sat by the fire, in his
new boots, and their shine angered me, for much of
his vanity lay in his foot.

Early on the following day, I heard some talk about
the county clerk, of marriage license, and my blood
turned chilly. There did not seem to be any hope;
but in the afternoon Wilbur went with the General
out to the meadow. I asked Nettie to take a stroll
with me, in the garden. She hesitated. She said
that the air was cold, and it was—becoming more so,
it seemed to me; but I saw that she was putting on a
wrap. Knowing that our time would be short, I was
much disposed to bid her make haste, but when I
showed impatience she reproved me with a light in
her countenance which she no doubt intended for a
frown.

We walked out toward the summer-house, and
though it was past the middle of March the air came
cold from the north. She was lively, joking with me
until we entered the summer-house, and then a sadness came upon her, showing how beautiful her face

" YOU SHALL NOT!"

could be when serious. She sat down, I beside her,
and I would have thought that she sighed but I had
lost too much hope for that degree of self-congratula-
tion.

"A long time has passed," she said, "since—"

"Yes, since—our lips met, in the candle light," I
boldly broke in, and she finished: "Since we together saw the old whale that swallowed Jonah."

"Ah," I answered, "and on that day a life was
swallowed. By fate—my life."

She sighed now, and our eyes met. She was wondrous calm, for her, and her face was pale. But she
smiled and said: "I haven't yet learned very many
big words, as I told you I would. They did not come,
with the long dresses. I like the simple words that
called us so close to happiness, in that dear time so
long ago."

"Yes, how much sweeter are the simpler words—
the words, 'Nettie I have always loved you and beg
you not to take a step that may make you unhappy.
We were born for each other; we have known it during these years. You must be my wife—you shall
not—' "

"Here comes Wilbur," she said; and her hand,
which I had seized, fluttered like a bird within my
grasp. She arose and was standing some distance off
when Page came to the door. "Several visitors are
at the house waiting for you," he said to her; and
without a word she left me. Page walked off with her,
having merely looked at me; and toward him my
anger arose, as it had arisen when I slapped Lismukes' face. But I was just enough toward him,
with all my boiling blood, to know that I had no real

cause for violence. He had simply insultêd me with a look of contempt.

When the candles were lighted and the guests began to assemble, the General came to my room. "Mrs. Jackson has just told me something which I suppose I ought to have observed, Richard. I am sorry for you, and by the Eternal, for her—but it cannot be helped. The southern woman, sir, is educated to believe that she was created to sacrifice herself. They are nearly ready. Come on, Richard, and bear it like a man."

As I entered the parlor Mahone seized my hand, and I remember Arabella's sad face. "Here is Chaplain Atcherson," said the Irishman. "Knowing that he would be welcome to all concerned, I took it upon myself to invite him."

Everything seemed to be in readiness. The clergyman selected by Page had arrived. At the parlor door Page stood waiting for Nettie. She was to join him there. But why did they wait so long? Suddenly Mrs. Jackson came swiftly through the door. "Miss Blakemore has fainted," she cried. Page leaped through the door into the room.

"By the Eternal, the wrong physician," Old Hickory roared.

Arabella hurried after Page. "Arrah," cried Mahone, "if there's any news she'll fetch it."

A few moments later Arabella came out. "Nettie has asked for you," she said to me.

I must have run over some one getting into that room. Nettie was sitting on a couch. She bade me sit down beside her, and when I obeyed she turned her glorious eyes full into mine. "You asked me to be your wife," she said, and she put her arms about my neck.

"I won't stand this," Wilbur Page cried out.

"Yes, you will," said Old Hickory. "It is the demand of the Eternal, sir."

Page bowed, and without uttering another word, strode out.

I was in a daze. I strove to speak—failed; and then I heard some one speak of sending to town for "a new license."

"Begorry, that is unnecessary," spoke up Mahone. "I have it here, together with Preacher Atcherson. I did not think the previous set would mature."

Old Hickory took my hand, Nettie's hand, and said to us: "This gives me great happiness. Colonel Mahone, by the Eternal, you are a genius, sir; and I wish to recall my reprimand for impetuosity."

I saw Atcherson standing in front of me—felt a touch upon my arm. The old earth, soloist of the spheres, was singing.